To [scribbled out]

Watermelon Road

by

Madeline L. Nowlin

Madeline L. Nowlin (signature)

RoseDog🐾Books

PITTSBURGH, PENNSYLVANIA 15222

The contents of this work including, but not limited to, the accuracy of events, people, and places depicted; opinions expressed; permission to use previously published materials included; and any advice given or actions advocated are solely the responsibility of the author, who assumes all liability for said work and indemnifies the publisher against any claims stemming from publication of the work.

All Rights Reserved
Copyright © 2010 by Madeline L. Nowlin
No part of this book may be reproduced or transmitted in any form or by any means, electronic or mechanical, including photocopying, recording, or by any information storage and retrieval system without permission in writing from the author.

ISBN: 978-1-4349-8189-9
eISBN: 978-1-4349-4433-7

Printed in the United States of America

First Printing

For more information or to order additional books, please contact:
RoseDog Books
701 Smithfield Street
Pittsburgh, Pennsylvania 15222
U.S.A.
1-800-834-1803
www.rosedogbookstore.com

For Tiny

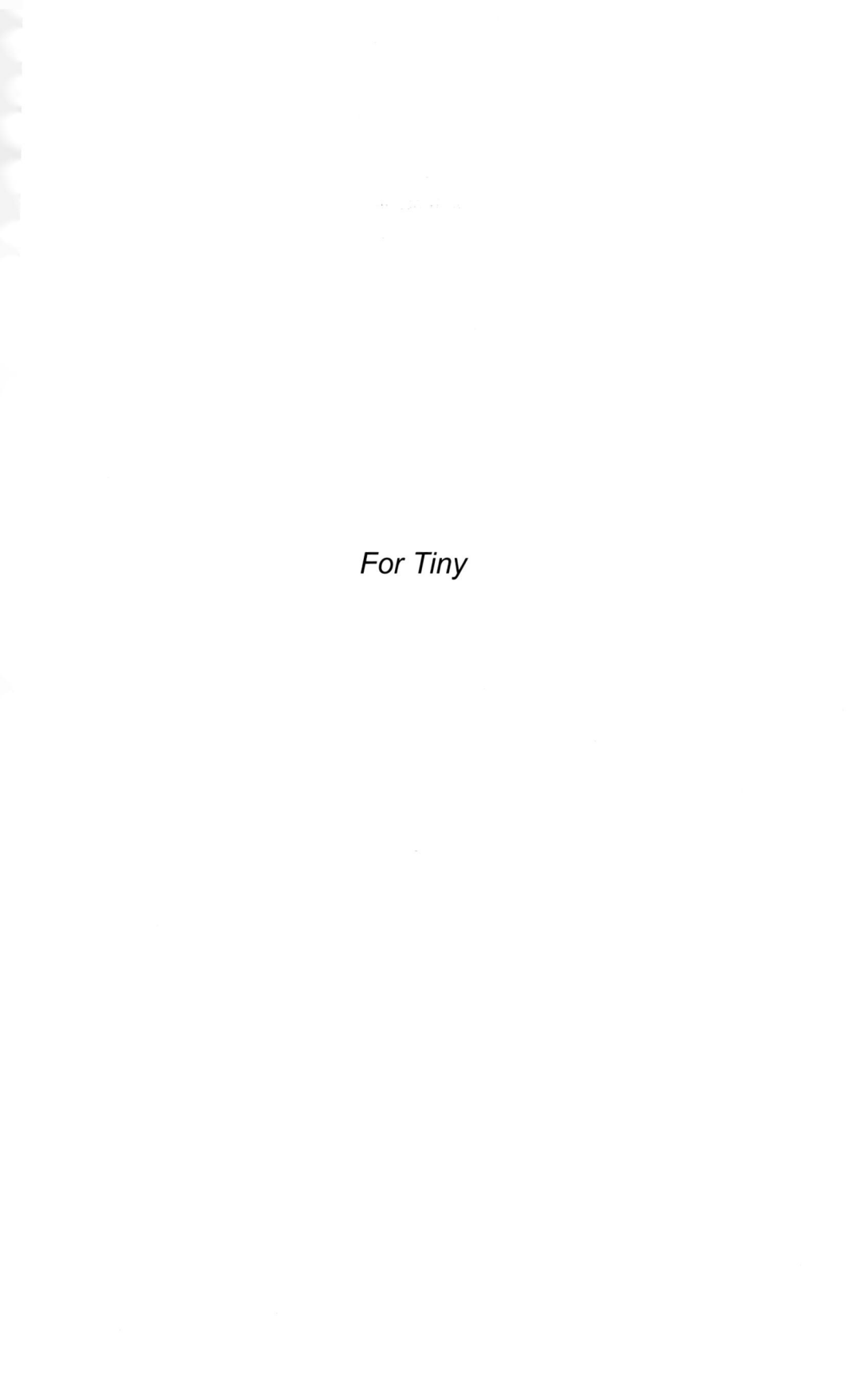

Watermelon Road
Chapter 1
Horace Graves, Alabama 1935

Petey and me hid in the bushes by the dirt road. The road is Fisherman's Lane but we call it Watermelon Road 'cause that's the way the melon man come when he sell his fruit. He name Mr. Miller. Them words on the sides of his cart say "Miller's Melons." We laugh hard every time we see them words. We call him "Old Melon Head Miller." He got melons and cantaloupes and them big green things that taste so sweet you wanna hold that juice in your mouth and never swallow. I think they's called honeydews.

 That old horse cart was coming slow like. We put our heads down so Mr. Miller cain't see us when we jump up on the back of the cart and kick off some of them melons. We can run faster than that old horse if we have to. "You ain't gonna believe how good this big ass fruit is, Nightshade, 'til that red juice is running down yo face." Petey grin them big white teeth at me.

 "You hush up," I says. "You know I had watermelon before."

 I was ten and Petey was twelve. He was my leader.

 "Not like this, Nightshade. Not like the ones he's bringing today. They's special melons today. You stay here and wait 'til I come back with a melon or two."

 I ask him "How come they's special today?"

 "Cause I said so." Petey give me that answer to most everything I ask him.

 He knows how to scare me. All he gotta do is say a thing is gonna be bad for me and I gets scared. I ain't scared now. I told him I'm jumping on the cart anyways.

 "Okay. When I puts my two fingers up like this, it mean we gonna jump up out of this ditch and run like jackrabbits to the cart."

 I watched the back of Petey's right hand he was holding up in my face while his eyes follow Mr. Miller's cart down the road. He showed his pointin' finger and the one next to it. He started running and I run beside him. We run bent over behind the cart. We keep our heads down but I can see the back of the cart easy. That old horse looked back at us and snorted. I guess he smelled us. Petey got close and grabbed the back of the cart and pulled himself up. Mr. Miller felt him 'cause he turned and sees Petey climbing over them melons.

Madeline L. Nowlin

Mr. Miller says, "I knew it was you, you little nigger thief."

Then he put his hand under his seat and brung out that horsewhip. He swung that thing at Petey and caught him 'cross his back. I hear Petey scream but that ain't stop him. He pushed a melon off the back and jumps down and runs like his mama is whipping him. I see this while I'm trying to get a melon. Petey was right to warn me. I ain't move fast enough and Old Man Miller got me on my arm with that horsewhip. It hurt like hell. I jumped down and left them melons right there.

I hear Petey yelling, "Run Shade, I gots the melon. Old man Miller is coming for you."

That lick with the whip scratched my left arm. A little bit of blood come up on my shirt sleeve. My arm sting like I stuck it in a beehive.

Mr. Miller come after us, swinging that whip and calling us names. I pretend I was a doe and run like the wind down the split in them trees through the woods. Mr. Miller is almost on me 'cause I can smell his sweat. He was swinging that horsewhip in one hand and shaking his fist with the other hand. He called us no good niggers and picaninnies and said he was going to kick our black ass when he catched us.

Petey took a left and I did too. So did Mr. Miller. Petey laughed at him and called him "Melon Head Miller" and some other nasty names I cain't write down or say out loud.

Petey say to old man Miller, "Hey you old fart, you so tired you can't even catch a nigger carrying a big fat watermelon."

My legs felt like rubber and I prayed I don't fall down. I run fast with my knees high and my eyes open big so's I don't run into no pine tree or them scratchy flower bushes on the path. I see Petey up ahead, running round things in his way and jumping over oak tree branches like he was a deer. He had that big fruit in his arms and he ain't fall down neither.

Mr. Miller give up. I look back and see him bent over trying to catch his breath. His gray white hair is shinning in that patch of sunlight through the trees. I see the sweat pouring down his face into all them wrinkles he got. He looks like a little old green man I seed once on a St. Patty hat I found near the white beer garden on Ash Street. I turn and laughs with Petey 'cause we got away.

Petey and me keep running fast 'cause Mr. Miller could still come for us. We keep going 'til we see our secret place in the woods. We call our secret place the "hole." Can't nobody find us in the hole. I love our secret spot. It's our freedom land. I says that 'cause I hear Uncle Sax talk 'bout freedom land once and I asked him what that mean. He say it's a place where people can do what they wants to and say what they wants to and cain't nobody do nothin' 'bout it. That's what our hole is, our freedom land.

There's a creek that runs along side it. It's about five feet deep and mo' when it rains a lot. Me and Petey swim naked in that creek with them little fishes. I don't know what you call 'um but they tickle your toes. Other cheerin swim further up the creek 'cause they don't know 'bout our spot.

Petey drop the melon on the grass.

Watermelon Road

He says, "Let's push this sucker."

Petey pushed with his right foot and I pushed with my left foot. We rolled that melon right up under the big cypress tree in our secret spot. Then he jump me like he always do, wanting to wrestle. I yelled when he done that 'cause my arm hurt. He don't know 'bout my arm.

He stop and look at me when I say "ouch."

"Nightshade, why you don't tell me you hurt?"

"Cause I ain't no crybaby," I says. I roll up my sleeve and show him my arm.

"Lawd Jesus, I thought your arm was cut in half. Ain't nothin' but a scratch."

He grinned at me and says, "Yo mama might need to put needle and thread to that."

I says to the funny man, "Ain't your back hurt too? I see Mr. Miller hit you with that whip."

"Yeah, but I'm use to it."

"Petey, what I'm gonna tell my mama when I come home with this blood on my shirt?"

"You tell her you fell on some glass from a soda pop bottle."

"Okay, that's good. You smart."

"Come on, Nightshade, let's eat."

Petey picked up that melon and threw it at a tree. Nothin' happened. He did it again and nothin' happened but the melon was dented in. He threw it again and it bust open. Melon went flying every place. I don't know why he loves to throw it. We could cut a hole in it and tear it open with our bare hands. We picked up chunks of the red stuff and pushed our faces in it and ate, spitting them seeds out our mouth.

"Sweet, red and luscious," Petey said. I look at him and his face looks funny with melon hanging from it. He look at my face and we laugh. Then we wiped our faces with our shirts. My mama's gonna kill me when she see my clothes. I'm thinking I can wash them myself when I get home. I know I won't remember when I get home.

My friend rest his back against that big cypress and watched me stuff myself with melon.

"This is what happens when you crack open somebody's head. They head can bust open jest like that there watermelon and blood and gray spongy stuff run out every which way. And, you sho' 'nuff don't want to eat none of it."

Petey says this so's I'd get sick and stop eating. I keep on eatin'. A cracked head don't bother me none.

Petey was like that. He says things he thinks will make me sick whiles I'm eatin'. Sometimes my friend ain't so funny like he thinks he is.

My name's Jesse but sometimes Petey call me "Nightshade" 'cause I'm dark-skinned. I told him I looked up nightshade in the dictionary in Mrs. Beaumont's class and it was a plant with dark green leaves, not black at all. Petey laugh and say that the word had "night" in it and I was dark as night. Then he say the word had "shade" in it and I blocked out the sun with my big black ass.

I let him make fun of me when ain't nobody else around. It's all right then 'cause we's friends and I know he don't mean it. He knows when to stop. He never make fun of me in front of our friends. Some of our friends call me "Fatback Blackjack" right to my face. It hurts when them other cheerin call me names but not when Petey call me names. It makes me feel good that he got his own special name for me.

We ate for awhile then Petey got quiet. He closed his eyes and hugged his self. Then he went dark. I say he went dark 'cause he had moods that sent him to another place in his head. Sometimes he moaned or cried when he went dark but I never tried to touch him 'cause he don't like to be touched then. He might forget who you was and beat you up.

I ate slow so Petey cain't hear me sucking the juice out of them melon pieces. When I see him feeling better, I got up and found some dry leaves he could rub between his hands. He liked rubbing stuff he can scrunch up, rags was too soft. Sometimes the rubbing made him feel better. Sometimes it don't work at all and he gets mean. He ain't look at me when I give him some leaves to rub, but I know he was thankful. His mama, her name Esther, told my mama, her name Lily, that Petey been having nervous spells since his brother, Joel, was killed back in 1933. That's what his mama called his dark moods, nervous spells.

Petey blew air through his lips. I hear him say, "I sho' wish I'd kept my boney ass in the bed that night. I was too nosey so I followed him."

I watched my friend leaning against the tree. His eyes looked funny, like he was looking at something I cain't see.

Even the woods got quiet. The birds stopped singing and things stopped buzzing round my head. I looked up to the tops of the trees and nothin' moved, not a leaf, not a bird, nothin'. I swear, it was like, them trees was waitin' with me to hear the story again.

Petey didn't say nothin' else for awhile. I looked around and see one of them bagworm nests in a tree by us. I see them slimy things wiggling. I hate them 'pillars.

The water in the creek made sounds like the fish was drinking it.

I was sittin' in the shade 'til the sun moved. I stayed in that sunny spot, any ways, so's I could hear Petey mo' better. The sun felt hot on my face. I wiped sweat off my forehead with my shirt. I felt sticky. My arm still hurt, but it ain't matter. I felt good right then 'cause it was the last Saturday in May and we had 'till next Friday afore school closed. Petey and me will have all of June, July and August for eating melons and swimming in the creek. I love summer 'cause it last a long time.

I watched Petey's face while he rested on that tree. He closed his eyes, but they still looked like they was moving under the lids. Petey's eyes looked funny anyway. They looked brown and green at the same time. Sometimes his skin looks like the color of honey in that jar sittin' in my mama's kitchen window. All gold and shinny like, but I can see right through it when the sun shines. Them

Watermelon Road

girls in town, it don't matter how old they is, is always trying to get him to look at them. They like his long eyelashes and his curly hair. His hair is the color of honey too. Mostly though he jest a skinny kid but he taller than me and I'm a lot fatter than him.

Mrs. Beaumont, our schoolteacher, winks at him a lot in class and let him stay after school to clean the blackboards. I ain't jealous 'cause he's my buddy. Them other boys in school hate him 'cause the girls like him. Them boys call him "lover boy," behind his back. They scared of him 'cause he don't take no stuff off nobody. Besides, Petey see them girls, but he never wants no female company.

Petey stretched his legs out and made a funny noise in his throat. He started talking again. He rubbed them leaves while he talked.

"Only I knows Joel sneaks out the house most nights after we went to bed. Mama made Uncle Sax look in on us afore she went to bed. He ain't our real uncle but mama made us call him uncle. Joel waited 'til mama and Uncle Sax was snoring and then he'd sneak downstairs and out the front door. Sometimes Freaky Joe and Lewis come by in Lewis' old Ford Coupe. You know, the one Lewis found beat up on the side of the road one night and fixed it up. They'd go to them dancing places and beer joints along the Proud Rock River. Most times, though, Joel would go off alone.

Mama and Uncle Sax was good-timing it like they always do on Friday nights. Uncle Sax catched some catfish for dinner, buyed some whiskey for himself and gin for mama with his paycheck, and had his buddies over for a fry-up. Joel knew Uncle Sax would be too drunk to look in on us so he bided his time 'til they got real noisy downstairs. When he heard Uncle Sax blowing on his saxophone, he knows he's good and drunk. They friends, Mrs. Bertie, Junior Rocket and Earl would go on and on 'bout Uncle Sax having balloon lungs and such. They be talking jive all night 'bout the blues, Bessie Smith, the jazz singer, and that saxophone player, Coleman Hawkins. They listen to band music on the radio half the night. They's three things Uncle Sax loves to talk 'bout. He loves jazz, blowing that saxophone and talkin' 'bout baseball. Most times they listen to him running his mouth 'bout all the Negro League baseball games he done gone to and that time he seed Satchel Paige pitch at Richwood Field over in Birmingham. I guess that's why he loved Joel so much. *That boy sho' can play some ball*. That's what he say every time Joel come around him and his friends.

I slept in the bed with my little brother, Peewee. Mama named him Simon Joseph when he was born. I was hiding in the closet in my mama's bedroom the night Peewee was born but mama and my real daddy ain't know that. My mama screamed out my daddy's name, *Amos,* so many times afore Peewee's head come out her butt that I wanted to hurt my daddy real bad 'cause he wouldn't help her none. Mrs. Bertie helped, though. I was only five but I still remember that night. I guess Mrs. Bertie was good at pulling babies out 'cause she got eight cheerin of her own."

I always feel sick at this part when Petey talk about Peewee coming out his mama's butt. I prayed that ain't happen to me when I was born.

5

Madeline L. Nowlin

"My big brother, Joel, had his own bed but the three of us slept in the same room. I guess you know how Peewee got his name?"

I laughed at that part, just like I always do.

Petey laughed too. After we laugh, he say....

"Lawd, I sho' 'nuff wished I'd kept my black ass in my bed. But mor'in that, I wish I could have stopped Joel from going. Like I said, while mama and Uncle Sax was in the kitchen, Joel tiptoed downstairs and out the front door. There was no tellin' what time our folks would go to bed that night so I guess Joel couldn't wait much longer. He went to the back of the house, pass mama's kitchen garden and beyond that, into the woods. I waited 'til he was in them woods and I sneaked out the house so's I could follow him. On the way out I see mama's grandfather clock in the hall say 12:30. It was already Saturday morning afore I went out the door.

Shade, I tell you I was scared to death to be in them woods at night. There wasn't a full moon and I couldn't see much in front of me. I heard Joel up ahead slashing bushes and crunching things on the ground, but that's all. Afore long he slowed down and started whistling. He come to a stop. That's when I looks for a place to hide. I found a good spot, too, in a patch of leaves behind Joel. I crawled up under them leaves and what not and thanked God it ain't raining. Next thing I hear somebody else whistle the same tune as Joel. Then I seed her parting some bushes near where Joel was standing. I couldn't believe my eyes. I rubbed my eyes to make sure. Like I say, there wasn't much moonlight but I could see her stringy white blond hair. It was that skinny white girl with the big tits that lived in that shack on St. Lucia Road, behind Mr. Batty's store. She live with her daddy and two brothers. Her mama dead.

She come out of them bushes shaking and rubbing herself and come up to Joel, still whistling. He kept on whistling, too. That tune they whistle sounded like that old song my mama always singing. Then it come to me. It was that song mama say two men wrote in the 1920's when I ask her 'bout it. Why you always humming that song? I asked her once and she say 'cause that Mr. Grainger and that Mr. Robbins can sho' make my feet tap. Besides, I like it because it ain't nobody's business what I do. If I want to drink, I drinks. She called it *'Tain't Nobody's Biz-Ness If I do.* Yeah, that's what Joel and that gal was whistling.

Joel bend down a little and kissed her on the mouth. I ain't know my brother did such things with girls. They started doing things to each other I sees mama and Uncle Sax do. I knows 'cause I hid under mama's bed once and that's when I find out Uncle Sax and my mama is nasty. Anyhow, they fell on the ground gruntin' and sweatin'. I cain't see nothing but I sho' heard a lot. That white girl got to moaning and groaning and yelling Joel's name. I think Joel must've put his hand over her mouth 'cause she stopped that noise. I hear him whisper to her to be quiet.

You don't want nobody catching us, do you, Mirabelle?

Them the last words I ever hear Joel say. Two white men come out of them bushes. They was carrying flashlights and shotguns. But I didn't see the light

Watermelon Road

from them flashlights afore they was up on us 'cause I would have warned Joel they was coming. I ducked my head down so's the light don't shine on me. Joel was still on top of Mirabelle. When they shine the light on Joel and Mirabelle, I could see her dress was way up her thighs and Joel's drawers was down round his knees. Her legs were wrapped around his back. She pushed Joel off her when she sees them men.

I didn't need a good look at them white boys cause I heard one of them speak and I knew they was Mirabelle's brothers, Calvin and Haley. I seed them before 'round Mr. Batty's General Store. They always call me nigger when I come to buy stuff for my mama. Sometimes one or the other makes fun of my mama too. One of them said, W*here is that drunken whore mama of yours?* I keep my head down and keep to my business. They looked something like Mirabelle, only they blond hair is shorter and they have the same crazy look in they brown eyes. People call them the lumberjack twins behind they back 'cause they got thick bodies and thick heads.

Joel was lying on his back when them boys come up on him. He screamed when he sees them two white men. I ain't never seed my brother so scared in my whole life. Joel tried to get up and that's when one of them hit Joel in the head with his rifle butt. I hear Joel's head crack. I knows he dead. Mirabelle screamed and cover her face. I put my face in the dirt and put my hand over my mouth so I don't scream none. I wet my pants. I can't tease Peewee no more. I was so scared, but I was mostly mad 'cause I cain't help Joel. Nightshade, I was a coward and you ain't never see me be scared of nothin'. I knowed mama was gonna blame me for what happen to him. She loved him more than me and Peewee. I know she hate me now.

Joel was quiet. He ain't move no more. One of them boys kicked Mirabelle in her stomach. She yell for him to stop.

I hear her say, *Stop it Haley, don't hurt me no more.* That's the one that always wear them bib overalls. Then Haley kicked her hard again. Then she say, *Please help me Calvin. Make Haley stop.* The one she call Calvin told Haley to quit it. I think Calvin was the oldest but I ain't sho'. Mirabelle got up off the ground crying and holding her stomach.

She say, *What you do that for, Haley? You got no cause to hurt me and Joel. You likely killed him.*

Calvin shined the light on Haley. Haley showed them rotten teeth in his mouth when he grin at Mirabelle. *Why you care? We've been following you for a couple of days and you been sneaking around with this nigger. We put up with you giving it up to every white man in town but you ain't gonna shame our family sleeping with niggers.*

Shame? You and Calvin think I shame you? Mirabelle was shaking her shoulders and pointing her finger in Haley's face. *Where were you and Calvin when daddy was sneaking into my bedroom after mama died? Huh? Maybe that's why I like fucking so much.*

Haley was still in Calvin's light so I see it in his eyes that he knows something bad 'bout his daddy.

7

Madeline L. Nowlin

Mirabelle say *I know something 'bout you two. You the ones done hanged them two niggers last month. You strung them up at night in the woods near Fisherman's Lane. I'm gonna tell Sheriff Richards so he can put your asses in jail.*

That's right, we done it, says Haley. *You can tell all you want 'cause ain't nobody gonna believe your dumb ass."*

Every time Petey tell Mirabelle's part of the story his voice gets real high and makes me wanna laugh. I cain't laugh 'cause I loved Joel too. He was like a big brother to me. I don't have no brothers or sisters. I put my hand over my mouth to make sho' I don't laugh.

Petey went on with his story.

"Joel moaned. I peeked from my hiding spot and prayed. I thanked God Joel was still alive. I ain't never prayed as hard as I did that night. I prayed to God to save Joel. I chewed my mouth up trying not to cry. Hell, Nightshade, I was 'bout your age back then and I didn't know what to do. I think I put some dirt in my mouth so's I'd have something that taste bad to keep me from crying out loud. The dirt in my mouth made me cough once and I hear one of them boys say, *Did you hear something*? I had to cough again but I held it down 'til my eyes water.

I hear them brothers talking. Haley say, *Ain't gonna be no fun hanging this one. He's half dead already.*

Calvin say, *Let's string him up anyway. The fun part is when them niggers find him in the morning. His mama be screaming Oh, Lawd', and people be crying and jumping around and holding their hands up to the sky, calling on Jesus. It's the best show in town.'*

That's when Mirabelle turned and run through them bushes, but they don't mind her none.

I hear Joel moan again. I wanted to go get some help but it was dark, and I didn't know my way back and they might hear me running away and shoot me. Calvin shine the flashlight over Joel's face, looking at him. Haley looked too. I seed Joel's head looking like that watermelon I busted open awhile ago.

Haley raised his rifle butt and beat Joel in his face and head some more. Then them boys left my brother lying there in the dirt.

I waited in my hiding spot a good while longer 'cause they might come back. I crawled over to Joel. I ain't never seed a dead person 'cept my daddy, but he was in the box when we come to look on him. I was afraid to touch Joel, but I did. I closed my eyes and touched his hand and told him I loved him and I was going to get help. I told him I'd tell Uncle Sax what happened and bring him back to that place in the woods. He wasn't breathing 'cause I felt his chest. I took off my shirt and put it over his face along with some leaves and then I got some more leaves and covered up the rest of him so's nobody could see him and none of them wood creatures could eat him. I cried the whole time I did this.

I found my way back home. On the way home, I tore off pieces of my clothes and left them on bushes so's I can find my way back to Joel. When I got there, I peaked in the kitchen. Uncle Sax and his buddies was playing gin rummy

Watermelon Road

at the kitchen table and mama was at the pail washing up dishes. I tiptoed upstairs and went in mama's and Uncle Sax's bedroom. Her table clock say 2:30 in the morning. Imagine that? It's like I sees Joel's whole life go by in a couple of hours. I picked up that heavy glass ashtray off the table by mama's bed and threw it across the room so's it would make some noise and somebody would come running. I prayed that somebody would be Uncle Sax. That ashtray was so heavy it ain't even break when it hit the floor but it made a big noise.

It got real quiet downstairs and then I hear Uncle Sax running up them steps, cursing all the way. He said a bad word on every step his feet touched.

I peaked out from they bedroom. It was dark at the top of the stairs but I hear Uncle Sax run right into our bedroom. He bust open the door and stopped dead when he sees only Peewee in our bed. He come out in the hallway and looked around. I stuck my head out and seed the cigarette he was holding glowing in the dark. I was shaking 'cause I was scared of Uncle Sax and shaking 'cause I left most of my clothes on them bushes. I ain't have nothin' on but my drawers and shoes and the June night done turned cool.

I whispered in the hallway, "Uncle Sax, I got something to tell you 'bout Joel."

I don't think he heard what I say 'bout Joel. Uncle Sax come in the bedroom, put that cigarette back in his mouth and put his hands on my shoulders and starts shaking the life out of me. I guess he thought I was trying to steal some money or something. You know he's a big man. I thought he was gonna kill me. When he gets angry nobody can pull him back 'cept mama. He ain't never hit us boys or my mama, though. This time was different 'cause he'd been drinking half the night. He stopped shaking me and lift me up so's we was face to face and I see his black eyes and his white teeth when he open his mouth. I thought he was gonna eat me. I knows I was gonna die afore I could tell him 'bout Joel. He held me in the air with one hand and with the other reached over and turned on mama's table lamp."

Why the hell you in here, breaking up shit?

"Joel is dead," I said. Then I started crying.

"He threw me down on the bed and stared at me, like I had turned white. He picked up the ashtray off the floor and put his cigarette out in it. He set the ashtray back on mama's table. His right hand was shaking and he put it to his mouth. He sat down beside me and covered his face with both his hands for awhile. I sat up on the bed looking at him. When he put his hands down he had tears in his eyes but they didn't come out. He clinched his fists real tight.

How you know Joel dead?

I say, "'cause I followed him when he sneaked out the house tonight. Them Lucas boys got him and beat him with they shotguns. They caught him messing with they sister, Mirabelle, in the woods and he ain't see them coming."

Uncle Sax was quiet. He took out a pack of Camels and took a cigarette for himself and give one to me. He lit us up. That's when I know that he knows that I been stealing his smokes.

Listen to me boy don't you tell your mama or brother nothin'. You let me tell your mama in the morning. You seen who done it and we is all in danger. Them Lucas boys belong to a white group of men that love to kill Negroes. Don't you say nothin' to nobody. We gonna go find Joel's body right now and bring him back and put him in the shed. I'll go over to Olivia's Diner as soon as she opens tomorrow morning and use the telephone to call the Sheriff. Olivia's Diner will be empty 'til the breakfast folks come in. I'll call Sheriff Richards over to Bison so he can come have a look at Joel and hear your story. Now remember, don't say nothin' when we go downstairs. I don't want Esther going crazy along with Mrs. Bertie, Junior Rocket and Earl. You go put some clothes on.

I got dressed and we went downstairs and out the front door. On the way out, Uncle Sax yelled at mama that he was taking me to the woodshed to give me what for.

Esther, I caught this boy in our room. He was looking for some cigarettes and knocked your ashtray off the table but it didn't break. I'm gonna teach him a lesson 'bout stealing my smokes and lighting up.

Mama come from the kitchen, hands on her hips, staring at me. Junior Rocket and Earl was standing behind her.

What in the name of Jesus was he doing looking for cigarette? I know he ain't been smoking. Not at no ten years old. I bet Joel put him up to it. I should go upstairs right now and give Joel a piece of my mind for teaching his brother how to smoke and he ain't mor'in ten years old.

Uncle Sax say, "*Don't wake Joel up, I'll find out what's going on. Me and Petey is gonna have us a man-to-man talk in the shed.*

We walked around the back of the shed and into the woods. I showed Uncle Sax the way. You know he not our daddy but us boys respect him. He treats my mama real good. He been with us for three years, 'bout a year after my daddy died from ptomaine poisoning when he ate a can of cold beans. Mama said our daddy was the best husband a woman could want. He was a good daddy too. Peewee don't remember much 'bout him but I do. He used to take me fishing. Uncle Sax do that sometimes.

While we was walking in them dark woods, I asked Uncle Sax if mama was gonna be mad at me for not helping Joel. He told me not to worry 'cause he would have a talk with mama after she calmed down from seeing Joel's body in the morning.

When we found Joel's body, Uncle Sax brush the leaves off him. He left my shirt on Joel's face for awhile. Then he took my shirt off Joel's face. I heard a low moan come from Uncle Sax and then he bust out crying. He cried real loud and he beat his chest with his fists like he wanted to make himself hurt like Joel was hurt. Some more tears come down my face too.

He quiet down and turn to me and said, *You did a good job of covering him up.* What he said made me feel better. He covered Joel's face with my shirt again and picked him up and carried him all the way back to our woodshed. I took my clothes off them bushes on the way home and hid them in my room. I burned them later.

When we got home, Uncle Sax told me to go in the house and get some blankets to cover Joel. I did that. After Uncle Sax covered Joel, we went back to the house and I didn't have to fake no crying to make like Uncle Sax whipped me. I was crying for real. Mama told me to go to bed and stay the hell out of her stuff.

I got back in bed with Peewee. He didn't even wake up. I was scared to sleep in Joel's bed. I could still smell him in the room. I lay in bed, looking up at the ceiling and listening to that noise downstairs. Uncle Sax was playing cards and joking with his friends like everything was just fine. I looked at Joel's empty bed. He ain't never gonna sleep in that bed again. I didn't know how I was gonna tell Peewee in the morning that I'm his big brother now."

Petey took a rest from talking. I got up and stretched and looked for more leaves for him to rub. I give him some more leaves and that made him easy. He rubbed them leaves so fast his hands turned green and smelled like pine.

He still looked kind of wild. I moved to some shade 'til Petey can finish out his story. Then he might not go dark for a long time.

"Uncle Sax went over to Olivia's Diner in the morning. I hear his shoes going past my bedroom door. I waited 'til Peewee woke up then we went down to get us some breakfast since mama was sleeping late like she do most Saturday mornings. I went out back and got some wood for the stove. I sliced up bread for toasting and give Peewee some milk. I made a pot of coffee for mama and me. I drink it black like a real coffee drinker. That's what Uncle Sax always say. *Drink it black like a real coffee drinker. You don't need to make it sweet with that milk and sugar. Otherwise, you might as well drink soda pop.* I still like soda pop too.

I sat in the parlor and looked out the window. It took about two hours afore Uncle Sax showed up with the Sheriff. Peewee was outside playing and I could hear mama stirring upstairs.

They drove up in the Sheriff's county car. Uncle Sax was sitting in the back seat. The Sheriff and his Deputy sat up front. I knows the people in town must've thought Uncle Sax done something wrong, sitting in the back of the Sheriff's car like that.

I took my third cup of coffee and went out to the porch. Uncle Sax got out the car and held up his hand for me to stay on the porch. Sheriff Richards and his deputy followed Uncle Sax to the shed.

How come the Sheriff is here? Peewee asked me. He was sitting on the porch with a box of crayons, coloring in that coloring book Joel give him. That boy loved to color and he was good at drawing stuff too. I told him that it was none of his business 'bout the Sheriff. I said the Sheriff and the Deputy could be friends with Uncle Sax and maybe they wanted to borrow some fishing poles Uncle Sax keeps in the shed. Peewee give me a long look then he went back to coloring.

They stayed in the shed for a long time. Uncle Sax come out and told me to come into the shed. I told Peewee to stay put. My legs felt heavy like tree trunks 'cause I didn't want to go into that shed and see what Joel look like now. Joel's body was lying on the workbench. They had a blanket over him, so I was calm 'bout that. Sheriff Richards told me his name like I didn't know it already. He said his Deputy's name was Rudy Cox. Both of them shook my hand. The Sheriff asked me three times to tell him what happened and I told him three times. He asked me something different every time I told my story.

When the Sheriff was done, Uncle Sax told me to leave the shed. He hand me three dollars and said for me to take Peewee to the picture show and then get something to eat. He said he was going in the house to get my mama and he didn't want Peewee and me around when she knows the truth 'bout Joel.

I took Peewee by the hand and left the yard. I told him we was going to the picture show. A little ways down the road, I say to Peewee I forgot something and had to go back to the house. I told him to stay put or he won't see no picture show. He said he was gonna sit right there on the side of the road 'til I come back. I sneaked back to the house and hid behind a tree in the front yard so Uncle Sax cain't see me. That's when I hear a loud scream come from the shed. It was the worse sound I ever hear from a person. It made my body feel cold.

Directly, Uncle Sax and mama come out of the shed with the Sheriff and Deputy Cox. The two men got in the Sheriff's car and drove off. Then I see Uncle Sax pushing mama towards the house. She walked like she had a spell on her from Miss Desiree what lives down by the swamp.

I went back to Peewee and we started walking. *What you forget?* My little brother asked me. I had to think fast so I say I forget to put some more wood in the stove so mama and Uncle Sax can have a hot breakfast. He was quiet while we walked then he asked me, *You see Joel this morning?* I say, *I ain't seen him. Maybe he done got up early and gone someplace. You know how Joel likes to get up early and go out with his friends.* He nod his head at what I say.

If we have some money left, I'm gonna buy you another nickel coloring book. He looked up at me and give me a big smile then he skipped ahead of me. I felt bad making him feel happy like that when I know he'll be crying later when I tell him the truth 'bout Joel.

I waited 'til we see two cowboy pictures and ate our bellies full of fried fish, potatoes and collards from Miss Olivia's, then I told him 'bout Joel. I told him that Joel got beat up by some white men and he died. Peewee didn't cry. He ask me what dead mean. I forgot he was only five years old when I told him 'bout Joel. I looked at my little brother and my heart hurt 'cause he looked more like Joel than me. I told him Uncle Sax would tell him what dead mean when we get back home. Peewee cried later when Uncle Sax tell him that dead mean you ain't never coming back home again."

That was the end of Petey's story. That's as far as he ever goes.

I picked up the rest of the melon and threw it in the creek. I don't want no ants crawling round our spot.

Petey jumped up and brushed his pants off. He started walking and didn't look back. I caught up and walked beside him.

He looked at me like he was himself again. "Remind me to tell you 'bout Uncle Sax's promise. Don't let me forget."

I ain't know that was coming. I told him, "I won't forget. I ain't heard that part before."

Watermelon Road
Chapter 9
Joel

A funeral in Horace Graves was more like a social function than a sad affair. A gathering of relations and townsfolk celebrated the life of the loved one with an abundance of food, liquor and socializing. The deceased ascended to heaven's gate with the help of loving tributes from family and friends.

That was not the case at the funeral service for Joel Nathanial Creek in 1933. On Monday, June 5, he was buried quietly in the back graveyard of the largest Negro church in Horace Graves. Reverend Xavier Beaumont, pastor of "Upon This Rock Baptist Church," presided over the funeral services. In attendance were Joel's mother, Esther Mary Creek; his mother's friend, George Johnston, called Uncle Sax by the children; his brother Peter Delroy Creek, Petey for short; and youngest brother, Simon Joseph Creek, also known as Peewee.

Before this funeral, Esther had received $500 from a life insurance policy on her husband, Amos, when he passed. She spent $200 on his funeral and the rest of the money had long since been spent on necessities. Sax paid for Joel's funeral. He felt that Esther's children were his children.

Sax made certain there was no "show" when Joel was laid to rest. He instructed John Birchwood, owner of Birchwood Funeral Home, to clean Joel up and put him in a pine box. Mr. Birchwood, a white funeral director, was the owner of one of the two funeral homes in Horace Graves. In fact, Mr. Birchwood was the only funeral director in the county proper that would attend to Negroes.

Sax expressed the family's wishes to Reverend Beaumont that Joel's burial be private; no viewing of the body by the congregation.

After the funeral, the family went home to their two-story clapboard house on Beaver Point Road and sat in a stunned silence of disbelief that Joel was gone. There was no repast as Esther was too depressed to fix or organize anything. The night before the funeral, Miss Olivia sent over a baked ham, macaroni and cheese, fried collards and two-dozen of her famous honey butter biscuits.

The Jackson sisters, Desiree and Patty, came to visit Joel's family, in their old woody station wagon from the other side of the Proud Rock River, about 20 miles outside of town. They came by after the family returned from the funeral, bringing a pineapple cake, a cherry pie, a jar of corn liquor for Sax and a jar of

Madeline L. Nowlin

gin for Esther. The liquor was made from their stills out back of their farmhouse. Both women had been well acquainted with Joel.

On their day off work, Joel and his two buddies, Freaky Joe and Lewis, would squeeze into Lewis' jalopy and chug out to the Jackson sisters' 20-acre farm near the swamplands surrounding Proud Rock River. There they would help the two women pick corn from the fields. On occasion the boys would help with the making of the corn liquor the women sold at nip joints around Bison County.

The three young men, each age 16, would use their muscles to grind the dried corn into meal. Gallons of water, malt, yeast, barley and hops were added to the mash. This mash would ferment behind the barn in huge barrels near a stream running off the river. Several weeks later the liquor was poured into glass canning jars, packed in old crates and stacked in the station wagon. Desiree and Patty took turns driving the wagon and selling the liquor throughout the county. The three young men took turns staying at the farm to keep an eye on the children so that the other two could help with the lifting of the crates while the liquor was being sold. Desiree and Patty never let the boys sell the liquor.

So far, the Sheriff and other county officials had looked the other way while Desiree and Patty sold their corn liquor, called white lightening. Often times the Sheriff and county officials bought liquor from the girls "just for a special occasion." Unlike the other still owners, the sisters had no trouble from the government tax agents that sometimes showed up unannounced at the farm. It was well known that the two women were very generous when male company came to call.

Desiree and Patty were also bold enough to make gin from the juniper trees growing on their property but not as often as they made the corn liquor.

As payment for the boys' help, the two women would give them each a bushel of corn to take home, along with a pail of fried chicken. Desiree would occasionally give them a pint of gin or corn liquor. Patty gave Joel a little more than that.

Other produce was grown on the farm besides corn. Fields of peanuts, soybeans and tobacco were grown and harvested in season. They also kept chickens, pigs, cows and two horses. The children took care of the animals. They did not attend school but were home schooled by their mothers.

Desiree had three boys, ages ten, five and one. The oldest was Thomas, called Tom for short. The middle child was Richard, who was called Dick and the youngest was Harry. She said she named them Tom, Dick and Harry because those names were easy to remember.

Patty named her three girls after her favorite fragrances. Jasmine, age eight, Honey S., short for honeysuckle, age six and Lavender, age two.

When it came to having babies, it was like a contest between the sisters, one had to keep up with the other. No one knew who the daddies were and no one ever asked. Most women in the county didn't want to know.

The sisters received hush money now and then from the children's fathers. They improved on the farm with that money. The house repairs were kept up and

Watermelon Road

they even had a bathtub. There was no indoor plumbing, except for what someone had rigged up at the kitchen sink that was hooked up to one of the two wells on the property. They kept the old cast iron, claw foot tub in a small room off the parlor. Hot water had to be carried to the tub when the sisters and their children took baths. It came in handy for washing clothes too. They usually bathed on a weekend, which took them the whole day if they all took baths on the same day. Everyone still used the outhouse but they were saving up for a toilet and piping when it came to their part of the countryside.

Sometimes Joel and his friends would drop by for a visit in between the harvesting and the making of the corn liquor. They all loved to dance. After downing a jar of gin, Patty would start banging out Fats Waller tunes on the old upright piano in the parlor.

The sisters inherited the piano from their paternal grandfather along with the farm. The piano needed tuning because the six children used it as a play toy.

Desiree, a tall, slim, light skinned woman of 32 was the oldest of the sisters. She had the prominent nose and full lips of her African ancestors. She wore her short kinky hair natural, framing her oval face. Desiree, like her sister, had beautiful almond shaped brown eyes. It was Desiree's duty to entertain Freaky Joe and Lewis. She would dance around the parlor with Freaky Joe and then Lewis. Patty and Joel would sit at the piano and play by ear popular songs of the day.

Joel wasn't as cute as his younger brother, Petey, but he was six feet one and built like a truck, all muscle and tough. He and Patty would slow dance around the parlor floor and hum their favorite Fats Waller tune, "Ain't Misbehavin," holding each other up after quenching their thirst with whatever was handy. Patty, at 28 was short, slight and the prettiest of the two sisters. She would run her fingers through Joel's curls and he'd grin sleepily and stare into her bedroom eyes. He loved the way her long frizzy hair moved whenever she turned her head to look up at him. At some point during the evening she'd take his hand and lead him to her bedroom off the kitchen.

Joel enjoyed a healthy sex life and he truly adored women. He could charm the panties off most of the women in town, black, white, married or single. Joel liked making love with Patty because she was generous with her body in bed. Her bedroom was always scented with fresh flowers and the sweet scent seemed to seep into her skin. The soft glow of the lighted candles shimmered on the walls as they undressed each other in anticipation of intense pleasures. Her bed, a beckoning rose garden of flowered sheets and plump pillows made him never want to leave it. Although she was 12 years his senior, he regarded her as an experienced teacher. He would be there in the morning for breakfast but Freaky Joe and Lewis would be long gone. Joel would have to walk along the main road and hitch a ride home.

When Joel and Patty disappeared from the parlor, Desiree took the children upstairs to their attic bedroom and tucked them in for the night. Afterward she would retire to her bedroom/workshop on the enclosed back porch where she kept her jars of dead garden snakes, dead toads, bird feathers, herbs and other secret ingredients she used in her magic concoctions. Many considered her a white witch as her potions and spells were always helpful and not considered evil.

Freaky Joe was called "Freaky" because he was a Negro albino and was cruelly teased by his friends. He had a bad habit of smelling his food before he ate it. Some people thought he had this distasteful habit because he did not see well due to poor eyesight. He did have poor eyesight but his smelling everything was just a nasty habit because the large eyeglasses he wore did improve his eyesight. Freaky Joe would follow Desiree out to the back porch and beg her for a potion or spell that would make him irresistible to the young ladies. This would make his friends laugh at him.

Lewis, a quiet, timid boy of average height, did not have any unique qualities to set him apart from his buddies, except his large head. His head was no larger than anyone else's, but it just looked that way because of its shape. He wore hats all the time, indoors and outdoors. He loved reading books, especially books about history. Lewis could hold anyone's interest with his knowledge of the past.

Still, no one was like Joel.

Joel, with his striped shirts, bright colored suspenders and creased dungarees, was now dead.

On a warm June evening in 1933 the Jackson sisters sat with Sax and Esther in their parlor and talked of Joel. Esther wept as Desiree and Patty spoke in soft voices, hugging her or rubbing her arm to bring comfort.

"He used to call me *Mother Dear*, you know. Not mama, like my other boys, but *Mother Dear*. He was such a sweet chile." Before long, Esther excused herself and retired to her bedroom, taking the gin with her. She sat peering into her dresser mirror. She undid the long black braid down her back and began to brush her hair. The mixed blood of her forebears showed in her face. The high cheekbones and the rosy glow of her complexion beheld some ancient birth of a tribe that roamed the plains a long time ago.

The tears started to flow. She left the mirror and lay on her bed. The sadness took over her body and the sobs exploded in her chest. A half hour later she slept.

Sax, now the host, offered the Jackson women some of the food sent over by Miss Olivia but the sisters declined, indicating they wanted to get back home before dark.

The Negro community in Horace Graves and many of the whites were enraged and horrified by the circumstances surrounding Joel's death. Everyone was aware of the brutal beating of the boy. All knew of the hangings and general mistreatment of the Negro men living in the area.

Reverend Beaumont, along with other Negro ministers went to see Sheriff Al Richards over in Bison, the county seat. They confronted the Sheriff with a list of injustices inflicted upon the Negroes in the county and demanded that he initiate inquiries and arrests. They were tired of the white man's laws that only applied to Negroes, and tired of the mistreatment and the killing of their youth. Sheriff Richards thought the men insolent and aggressive. However, he informed them that he was keenly aware of their plight and that he was doing the best he could at the time with such a limited police force.

"I have contacted those in charge in Montgomery about the situation in the county and especially in Horace Graves. They have assured me that they are doing everything possible to send me some help to find the person or persons guilty of these crimes."

The men knew they were being patronized but they listened in earnest at what the Sheriff had to say.

One thing the Sheriff said stuck with them.

His last remark was, "I have to let you men know that you cannot come to me in a group like this unless you are personally invited by me or someone of authority in this office. Let one of you be the spokesperson and I will communicate with that elected person. Please do not come to Bison to see me unless I ask you to. My first priority is to maintain order at all cost and I think you men get my meaning."

It was time to go over the Sheriff's head. Some of the Negro ministers in the town, including Reverend Beaumont, wrote letters to law enforcement agencies in Washington, D.C. Ultimately, they received the same old "Be patient, somebody's working on it," statement that was written or said in so many different ways but always meant the same thing.

Sax never told anyone else in town that Petey had witnessed the murder of his brother. Besides Esther and Petey, only Sheriff Richards and Deputy Cox knew about Petey witnessing Joel's murder. Even after Petey's statement in the shed the morning of Joel's death, Sheriff Richards gave Sax no indication that he would arrest Calvin and Haley Lucas. Sax told the Sheriff that he did not want Petey involved in the arrest and conviction of the Lucas boys. The Sheriff told Sax that without Petey's testimony, there was not enough evidence to bring the Lucas brothers to justice unless he caught them in the act of another killing. He indicated that his hands were tied because Sax refused to let Petey get involved and wanted Petey's name kept out of any proceedings that would follow. Sax knew he had to keep Petey out of it to keep him safe. It was a no-win situation for him. Bringing Joel's killers to justice could mean the death of Petey. If the Lucas boys didn't get to him first the hate group would.

The Sheriff, along with other whites in the county, had liked Joel. He was always polite and soft spoken. Jonas Batty trusted Joel enough to let him work in his general store on Main Street. Joel had gone as far as the eighth grade in his education. He had dreams of becoming a ball player and being accepted into the Negro League. Joel decided to work at Batty's store until he could think of a plan for his life. Working there was not a waste of time because the money helped Esther maintain the house, especially during the times Sax couldn't find work.

The work at the store was strenuous, involving the lifting of heavy sacks of feed, sugar and flour among other things. Some of the sacks weighed 50 pounds or more. When the stacking was completed, Joel was expected to sweep the floor, stock shelves with goods, and in general, keep the store clean. The work

Madeline L. Nowlin

was hard but he enjoyed it. It filled out his six foot plus frame and the young ladies approached him, "just to feel those muscles."

"The Pointer," the county newspaper, printed a short obituary a few days after Joel's burial. It read as follows, "Joel Nathaniel Creek, a Negro male, died on June 3rd at the age of 16. He was buried on June 5th." Nothing else had been added to the two sentences.

Sax stopped looking for someone to do the right thing. It took him two years to come up with a plan of his own.

Watermelon Road
Chapter 3
Daddy's Gift

"Where you been, boy? You been around that crazy Petey again? You know I don't want you hanging around him. There's something wrong with that chile, always rubbing stuff between his hands."

"We jest been playin' in the woods. That's all. Petey ain't crazy none either." Jesse corrected his mother.

"Hey, don't you be talking back to me, you hear? I'll whip your behind so you cain't sit down for a week. Then I'll turn you over to your daddy."

"I'm sorry, mama. I ain't mean nothin' by it. Uncle Sax had a gig over in Bakerstown, so me and Petey stayed near the house to keep an eye on Miss Esther and Peewee."

"Oh, that po' woman. Lawd only knows what Miss Esther has been through, losing a chile like that. I believe that's why Esther drinks so much and Petey's so messed up in the head. You be careful, baby, cause' you my only chile. I don't want to wake up one morning and find your head bashed in or you hanging from no tree. You hear me?"

Lily noticed the blood stain on Jesse's shirt.

"Lawd Jesse, what happened to you?"

"Me and Petey was rolling in the grass and I rolled over a broken bottle. Ain't nothin' but a scratch. See?"

Lily looked at the small cut and decided it wasn't serious.

"What's for dinner? Is it ready?"

Swinging her son's hurt arm, Lily said "You is just like your daddy, only interested in your stomach."

Lily Hammond, wife and mother, was treated with respect among the residents of Horace Graves. You could always count on her willingness to help wherever needed. She was easy to confide in and knew not to judge or give unsolicited advice. Mrs. Bertie Philips, who lived across the street with her husband, Bumpy, and eight children, often depended on Lily to babysit. Sometimes, but not often, Mrs. Bertie asked the Hammonds for financial help when Bumpy was laid off or laid up. Bumpy was the town drunk.

When inspired, Lily sewed beautiful outfits for the women in Horace

Graves. Even Marie, the white lady who owned Marie's Dress Shop on Main Street, bought several of Lily's creations to wear and to sell in her store. Lily was commissioned several times a year to make dresses for Lydia Beaumont and her daughter, Mimi. Twice, Lydia had asked Lily to make matching mother and daughter dresses for herself and Mimi. Mimi disliked dressing like her mother. She had her own unique style of dressing. Sewing clothes for the pastor's wife and daughter resulted in Lily getting more sewing work from the church congregation. Lily loved sewing dresses for Mimi. She didn't have a daughter and wanted to make pretty things for a girl. Jesse had a crush on Mimi, and was always home when he knew Mimi was coming over for a fitting.

Francis, the patriarch of the Hammond household, was a proficient carpenter. He found lucrative work in Horace Graves and the surrounding counties. Like Sax and other Negro men in the area, he worked in the lumber mills down river when things were slow. At present, he worked at a large salvage yard two miles outside of town. Tim West and his son, Bobby, were the owners of the salvage yard. Francis repaired items for resale by Mr. West. Bobby kept the books and showed up for work on occasion. Mr. West had a daughter, Margaret, who was a single mother with three children. Sometimes Margaret would come by the junkyard and bring her father lunch. She took care of her father and brother after her mother died of a stroke a few years back. Tim doted on his grandchildren. His son-in-law ran off with a waitress who worked at a beer joint in town and left Tim's daughter to care for her three children by herself. Although he had the two grandsons, he doted on his granddaughter, Suzy. She could wrap her grandfather around her little finger.

Francis enjoyed his work at the yard. What he liked most about his job was the fact that Mr. West treated him with respect and never hesitated to ask his opinion on what to do with the items that were brought into the yard. The pay was sufficient to support his family. They were able to put away the money Lily made from her sewing.

"Go on Rufus, go pick up the stick," Jesse prodded his dog. He'd been unsuccessful at teaching Rufus to play fetch. Rufus, a hybrid of a cocker spaniel and some inconspicuous stray mutt was found roaming the junkyard by Francis and given to Jesse as a birthday present a year ago last March. Rufus looked somewhat like a cocker spaniel with tan and black markings. He was short and furry and very pleasant around children.

Jesse's father appeared in the front yard.

"You cain't teach that old dog nothin."

"Daddy!" Jesse hugged his father. "You bring me something from the yard?"

"Just this." Francis held out a pocket knife he found that morning in a bucket of items Mr. West purchased from an estate sale. He tried each day to bring Jesse a little surprise from the discarded items at the yard.

"Here, take it. Mr. West gave it to me 'cause I did a good job repairing some chairs. He sold them chairs for a good price."

He handed his son a pocket knife with a four-inch blade, encased in a handle covered in treated rattlesnake skin. The blade was an inch across its widest

Watermelon Road

point at the beginning and tapered to a thin sharp point at the top. The black and brown marking of the rattlesnake skin was stretched over the handle of the knife. At the end of the handle was a small replica of a snake's head with a black glass eye on each side of the head.

"Wow! You ain't bring me nothin' this good before. I thank you, daddy."

Jesse danced around the front yard. Their one story house was rented from Jonas Batty, who owned several houses in town besides his store. The small house sat back from the road on Lawrence Street, a half-mile from Main Street. Francis kept the house in good condition. Lily made the grounds beautiful with plants and flower seeds she purchased from Mr. Batty's General Store. The Hammonds were proud of having their own place.

"Look at this knife, Rufus. Now we got to find some wood to carve up." Jesse called to his dog.

"You be real careful with that knife, Jesse. Don't lend it to nobody," said Francis. " I'm only giving it to you 'cause you might learn to carve something with it. If you get good at it, you might take some of your pieces down to Mr. Batty for him to sell for you." Francis hoped the knife would help Jesse learn to carve wood and thereby make him want to become a carpenter like his daddy, provided Jesse didn't become a great baseball player.

"Don't let your mother see that pocket knife for awhile. And, don't go doing something stupid with it and hurt yourself."

"Yes sir. Ain't nobody gonna touch my knife," Jesse promised his father.

Lily yelled from the front steps of the house, "You boys come on in for dinner. I fixed smothered pork chops, mashed potatoes, peas and rice and poke salad. Don't forget to wash up."

At the kitchen table, the family held hands and Lily said grace.

"Honey, where's the cornbread?" Francis inquired after looking over the table and finding the cornbread missing.

"It's still on the stove, be ready in a few," Lily said as she fixed Jesse's plate.

Jesse was pointing to every dish on the table so his mother could put a portion of each on his plate.

Francis protested. "Stop that. That's why this boy is so big now. You feed him too much and he eats too much."

"Oh, let the boy eat. The way he and Petey run around town, he's bound to work it off later." Lily was perplexed by Francis's growing concern over his son's weight problem. He had dreams of Jesse playing professional baseball one day and she did not want him to pressure Jesse into that kind of career. At present, Lily had no inkling as to the form of greatness her son's life would take once he was grown. She did know it wasn't going to be in baseball.

Lily placed her hands on her hips and stared at her husband. "I guess you think I'm too big too?"

"Woman, you know you ain't ever gonna get too big for me to stop reaching for you at night. Don't you know that?" Francis winked at his wife. He watched her pretty round face as she gathered up a fork full of poke salad. He had loved that face dearly for the past twelve years. When he said the words,

Madeline L. Nowlin

"Until death do us part," he meant it. Francis reached over and touched his wife's cheek. It was warm to the touch. Her dark brown eyes and dimpled cheeks caused his heart to flutter.

Francis was of average height but well built because the carpentry work kept him in shape. He was not handsome but had a kind face and smiled easily.

He first met Lily when he traveled from Atlanta to Charleston, South Carolina with his aunt to visit distant relatives. Francis's mother died giving birth to him, and Francis senior, unable to cope, gave the newborn to his married sister to bring up. Aunt Rose did the best she could to raise him along with three daughters of her own. Her husband, Arthur, was a gifted carpenter by trade and taught Francis everything he knew about carpentry.

Francis was 19 when he first saw Lily. His cousin, Stewart, lived next door to the Green's and he watched from an upstairs window as the short woman, with the big butt, hung clothes on the line in her backyard. He was introduced to her that evening when his cousin had a get-together in the backyard and invited Lily Green, her parents and two younger brothers over for fried chicken and potato salad. It was August and the breezes were soft like distant music and the fireflies were lighting up the sky. They were married two years later and settled in Alabama because he wanted to be near the lumber mills. Carpentry work was good in the areas around the mills. He was 21 and she was 23.

Jesse stopped eating and watched his parents in anticipation of hearing something he shouldn't in their otherwise boring conversation.

"What you looking at boy?"

"Nothin' daddy. I was just thinking 'bout my knife."

"What knife?" Lily asked, looking concerned.

Francis gave Jesse a stern look.

"I said what knife?"

Jesse showed it to her. She looked at her husband with an angry expression and shook her head.

"We gonna talk about this gift after dinner," Lily declared.

"Let's finish eating and get this kitchen cleaned up, we got church tomorrow," Lily ordered as she started clearing the table. "I have to make fruit pies for the church picnic."

"You're right, we're having a picnic right after the service out on the church lawn. Jesse can get in on the baseball game," added Francis.

I hate running around them bases in the hot sun. All I want to do is be with Petey and show him my knife. I can't wait to see his face when I shows it to him. Jesse kept his thoughts to himself.

Lily got busy making pies and forgot about the knife.

That night, Jesse sat up in bed in his room. He turned on the night table lamp and took the knife out from under his pillow. He pulled the blade out and pushed it back into the snakeskin handle several times. He touched the eyes on each side of the snake's head. *This is the best surprise I ever got. Petey's gonna be so jealous of me. I can't wait to show it to him. I'll let him keep it for a day or two if he wants to. He's my best buddy and we share everything.*

Watermelon Road
Chapter 4
My Brother's Keeper

Petey brought Peewee to the front steps of the church.
"You go in afore you late for Sunday school. I be waitin' when you come out. You better be good 'cause I can see you through the window and I be watching." He was already mad at Peewee for wetting the bed last night. He would have to go home later and change Peewee's bed.

Peewee ran up the front steps and went into his Sunday school class. Today, they were holding Sunday school classes in the sanctuary. Lydia Beaumont was their Sunday school teacher as well as their public school teacher during the week. Sunday and regular school were usually held in the church's basement. Often, in good weather, Mrs. Beaumont held classes on the veranda of the parish house but it was too warm to hold the classes there this Sunday. Sunday school was for one hour starting at 9:00 a.m. Worship service began promptly at 10:00 a.m. If a worshiper strolled in a little after Sunday services started, Reverend Beaumont would embarrass the tardy person or persons by stopping the worship service and inviting them to take a seat. The congregation made it a point to be seated before 10:00 on Sunday mornings.

The Reverend didn't look like a preacher, but he was, and walked around in preacher mode all the time. He wasn't tall but appeared taller when standing in the pulpit on Sunday mornings, preaching fire and brimstone. He was of medium complexion with smooth skin and a thin mustache above his top lip. His black hair was brushed neatly against his head. Women adored Reverend Beaumont. He treated them with respect and was willing to listen to their complaints about their relationships and their troubles at home. Men seldom made eye contact with him because they felt he was always looking for some sinful secret no one else could see in their eyes. The men sat in the hot sanctuary on Sunday mornings so they could later enjoy peace and quiet the rest of the day with a newspaper and a baseball game on the radio.

Reverend Xavier Beaumont was passionate about his religion and no one wanted to start up a conversation with him if they ran into him outside of church. He always had a sermon ready. His father, a Creole from New Orleans, Louisiana married his mother, a Negro woman from the Caribbean islands. They

Madeline L. Nowlin

both loved to cook and opened a café called "The Shrimp and Grits Café" in New Orleans. They had three sons, Charles Junior, Ramón and Xavier. Xavier was the youngest. Neither parent was well educated but they made sure their boys had a good education. They were overjoyed when Xavier chose to attend a divinity school established by a group of ordained ministers not far from home. His parents, both Catholics, did not discourage him from becoming a Baptist minister, which was Xavier's wish. His father managed the business side of the café and Viviane, his mother, did the cooking and managed the day-to-day chores of running an eatery. Charles Junior worked with his parents in the café and later opened his own restaurant in New Orleans. Ramón also stayed in New Orleans and became a schoolteacher.

Reverend Beaumont met Lydia while visiting Ramón at his teaching school, Teachers Union College, established ten years earlier by Negro businessmen. The college was 20 miles outside of New Orleans. Lydia was there working on her teaching degree. Ramón was a member of her study group and he introduced Xavier and Lydia to each other. The two became friends first and it later developed into a relationship. They were married right after Lydia graduated and moved to Alabama where the newly ordained Reverend answered a call to become the pastor of "Upon This Rock Baptist Church."

Petey stood in a clump of trees near the church smoking one of Sax's Camels. As soon as Sunday school was over, he'd take Peewee home and bring him back later for the picnic after the worship service. He leaned against a tree and winced. His back was still sore from Old Man Miller's whip and from the whipping Esther had given him when he returned home yesterday after eating watermelon with Jesse in the woods. Esther had gone into a drunken rage and whipped him with one of her clotheslines when he didn't move fast enough after she told him to sweep the kitchen floor. Sax tried to stop her, but she turned on him, striking him across the face with the strong hemp. Sax calmed her down and helped her upstairs to sleep it off. She never hit Peewee, only Petey. He never cried or tried to run when she beat him. He knew she was still angry about Joel's death and blamed him for not saving Joel or running for help. Esther never said it, but he knew how she felt.

Esther and Sax never bothered with church. Neither cared much about religion. Esther hated God because he took Amos and Joel. Sax never gave God much thought, period. Petey liked to take Peewee to Sunday school because Peewee wanted to go. The church served the children a light breakfast before their Sunday classes, so Peewee got fed. He also liked the planned activities. Peewee loved to draw and color pictures. In Sunday school, he was given a picture of Jesus or a scene with animals in it from Mrs. Beaumont, and two pieces of crayon to use for coloring. Peewee drew pictures on any paper he could find around the house. He amused himself on rainy days by coloring the characters in the funny pages of the newspaper that Sax brought home. His masterpieces were tacked to the wall above his bed. The pictures he colored of Jesus Christ hung on the wall over Joel's bed, where Petey now slept. Petey didn't mind.

Watermelon Road

Through the opened church window, Petey heard the children singing and clapping their hands as they sang a song about Jesus loving them.

That made him laugh.

Watermelon Road
Chapter 5
The Church Picnic

"What you doing out here?"
Startled, Petey jumped when he heard Mimi's voice. "I'm jest waiting for my little brother."

He hated for anyone to sneak up on him like that. Mimi Beaumont was very good at it. He looked at the young girl's face. He could see why Jesse was so enamored of her loveliness. She was not pretty in the usual sense but more striking like. Her dark, flawless skin glowed as if fire was underneath it. At twelve, Mimi was well on her way to becoming a beautiful and elegant young lady. Her features were a composite of both her parents, taking the very best from each. She had long straight hair and the finer features of her father, sharing her mother's radiant darker complexion and build. She came with her own unique personality and mannerisms. Petey admired her because even though she wore frilly dresses, she was like him and didn't take no shit. She was tough and always spoke her mind to adults and children no matter what the consequences. Mimi was not a prim preacher's daughter, she had had a few fist fights with other girls in the church's schoolyard.

Mimi wore dresses, pretty ones, every day no matter what the occasion. She kept her hair in a ponytail, pulled back and tied with a colorful laced ribbon to match the dress she was wearing at the time. Some hair was left in front to form bangs down to her eyebrows.

Mimi had a crush on Petey.

Finding him in the church yard on her way to Sunday School, Mimi could not resist speaking to Petey. She ran her fingers through her bangs and batted her eyes at him. Petey was immune to her seductive behavior, except for her smile. Mimi's smile was what caused little stirrings in Petey and heart palpitations in Jesse and the other boys. Her smile was a treat, all straight white teeth and pink gums. He knew of no one else in Horace Graves who could produce such a smile.

As far as Petey could tell, Mimi had one or two big problems, depending on how you looked at it. She had identical twin brothers, Jimmy and Danny, and most of the time they were attached to her hip. The boys were seven years old,

Watermelon Road

the same age as Peewee but bad to the bone. They were standing on each side of Mimi that morning as she stood talking to Petey. He couldn't ever remember seeing her without the boys. She had taken charge of them from the time they could walk even though she was a young child of five when the boys were born. They had been her real life dolls. Looking down at the boys, Petey remembered some of the remarks about the twins he had overheard around town. "Chile it makes you wonder don't it? With a father for a minister, you'd think them boys were better behaved than what they is."

"Let me have a toke," said Mimi, pointing to Petey's cigarette he had between his fingers.

Petey took another drag on it and then handed it to her.

"Here, keep it."

"I'm gonna tell daddy," said Danny.

"If you do, I'll pinch you so hard you'll bleed," said Mimi.

With that threat in mind, Danny decided to take his anger out on Petey so he kicked him on his right shin. Not wanting to be outdone, Jimmy kicked Petey on his left shin. They were wearing their hard leather Sunday go to church dress up shoes.

"Ouch, dammit," Petey yelled. He bent over to feel his shins and the two boys slapped him on the top of his head. Petey was trying to hold his head and his shins while jumping around in pain. Mimi and the boys laughed as they ran towards the church. She looked back at Petey and bestowed on him that wonderful smile and blew him a kiss.

After worship service was over, some of the men carried the long tables, normally used for school desks, out to the lawn for the picnic. Petey and Jesse helped Sax and Francis bring out some of the tables. The ladies, including Lily and Mrs. Bertie, helped place a crisp white tablecloth over each table along with stacks of plates, cups and utensils. Choir members set out large jugs of sweet tea, lemonade and cold well water in the center of each table. Chairs were placed under tables and some were put under shady trees for sitting, eating and good conversation. Fellowship was the purpose of the day. School would be closed on the coming Friday, May 31, and the congregation always held a picnic around this time of year before children were farmed out to relatives up north or further south for the summer months.

Sax showed up to initiate a baseball game, which was as close as he ever got to the church building. Reverend Beaumont had helpers bring out the baseball equipment and before you knew it, everyone was cheering on some catcher, pitcher or batter who was out on the field. Bets were placed all around and Sax was in his glory.

The lumbering ice wagon turned into the churchyard. There was an old horse trough on the church grounds that had been cleaned out so that huge blocks of ice could be put into it. After three large blocks of ice were deposited in the trough, men pulled out hammers and ice picks to break up the ice into smaller chunks. Jesse and Petey watched the men chip away for awhile. Because children were not allowed to take part in the ice crushing, the two boys went off to find their own amusement. Jesse touched his pants pocket to make sure he had his pocket knife. He would show it to Petey when the time was right. He wanted to make sure he showed his friend the knife while his parents were not around.

Once the ice was chipped into smaller pieces, half the trough was filled with bottles of assorted soda pop and the other half with tubs of homemade peach ice cream. The sodas and ice cream would be sold, along with fresh slices of homemade apple, cherry and blueberry pies. The quarter donations would go toward school supplies for the next school year.

Petey heard screaming coming from behind the church and ran over to see what was going on. Danny and Jimmy had found two empty soda bottles and filled them with water. They were shaking the water from the bottles onto Peewee as he ran around the yard. Peewee was soaked. Mimi got to the twins at the same time Petey did. She took the bottles from her brothers and they ran and hid from her. Peewee was crying and shivering.

Petey said to Mimi "I gots to take him home for a change of clothes. The ladies ain't got all the food out on the tables yet, so I got time to go home and bring Peewee back."

"I'll walk with you," Mimi offered.

"Me too," mumbled Jesse, breathing heavily after catching up to Petey. He kept staring dumbfounded at Mimi. She was dressed in a short-sleeved summer dress with tiny white daisies printed over the entire dress. A red belt cinched her small waist. A red lace ribbon was tied around her ponytail. Her nails were painted red.

Petey and Mimi burst out laughing at Jesse because his eyes were bugging and he was working his mouth like a fish.

"Why don't you take a picture, it will last longer," said Mimi.

Jesse looked away and walked on ahead with Peewee.

She don't know it but I'm gonna marry her someday. He thought.

"Why don't you ask my daddy if you and Jesse can come with me to Grandmother Mimi's when I go up to Baltimore after school closes?" Mimi asked Petey.

"You mean ride the bus up north with you and your father?" Petey asked, trying to keep the excitement out of his voice.

"If you really want to come, I can ask my daddy for you, and he can talk to your folks and Jesse's folks. Daddy takes us children up to Grandmother's every summer. He stays for a few days and heads home again so you boys can ride back with him too. He'll tell your parents that it's only for a few days, not the whole summer. Daddy comes back to get us in August. Grandmother Mimi has a big house on Bottom Street with plenty of room for company. Mimi leaned into Petey and whispered "Daddy said she bought that big house with the numbers money."

"I knows 'bout them numbers. My mama and Uncle Sax always give Slew Foot money when he comes by and he writes their numbers down in his book."

Jesse looked back at the two children whispering. His face felt hot. He wanted to punch Petey in the face. *"Since he wants to be a lover boy, I'm not*

Watermelon Road

showing him my surprise."

Petey looked over at Mimi and asked "How come your grandmother got the same name as you got?"

"That's cause my mama wanted me named after her mama," replied Mimi.

When they reached the house, Peewee ran in to change his clothes. The children sat on the front steps and waited. A sober Esther came to the front door and asked why they were there instead of at the picnic. Petey explained everything and she went back inside and closed the door.

Petey and Mimi told Jesse about their plan to have Petey and Jesse ride up to Baltimore with Reverend Beaumont. Jesse was all for it and showed unabashed excitement at taking a trip with his best friend. He tried to skip all the way back to the church which caused Petey, Mimi and Peewee to laugh because Jesse couldn't do it properly. He didn't care. He had the best gift in the world in his pocket and he would be taking a trip with his best friend and the girl he loved.

The children were happy to see that the tables were laden with every dish they could ever want, all made from scratch. Fried, baked, grilled, and smothered meats had been placed in large wooden platters on every table along with casseroles, and fried and sautéed vegetables. The smell of fresh baked breads from the parish next to the church filled the air and sailed like a food cloud over the town. That smell always made some of the white folks in town drop by for a plate. They offered to pay but were given the food freely and with love.

Lydia and Mimi brought forth trays of cakes and baked cookies and placed them on the dessert table along with Lily's pies. The congregation held hands while Reverend Beaumont delivered the prayer and unity grace over the food. After that, everyone filled their plates and looked for a cool place to sit and eat.

Peewee, Danny and Jimmy ate at a table across the yard from their older siblings. Children closer to their age were also seated at the table. The grandmothers in the congregation watched over them to make sure there was no fighting or throwing of food. Mimi found a shady spot under a large pine tree and spread a blanket under it. Petey and Jesse joined her. They spent a good deal of time watching Jesse eat. Jesse exhibited no shyness then. He ate like it was his last meal. Everyone did.

While they were eating, Petey and Jesse heard a familiar sound. It was old Mr. Miller's horse cart coming up the road towards the church. Mr. Miller knew about the picnic and took advantage of the occasion to sell his fruit. He stopped the horse in front of the church and called to the congregation to come over to the cart. Some of the people walked over to look at the melons, which would be good eating for the picnic.

Jesse and Petey took off running with their plates in hand and hid underneath one of the covered picnic tables. Mimi, taken by surprise, assumed it was some stupid game the boys were playing. Unfortunately, Jimmy and Danny saw the boys hide under the table. They followed Petey and Jesse. Each twin took a part of the tablecloth and raised it so everyone at the picnic could see under the table. Petey and Jesse ran to another table further back. The twins followed and held up that tablecloth. They ran again and the twins followed. Everyone was laughing by now, but, Mr. Miller was so busy selling his fruit he never noticed the two melon thieves.

They went back to sit with Mimi once Mr. Miller left the church yard. Feeling this was an opportunity to impress both Petey and Mimi, Jesse decided to show the two of them the pocket knife. His parents were occupied elsewhere. He removed the gift his father gave him from his pocket. "Looka here," he whispered. He showed both of them the pocket knife and made them swear never to let on that he had brought it to the picnic. They both swore. The look on Petey's face when Jesse handed him the beautiful pocket knife surpassed the reaction Jesse had expected.

"Wow! Man oh man." exclaimed Petey. Petey fondled the knife. He kept turning it over and over, opening and closing it, running his fingers over the snakeskin and touching the snake's eyes.

Jesse was pleased. Mimi could have cared less. She wanted to put her arms around Petey and kiss him on the mouth like they did in those romance novels her mother kept under her bed. She sat with her dress spread out over her legs, showing her shins with the pretty lace top stockings she wore with her white Sunday shoes. Neither boy noticed.

A reluctant Petey returned the knife. Just then Sax and Francis called out to them to come play ball. Jesse put the pocket knife back in his pocket. They left Mimi sitting alone.

"Boys," she thought as she went in search of the twins.

The boys joined Sax's baseball team. To Jesse's dismay, some of the children from the other team called out "Run Fatback Blackjack" whenever he ran the bases in the game. When it was Petey's turn, he punched each boy on the arm, who was on the other team, with his fist whenever he got a chance to run bases. He knocked the boy guarding second base to the ground. That stopped the teasing, although the parents of the other team members were angered by Petey's behavior and wanted him off the team. Sax told the parents to take their wimpy children off the team because Petey wasn't going anywhere. Petey was almost as good as Joel when it came to batting. Because of the heat, the players grew tired after five innings and Sax's team was declared the winners. Petey and Jesse retreated to the pine tree they had shared with Mimi to cool off. Mimi and the blanket were gone.

Sax was full of himself. He sat with a group of men at one of the tables. Junior Rocket, nicknamed after his daddy, who could run any race on foot and win, and Earl were sitting with Sax. Joel's old friends, Freaky Joe and Lewis were also at the table. They were talking jive and playing "top this" with stories that no one at the table believed. Every now and then Reverend Beaumont would come by the table and they would nod at him and tip their hats. They hid the betting from the Reverend. Sax had done well betting on his own team. He gave Petey and Jesse two quarters each to buy soda pop and ice cream. After the boys left the table, Sax reminded his two friends about the promise they made to him two years ago. He then related his promise to Freaky Joe and Lewis and invited their help in killing the members of the Lucas family. He told them that his plan involved killing the Lucas boys first, and after that incident died down "Miss Whoring Mirabelle" and her daddy were next.

"There ain't been no hangings in awhile," said Junior Rocket.

"That's 'cause them Lucas boys done found something else to do with their spare time. They been going out of town a lot, so maybe they been doing hangings in other places," Sax remarked.

"Maybe they done stopped," put in Lewis.

"Ya'll backing out on me? If they don't show up here soon, I plan to hunt them down and I thought you so-called men were in this with me. After all, didn't they kill some of your kin? Didn't you come up on your cousin hanging from a tree branch not a month after Joel was murdered, Freaky Joe? What's the matter, now? Speak up. You know who done them killings. You all owe it to Joel to help me."

Earl looked around the table and said "Sax, don't be getting mad at everybody. We ain't going after these white boys. We all sorry 'bout Joel and our kin but we got other people depending on us just like you got Esther and the boys. We don't want to end up gittin' strung up like them others. We don't want to end up in jail either."

"If the town found out we hurt them white boys, they will kill us and the rest of our kin and maybe some other innocent folks in this town," Lewis spoke with authority.

"Well now, Lewis. That's the most I ever heard you say. I guess you speaking for the others. Even so, this ain't gonna stop me. A promise is a promise and I'm gonna get my revenge with or without you." Sax put on his baseball cap and walked away from the table.

After Sax left, Earl said "I seen them Lucas brothers the other night going into Batty's store with some boxes in their arms. The boxes looked heavy too."

Junior Rocket said "They probably stealing stuff and selling it to Jonas Batty. I'm sure those two got something dishonest going on. Either way, I ain't getting myself in trouble 'cause Sax wants revenge. It's been over two years now. I thought he'd forget about that promise." The others at the table nodded in agreement.

Freaky Joe said "Man that Lydia Beaumont is a cool chic. Look at that behind in that tight skirt." They all laughed and soon forgot about Sax and his revenge.

Petey bought a soda for himself and ice cream for Peewee. Jesse bought a soda, and a slice of blueberry pie.

While they were eating, Sissy, one of Mrs. Bertie's girls walked by holding hands with a little white girl about eight years old. The white girl was an unattractive child. Everything about her face seemed askew. Her eyes were close together with droopy lids. Her nose had a bump and leaned a little to the left. She had a funny way of moving her mouth to the left when she spoke as she was doing now with Sissy. The little girl kept reaching into her dress pocket and taking something out and looking at it and then putting it away again.

Madeline L. Nowlin

"Who's that with Sissy Philips? Petey asked Jesse. "What she doing bringing that scrawny little white girl to the church picnic? Must be another one of them white children her mama keep. Mrs. Bertie ain't nothin' but a mammy. Cooking, cleaning and babysitting for them white folks. I bet that chile's family ain't no better off than Mrs. Bertie and she got eight cheerin. She look like po' white trash to me with that mousy brown stringy hair. Eyes so close together they look like they looking at each other."

Jesse laughed at Petey's comments about the little girl. However, he was surprised at his friend's annoyance over the girl's attendance at the picnic – a child he would never have noticed if it were not for Petey's unkind comments.

"Oh she just some chile Mrs. Bertie keeps while her mama works over in Bakerstown. I know her name is Suzy cause Mrs. Bertie asked my mama to watch her once when she had to take one of her cheerin to the clinic. Ain't no cause to worry 'bout that mousy little thing," Jesse assured Petey.

"What's that she keeps taking out of her pocket and looking at," Petey asked.

"She likes little turtles and her mama brought her one she found outside that restaurant she works at. She carry it with her all the time. An ugly little thing," Jesse said shaking his shoulders, not liking turtles himself.

Something shifted in Petey. Something deep inside moved. The thing tried to fight its way up out of the darkness in the pit of his stomach but he wouldn't let it. He fought it and got control. He got up to look for something to rub between his hands. He found a brown paper sack near one of the tables and tore it into strips. He then rolled pieces of the paper sack between his palms. He sat back down near Jesse. Petey became so quiet that Jesse thought he might go dark. He didn't want Petey to go dark, especially right there in front of everyone at the picnic, even though most of the Negroes in town knew about Petey's mood swings. Sometimes Jesse was embarrassed because his friend was different. He put his hands on Petey's shoulders and shook him. It worked. Petey came out of that dark place he was slipping into and smiled at Jesse.

"I'm all right. I jest got dizzy for a minute. I'm gonna get Peewee and go home. I'll see you later."

Watermelon Road
Chapter 6
The Promise

During school the next day, Jesse and Petey decided to meet in their secret hole in the woods right after school. Petey thought it was time to tell Jesse about the promise he had mentioned the last time he told the story.

I got to our secret place first. I tried to climb the cypress tree we always sit under so's I could surprise Petey when he showed. Maybe make a loud fart and scare the mess out of him. I tried to climb the dumb tree but my shoes keep sliding.

I got tired of waitin' for Petey at school 'cause he stayed to do a favor for Mrs. Beaumont. Mimi was hanging around, too. I hope he don't bring Mimi with him. We showed her our secret spot once and she talked the whole time 'bout how dirty it was and she ain't have no place to sit. Petey tried to get her to take her dress off so's she could swim with us in the creek. She run off screaming something 'bout boys being stupid and some other names she called us. I can't remember none of them names right now but it'll come to me directly.

I ain't hear nothin' else 'bout us going up to Baltimore. I know Mimi's daddy better ask my daddy soon.

I walked over to the creek and looked down. Some of them little fishes was swimming around and then a big fish come along and ate them. That was fun to watch.

Frogs started making croaking noises. Petey and me measured the creek once after it rained. It was over seven feet deep. The water is calm today. It can get real rough when it rains. I took my shoes off and sat on the edge of the grass and put my feet in the water. It felt good. Once I seed a snake in the water.

Directly, Petey come down the path whistling that stupid song Joel used to whistle. I got up to look for some stones to throw in the water. He sees me and comes down to where I'm at.

He says, "Hey, Shade."

Then he picks up some stones and starts throwing too. We got tired of that after awhile so we sit down and put our feet in the water. Then Petey told me 'bout the promise.

"One night after Joel's funeral, I comes downstairs for a drink of water. It was after midnight and I don't expect nobody to be in the kitchen. I hear voices when I reach the bottom of the stairs so I stop and listen. I hear Uncle Sax talking. I think he was talking to Junior Rocket and Earl 'cause Earl spoke once and I know his voice. Uncle Sax said he had a plan to get revenge on the Lucas family. He told them that he was going to wait a couple of years 'til everybody forgot 'bout Joel being murdered and he was going to kill the whole family. He asked Junior Rocket and Earl to make him a promise that they would help. They promised they would."

Jesse thought, *I got nervous when I heard Uncle Sax's promise 'cause I didn't want nothin' like that in my head.*

I says to Petey, "They's all still living. The Lucas family is still alive. It's been two years since Joel's been gone."

"Yeah, but you know why I'm telling you 'bout the promise?" He asked me.

I stayed quiet 'cause I don't know why he told me 'bout the promise.

"I just want you to know my secret. If Uncle Sax don't do nothin' I'm gonna carry out the revenge all by myself. You can help if you wants to," Petey said.

"You know my mama and daddy would kill me if I hurt somebody. Ain't you afraid of Sheriff Richards? You know he got them dogs and they will hunt you down if you try to run. I ain't getting ate up by no dogs or shot down by no Sheriff. I sho' hope you don't do nothin' bad either. You need to make me a promise that you won't kill nobody. You jest let Uncle Sax take care of stuff like that," I begged him.

"Awe shucks, Nightshade, I'm just fooling with ya. I jest wanted to scare you, that's all. I ain't mean nothin by it. I'm only twelve years old, what can I do to hurt somebody? You believe everything I tell you. You ain't nothin' but a baby. That's all you is."

I got mad 'cause he called me a baby. I ain't like him right then. He put his hand on my shoulder and started laughing. I acted like everything was all right and I laughed, too. He was my best friend in the whole world.

"Let me see that pocket knife again."

I give it to him. Then he ask me if he can keep it for a couple of days. I told him my daddy told me not to let nobody touch that knife but me. He promised to bring it back in two days. I told him I wanted to carve something with it. I was gonna look in the woods for a good piece of driftwood that very day.

"I thought we was friends. You know I'd let you hold my knife for awhile if I had one."

I know he was telling the truth. He shares everything with me. I told him I had to hold on to the pocket knife for awhile longer just in case my daddy asked to see it. "I tell you what," I says to him, "I'll give you the pocket knife this Friday 'cause it's the last day of school. You can keep it for two days then I want it back. You got to promise me that you will give it back after them two days."

Petey promised.

Watermelon Road
Chapter 7
The Snake

"Come here gal, I want to talk to you 'bout something."

"My mama told me not to talk to no strange nigger boys. I don't know you. It's getting late and my mama told me to come straight home from Sissy's house after school. If I go this way I can get home faster. You get out of my way and let me pass. I don't want to be in these woods after dark," said Suzy.

"You know me. I ain't no stranger. You saw me at the church picnic last Sunday. I seed you with Sissy. I'm a friend of hers. My name is Petey. Your name is Suzy. Today was the last day of school for us Negro cheerin. Is today the last day for you white cheerin too?"

Suzy didn't answer but kept her head down and tried to get past Petey. He blocked her exit, making her stand before him. She wanted to turn and run back the way she had come but she was afraid he would catch her before she made it to the main road.

"Don't be scared of me. You still got that cute baby turtle in your dress pocket?" Petey asked politely, smiling down at her. Suzy looked up at him and searched his face, making sure that he was not some evil demon she might have seen in her dreams. She was used to Miss Bertie's children and trusted them.

"I don't remember you at the picnic."

"I seed you. You had on a blue dress and you had a little turtle in your pocket."

"Come on, let me show you something I caught in the creek a ways from here. It's just a little ways further into the woods," Petey said.

"What you want me to see, is it a turtle?" Suzy asked.

"Yeah, that's what it is. In fact I got a couple of them in a sack. It's just a little ways mo' to go."

Suzy followed Petey deeper into the woods.

"The sack is behind that big rock over there. You walk real soft so you won't scare them. Put your hand in the sack slow so they don't bite you."

Suzy hesitated. She looked back at Petey. He gave her his most brilliant smile and motioned for her to move on. Suzy started toward the large rock he had pointed out to her. She looked over the rock and saw a sack behind it. As warned by Petey, she put her hand slowly into the sack and retrieved a rock. Suzy was confused but she placed her hand into the sack again and came up with another rock.

"This bag is full of rocks," she said, still not getting the point that Petey had lied to her. While she was searching the sack for turtles, Petey stripped down to his bare feet to avoid getting blood on his clothes.

He came up behind Suzy and put his left hand over her mouth and nose and held her upper torso tight against him with his right hand and arm. He had Jesse's knife open with the blade snapped in place in his right hand. She was shorter and thinner than him. It was easy for him to lift her off the ground and drag her behind the rock. She fought him — hitting him in his groin with her fist and kicking backward at him. Her hands went to his face, trying to find his eyes. He went along with her struggling and tightened his hold on her. When he got control, he took the pocket knife blade and jammed it down between her neck and shoulder blade. No one heard her muffled cries. Blooded, weakened and in great pain, Suzy slid to the ground on her stomach with Petey on top of her. Losing strength, she struggled to breathe. Petey turned her over on her back. He took part of her dress and wiped the blood from his face. She stared up at him with dazed eyes. Her mouth worked but not a sound escaped. Suzy's body began to shake.

Petey gave the thing inside him permission to proceed. The voice in his head that mimicked the hissing of a snake was talking to him now. It was screaming Joel's name. "Joooeeel" it hissed. Petey knew the snake in his stomach and the pocket knife were one and the same. He began to stab Suzy's chest with such force that he pierced her heart and a lung. He stopped only because he was afraid he would break the blade of the pocket knife. When his anger abated the hissing stopped. Covered in blood, he pulled himself up in a sitting position and leaned against the rock.

He wept.

His body racked with sobs.

It began to rain. He stood in the rain until he was washed clean.

He covered her with leaves and got dressed.

It rained for three days.

Watermelon Road
Chapter 8
The Bus to Baltimore

Jesse felt the tight string that tied him to his mother weakening as he waved to her from the back of the truck. Lily, now dry eyed, waved her hanky at him and he missed her already. His parents had one of the worst arguments he had known them to have and it was about him going to Baltimore. Francis had won the argument by convincing his wife to "let the boy go." Lily knew he meant more than just letting Jesse go to Baltimore. Her son was growing up and sooner or later she would have to cut the apron strings. And now, in her 30's, she felt the longing to have more children, which was not possible. A year after Jesse was born she contracted an infection that spread through her uterus. She sought treatment. The medication cured the infection but left her sterile. She was only 25 at the time. Francis had helped her through that ordeal and he was with her now, his hand rubbing her back in comfort as they watched their only child go off on a new adventure. Jesse would be gone for only five and half days but it would be a lifetime to Lily.

It was 7:00 a.m. on June 3 and the windows were already open on the bus in speculation of a record-breaking hot day.

Jesse had a window seat with the Reverend sitting next to him. Danny and Jimmy sat in the two seats ahead of them. Petey and Mimi sat across the aisle from Jesse. Mimi had the window seat. It didn't matter to the children that they had to sit in the back of the bus in the last seats behind the rope. The engine at the front of the bus roared so loud that no one paid any attention to the children making noises in the back. They could yell at each other, play games and eat their lunch in peace without being scrutinized by the whites sitting up front. Only Reverend Beaumont was uneasy about having to sit in the back, which he overcame with humble prayer.

Jesse looked down at the box of food in his lap. His mother had packed a huge lunch for him. She filled the box with his favorite foods and extras in case the bus broke down or something went wrong to prolong their trip. He thought about the pail of potato salad, the chicken sandwiches, ham biscuits, hardboiled eggs and the thick slice of apple pie. Lily had also packed two small cakes, one sweet potato and the other apricot, for him to share with the Reverend and the children. He would have to pace himself and not eat everything all at once. He was still considering whether to tell the others about the cakes he had for them or eat them himself.

Reverend Beaumont had a large box of food items under his seat for all of them. Lydia had stayed up late the night before frying and baking some of their favorite foods for the long trip to Baltimore. Everyone shared their food with Petey who brought only a chicken sandwich in a greasy brown sack.

Petey had washed and packed his clothes, and was standing in front of the church when Junior Rocket and Earl came to pick up everyone for the 40-mile ride to the Travel Light bus station on the other side of Birmingham. Earl borrowed a truck from the lumber mill where he and Junior Rocket were employed at present. Francis squeezed into the cab part of the truck with the two men. Lily stayed behind with Lydia. She could not manage another goodbye to Jesse at the bus station. The children sat in the flat bed of the truck with the suitcases and bags. The Reverend sat with the children to keep an eye on the twins, since they might get busy and accidentally fall over the side. No one came to see Petey off.

Reverend Beaumont was lulled into dozing by the rhythm of the bus on the long stretch of highway. The children could no more go to sleep than if it were Christmas Eve. Jesse could overhear some bits of conversation between Mimi and Petey. Petey was telling her a funny story about Peewee that Jesse had never heard before. He started mimicking his friend by pretending he was talking to someone, gesticulating and faking laughter. Petey caught him in the act and glared at him. He turned his face to the window and chided himself for acting stupid and being jealous of Petey. Mimi liked Petey and there was nothing he could do about it. To quiet his rage, he had a mental picture in his mind of throwing his hard boiled eggs at Petey's head but that would have been a terrible waste of food. To make matters worse, the twins had noticed their father napping and were now looking over the backs of their seats, mouthing the words "Fatback Blackjack" at him.

Four hours later, they pulled off the highway into the first stopover in Atlanta where they would transfer to another bus going north. There was a diner near the small bus station where the passengers got snacks and used the public bathroom. The diner and the bathrooms were off limits to Negroes so the Reverend, boys and Mimi went behind the diner to a clump of shrubs to do their business. Reverend Beaumont and the boys didn't mind but it was hard for Mimi. She wore one of her prettiest dresses and didn't want to get pee on it or on her shoes and socks. She found a private place to squat. She removed her underpants, shoes and socks, and relieved herself. She appreciated the little packs of tissues her mother had packed for her for this purpose.

They washed their hands at a pump in back of the bus station and cupped their hands to drink water from the pump. Reverend Beaumont asked a young white boy outside the diner to go in and get sodas for him and the children. The boy was kind enough to oblige and the Reverend bought the child a soda pop for his helpfulness.

Jesse kept patting his pants pocket to make sure the pocket knife had not fallen out. Petey kept the pocket knife an extra day and did not return it to him until that morning while they were waiting at the church for their ride to Birmingham. He was happy to see the pocket knife again. He was even happier that his father had not mentioned the knife since he gave it to him.

While the Reverend slept, Jesse's mind began to wander. He found himself thinking about the murder of Suzy Fletcher, Tim West's only granddaughter. He gave no thought to the fact that he and Petey were talking about Suzy at the church picnic a week before she was murdered. Jesse had heard rumors, like the rest of Horace Graves's residents, that Suzy had been stabbed to death with a big knife. He shivered at the thought of a huge butcher knife going through his stomach and coming out his back.

Jesse overheard his parents talking about the fact that Tim West was so overcome by Suzy's death that he told Francis the junkyard would be closed for a month. Francis had to find work elsewhere for the time being. Jesse prayed that his father would find another job before he got back from Baltimore.

Jesse grew sleepy and dozed off, holding tight to the box of food in his lap.

The bus traveled on into the night, filling up a little more with Negroes and whites after each pickup stop. The schedule called for stops in Georgia, South Carolina, North Carolina, Virginia, Washington, D.C. and finally Baltimore. Jesse and the twins had attacks of nausea from motion sickness during the trip and the three of them would run for the door whenever the bus stopped. This was a source of amusement for Petey and Mimi. They were overcome with laughter each time Jesse and the twins rushed past them on their way to the woods or to backs of stations where they would stick their heads into trash barrels or bushes and throw up. The constant motion of the bus and the exhaust fumes coming through the window took the fun out of the long ride for the children.

At the end of their trip, Grandmother Mimi had secured a taxi for them and the driver was ready and waiting outside the Travel Light bus station in Baltimore. She always did this and used the same driver. It was because of her that they all were able to make the trip. She had sent the money for all their tickets.

Watermelon Road
Chapter 9
Grandmother Mimi

Grandmother Mimi and Reverend Beaumont had an agreement. He knew she made her living from running numbers, and in a prostitution establishment on the other side of Baltimore. The agreement was that her grandchildren must never know the truth about their grandparents. Vincent Laurent, her deceased husband, started the illegal businesses thirty years before in Louisiana where he and Grandmother Mimi were born. They married early and had three children, Lydia, William and Franklin. To escape eventual arrest and prosecution, Vincent and Mimi Laurent relocated their family to Baltimore and set up their old businesses in that city. For a long time, their own children never knew of their parents' illegal activities. Mr. and Mrs. Laurent owned another house on the other side of the city. Lydia and her brothers were told that their father was a salesman and had to travel often because of his job. Lydia, several years older than her brothers, found out before she graduated from high school. Her father simply told her the truth because he didn't want her to hear it from someone else. He begged her not to be judgmental of her parents' lifestyle.

    Disappointed in her parents, Lydia went off to college fearing that they would be arrested and sent to prison and she would have to leave school and come home and finish raising her two younger brothers.

    Her college years were filled with unbearable stress from worrying about her parents. Nothing happened to threaten her college days. However, things did not improve after her graduation. Some years after she married and moved to Alabama with Xavier, her father passed away. Her grown brothers decided to go into the family business and worked with their mother's boyfriend who they called Uncle Theo. Theodore Cooke had been Vincent Laurent's best friend. He came to Baltimore from New Orleans to work for Vincent. William and Franklin did not object to Uncle Theo taking their father's place. He was doing a great job in keeping their mother happy and making the business profitable. The brothers left home and moved closer to the family business.

    The large house Grandmother Mimi owned at 337 Bottom Street was bought with money from her illegal activities. The standing agreement with her son-in-law was that, if she wanted to see her grandchildren, she would have to refrain

Watermelon Road

from her immoral lifestyle as long as the grandchildren were present in her home. Grandmother Mimi kept her word and cleared out the five-bedroom house, which was sometimes used as extra space in a pinch for her downtown girls.

This extraordinary and complex woman was standing on her front steps when the taxi pulled up to the house. Mimi and the twins nearly jumped out of the car while the driver was trying to park. They flung open the doors to the taxi and ran up the seven steps to greet their Grandmother. She was a tall, big boned woman, standing 5'10" in her bedroom slippers. Her 257-pound frame embraced her three grandchildren as they cried out for joy at seeing her. She spoiled them rotten. Petey's and Jesse's first impression of Grandmother Mimi was that she was a giant wearing a circus tent. The two boys hadn't spent much time together on the bus but they stood together now looking up at who would be their large but congenial host for the next few days.

Grandmother Mimi was 60 years old and in good health. She wore her grey streaked hair in a chignon, with a beautiful lacquered Chinese comb at the top of her head. Her make up was heavy with rouge and face powder complimented by blood red lipstick. She never went without her makeup or her long, thick false eyelashes. There was a fake mole on the right side of her face just below her bottom lip. Jesse fell in love with her at first sight. She was the most colorful person he had ever encountered. Petey reserved judgment for later. Grandmother Mimi was everything their mothers were not. She was loud and flashy. A lovely red lace shawl was around her shoulders, complimenting the multi-colored flowered blouse and long yellow pleated skirt she wore. Her outfit gave her, if possible, the look of an overdressed gypsy. Gold earrings dangled from her ears and gold and silver bracelets circled her arms. Each of her fingers held rings made of precious stones.

Petey never knew his maternal grandmother, or anything about his mother's side of the family. Esther never spoke about her family and he assumed everyone was dead. Once, while on a fishing trip, Uncle Sax told him Esther was of mixed blood because of her features. Esther didn't have any written proof but was told this by the Methodist missionaries who raised her. When she was old enough to ask about her heritage, they told her that one of her parents could come from the ancestry of a Creek tribe that lived along the Proud Rock River in Mobile, Alabama back in the early 1800's. As an infant, she was secretly left at the missionary farm near Mobile. They never found out who left her at the church steps on the missionary property. This was back around 1900 or so. "We really don't know how old your mother is 'cause she don't have a birth certificate," Uncle Sax had told him.

Jesse had seen his maternal grandmother only once in his short life. His mother's people were from Charleston, South Carolina. Lily had taken him to visit his relatives there twice, once when his grandfather died and again when his grandmother passed away. Those were the only times he had ever met his mother's brothers. His paternal grandfather came to the house on a visit when he was younger. Francis introduced him as "Papa Hams." Papa Hams had stayed a few days and then moved on. No one ever talked about his paternal grandmother.

Madeline L. Nowlin

Grandmother Mimi looked down at the two boys still on the pavement and said, "Ya'll come here and give your play Grandmother a hug." Not knowing what to expect, the two terrified boys started walking up the seven stone steps of the huge redbrick house.

Jesse whispered to Petey, "I'm scared to death but I like her."

Petey whispered back "Lawd Jesus, how in the hell can this woman be the mother of Mrs. Beaumont? I can't believe this is the mother of that educated, high-class woman."

She gathered them into her arms and squeezed them to her breast, cutting off their air supply. After that warm reception, the boys felt welcomed. Mimi was smiling at them as her Grandmother put them back on the step in front of the house. "Call me Grandmother," she said. She opened the door and they all stepped into a large circular room. Grandmother Mimi referred to it as the "vestibule."

Standing close to their friend's grandmother, Jesse and Petey noticed her welcoming smile included teeth that were stained brown and yellow. Grandmother Mimi had a disgusting habit. She took to dipping snuff. She carried a small round silver container of the ground tobacco in her skirt pocket along with a small silver spoon. Several times a day she would place some of the snuff on the spoon, pull out her bottom lip and put the tobacco between her bottom lip and her gums. She rubbed it along her gums. A brass spittoon was hidden in most rooms of the house so that Grandmother could spit out the liquefied tobacco.

Petey and Jesse avoided the spittoons and prayed that they would never be asked to clean one. They didn't have to worry. Althea, the housekeeper, took care of that.

As far as Mimi, Jimmy and Danny knew, their grandmother lived happily in the big corner house with her boyfriend, Uncle Theo. He told the children he worked at a bakery on the other side of town and that was why he had to leave the house early every day of the week. Sometimes Uncle Theo didn't come home at all. Grandmother Mimi told her grandchildren that she was retired from working in a hat factory in Baltimore. She owned a lot of hats so the children never questioned her about her life before they came into the world. She also mentioned that their grandfather had worked in the same factory and that was how they met. Reverend Beaumont and Lydia did not dispute Lydia's mother's account of her past life.

Upon entering the house, Petey and Jesse were mesmerized by the size and beauty of the vestibule. The entrance was half as large as Jesse's whole house. The floor was made of marble and there was a spiral staircase in the center of the room. Two large mahogany tables with marble tops stood on opposite sides of the hall. Resting on each table was a set of tall matching crystal candelabras and a large mirror was above each table. Beyond the vestibule was the parlor on the right. Overstuffed couches and settees covered in chintz or a garden blue and yellow toile patterned fabric, were placed around the room for formal seating. The wallpaper was also in a toile garden pattern. A huge fireplace was the focal point at the end of the parlor. Gigantic potted plants stood like sentries on each side of the fireplace.

A cherry wood paneled library was across the hall from the parlor. Books lined the walls in built-in cherry wood bookcases that stretched from floor to ceiling. There was a large antique oak desk facing the bay window. Further down the hallway, on the right, was the dining room. The ornate gold plated, encrusted African mahogany wood table had ten matching high backed chairs. Those invited to dine in this room considered it a privilege to sit in the beautiful chairs at the exquisite table.

The back of the first floor opened onto an enormous kitchen with a Spanish tile floor. Oak cabinets were placed conveniently above and below the marble countertops. There was indoor plumbing so the two sinks were ideal for preparing meals and the washing up afterward. The kitchen included a large gas stove and a wood stove. Althea loved Mrs. Laurent's kitchen and often told her friends that she could work in that kitchen all day and be happy.

The icebox was kept in the butler's pantry. Behind the butler's pantry were stairs to the third floor attic where two bedrooms and a bathroom were located. Under the stairs was a water closet with a sink and a toilet.

The round oak table in the kitchen was used for informal eating. Grandmother Mimi rarely had a formal dinner so most of the eating was done at the kitchen table. The best part of the house was a magnificent screened in porch encompassing the entire back of the house. The floor was made of wide pine planks and the room was decorated with pieces of comfortable wicker furniture. Grandmother Mimi used the enclosed porch for as long as she could each year. Her favorite time of day was dusk when she would sit on the back porch dipping snuff, drinking gin over ice and feel the warm evening breezes blowing through the screens and across her memories.

Jesse and Petey followed Mimi up the back staircase off the kitchen to the finished third floor attic that housed the two bedrooms and a hall bathroom. The older boys took the bedroom facing the backyard. Each room had twin beds in it. Jimmy and Danny had the bedroom facing Bottom Street. Mimi told the boys to unpack and wash up for lunch. Jesse and Petey were impressed with the indoor plumbing when they took turns washing up and changing their clothes. Everything was perfect except for their neighbors across the hall. They did not relish sharing the attic with the twins but they had no choice. Mimi's bedroom was on the second floor along with her father's bedroom and the master bedroom where Grandmother Mimi and Uncle Theo slept. There was no basement to the house, only a stone cellar cut into the foundation.

Jesse looked around their bedroom, noticing the rich dark wood of the furnishings and that all the pieces of furniture matched. The room was painted a pale blue with checkered navy and white curtains at the windows. The comforter on each twin bed was navy blue with a print of sailboats. The dresser on the wall facing the bed had a large round mirror attached to it. A small night table with an inexpensive lamp was wedged between the two beds. A little desk and chair had been placed in a corner of the room. The hardwood floor was partially covered with a red woven rug. Because of the high ceiling, the room seemed airy and larger than it appeared. The bedding and curtains were new.

Jesse loved the room and said so with enthusiasm: "This is what a palace must look like. I ain't never been in a bedroom this good. Grandmother Mimi must be rich." He began to unpack and place his clothes neatly in one of the dresser draws.

Petey's negative response was "It's all right, but I seen better."

"Where you seen better? You ain't been no place just like I ain't been no place. This is the best bedroom I ever been in and it got two beds so we don't have to sleep together. We got our own bathroom up here and don't have to go outside and put our butts over no smelly hole."

"Maybe I seen better in a picture book. This is nice though."

Petey changed into a clean shirt and pants. Jesse did the same and then circled the room, touching and admiring the items that held his interest. He paused to look out one of the windows. He liked the tall oak trees in the back of the house. They provided shade from the hot sun. Pretty flowerbeds stretched out on each side of the fence. A black iron gate at the end of the yard opened up onto an alley. The alley was unpaved, and wide enough for an automobile to drive through. If you stood in the alley, you could see how it extended to the next block and beyond that with houses backing onto it and trashcans lined up along its borders. Inside Grandmother Mimi's backyard was a 12 x 12 wood shed resting on a poured cement platform. Jesse thought about him and Petey exploring the shed later.

Petey sat on the bed with his head in his hands. He looked tired and unhappy.

"What's wrong with you, Petey? You ain't had much to say the whole trip. I thought you'd be happy to come. We ain't ever been this far from home before."

"You should be happy, you ain't have to sit by Mimi for a whole day and night listening to her talkin' and talkin' and talkin' some more. That girl sho' can run her mouth. I got a headache now 'cause I didn't take a nap like you did and I couldn't sleep none last night. My eyes are burning and I feel sick to my stomach."

"I knows how you feel. I was sick the whole way too. I couldn't keep down none of that good food mama packed. Besides it cain't be that bad sitting by Mimi. I would've took your seat if you asked me to."

"It's all right Shade. I don't feel so bad now. You go on down and get your lunch. I'm gonna lay down on this bed right here and rest my head for awhile."

Hearing Petey call him by his familiar nickname, Jesse felt better inside and went down to lunch.

Petey looked around the room for something to rub. Finding nothing in his room, he went down the hall to the bathroom and found a stack of magazines on a shelf. He removed one and brought it back to his room. He tore out some of the pages and rubbed them between his hands. That gave him some relief.

The twins had found the glider swing on the back porch and were swinging hard in it, making it creak.

Grandmother Mimi, with her granddaughter's help, had set up lunch out on

Watermelon Road

the back porch. The small wicker table with a glass top was set with a platter of tuna sandwiches and ham sandwiches, deviled eggs, and a garden salad with creamy homemade cucumber dressing. A pitcher of lemonade and a pitcher of sweet tea along with drinking glasses, plates, utensils and a basket of fruit were placed on another small table on the porch near the kitchen door. An iced coconut cake rested on the kitchen table, ready to be sliced after lunch.

"Get your dumb asses off that swing and get over hear and eat your lunch," Grandmother yelled at Danny and Jimmy. They stopped swinging and eased past their Grandmother and sat down to lunch. Reverend Beaumont shook his head in disgust at his mother-in-law. He firmly believed that nothing could clean up her act.

Everyone, except the twins, showed concern for Petey; when Jesse appeared alone on the back porch.

Grandmother Mimi asked Jesse why Petey was taking so long to come down to lunch. Jesse told her that Petey had a headache and felt sick in his stomach. She knew it was probably motion sickness. After all, they had been on a bus for 24 hours.

"I'll have Althea take him up some sandwiches and tea and give him some aspirin for his headache. He needs to eat something," she said, getting up from her wicker chair.

Mimi volunteered. "Let me do it. Just tell me where the aspirin is."

Grandmother Mimi looked over at Reverend Beaumont and he winked at her. She smiled and went to get the aspirin.

Mimi had changed her dress for lunch and now paused to look in the mirror in the hallway outside the boys' bedroom. She smoothed her bangs and adjusted the ribbon tied around her ponytail. She picked up the food tray she had placed on the small table under the hall mirror and knocked on Petey's door.

"Come in," said Petey.

"I come to bring you some lunch in case you get hungry later. I brung up some aspirin too," said Mimi.

Petey sat up on the side of his bed and took the tray from Mimi and placed it beside him on the bed. He took the two pills from her outstretched hand, put them in his mouth and washed them down with the sweet tea. Mimi sat down beside him and leaned over and felt his forehead with the back of her hand. Petey pushed her hand away.

"What you think you is, my mama?" He asked playfully.

"I jest want to see if you are really sick or if you jest don't want to come downstairs."

"I gets these headaches sometimes, that's all. I'm better now and I want to come down and have lunch with everybody else." Petey took the tray and walked towards the open door. "Come on," he said. Mimi sighed and followed him.

Yapping sounds came from under the back porch while the children were eating. A Jack Russell terrier came bounding up the porch steps. The little dog hesitated when he saw the strangers then he jumped onto Grandmother Mimi's lap and licked her face as she sat in the glider.

Madeline L. Nowlin

"Everybody, this here is Baby Boy. Digs gave him to me a year ago. He said he found him wandering the streets, if you can believe that. Anyways I love this little guy. He's real friendly and likes to play catch with his red ball. You children can play with him but I don't want you opening the back gate none so he can get out. He might run off. Ya'll hear me?"

"Yes Ma'am," the children spoke in unison.

"Don't ya'll feed him people food either."

"Yes Ma'am," they responded again.

Grandmother Mimi petted her precious Baby Boy as he began to fidget to be let down. Once on the wooden boards of the porch, he ran over to the children and started sniffing their shoes. Except for Jesse who had Rufus, none of the other children had pets. The terrier was white with a few brown spots on his back. He had two patches of brown over both eyes that extended upward into his brown ears. He looked as if he was wearing a mask that had been split into by his nose. Jesse petted Baby Boy and talked to him. The little dog wagged his tail and licked Jesse's hand. They became instant friends.

"Grandma, where yo cat? Do he fight with Baby Boy?" That was Danny asking. The twins were already planning something. Jimmy kicked his brother under the table.

"You mean Lucky? He's around here someplace. You know he's always hiding when ya'll come. He'll crawl out from his hiding place later. Just give him time to get used to you. He's a big cat, so don't go trying to pick him up. He weighs 'bout 20 pounds," she warned.

"What kind of cat is he?" asked Jesse.

"He's a Maine Coon cat and they grow pretty big," Grandmother Mimi replied.

Jimmy asked "Does he eat people food?"

"Don't be a smartass."

"And, I better not catch either one of you boys doing something bad to my animals. If I do, I'm gonna pack your asses up so fast and put you on a bus for home, you won't know what happened 'til your mama pick you up at the station."

All the children answered, "Yes 'Ma'am."

Reverend Beaumont flinched at Grandmother Mimi's language.

Petey opened the door to the back porch.

"There he is, Mr. Handsome," Grandmother Mimi exclaimed.

Mimi went over to the glider and sat beside her Grandmother so Petey could have a seat at the table along with Jesse, the twins and the Reverend. Jesse gave Petey a friendly tap on the shoulder, happy to see he felt better.

On his way into the house to take a nap, the Reverend looked down at Petey. "I'm glad to see you feeling better, boy," he said. "You children amuse yourselves until dinner time and after that it's straight to bed. Don't go running through this house like you crazy, either. Ya'll hear me?"

"Yes sir." The children answered.

Watermelon Road
Chapter 10
A Visitor

Digs, Grandmother Mimi's numbers man, was the only person to come by the house when the grandchildren were present. He addressed their grandmother as "Mrs. Laurent." He had worked for the Laurents for years and continued after Mr. Laurent passed away. He handled the numbers running part of the business.

Digs collected the written numbers and money daily from those who played. He was also responsible for payoffs to winners. Grandmother Mimi looked the other way when Digs skimmed money off the top every now and then to keep his loan shark business going on the side. People trusted him to pay in full if they hit the number. His loan shark business was another story, however.

He showed up on Bottom Street in a fancy car with a young, high-yellow woman sitting in the front seat. It was the day after the children arrived. He was rude and vulgar, disliked by everyone who knew him. His given name was Cleveland Owens but he was called "Digs" for short because it was rumored that he would make you dig your own grave before he killed you if you reneged on your loan.

Everyone had just finished breakfast when Digs came to visit, leaving his "pussy of the month," as he referred to his girlfriends, waiting in the car. She was young enough to be his daughter.

Althea took him out to the back porch. He stood on the porch, watching the children play with Baby Boy. Digs, a hard looking man, was short and slight in stature. He was dressed fashionably in the latest style for men at that time. He had on a pair of pinstriped slacks with a white dress shirt and suspenders. He wore a straw fedora on his short-cropped hair. Reverend Beaumont was in the library reading the morning newspaper when Digs arrived.

A few minutes later Grandmother Mimi came out on the back porch and handed Digs a small piece of paper with her favorite number to play written down. Right in front of everyone, she bent over and lifted up her red and white flowered skirt from her ankles up to her knees. She rolled down her left stocking and removed a white handkerchief, untied it and took out a fifty-cent piece and handed it to Digs. "Wait a minute," she said. She took out another one and handed that to him also. "I feel real lucky today."

Madeline L. Nowlin

Digs took the money and opened the folded piece of paper she handed him. "Three thirty seven. Now that number sho' has been good to you. It got you this house when you hit big all them years ago. I bet you got money stashed all over this place. I bet you don't even need the money from the whorehouse. Ain't that true Mrs. Laurent?"

Grandmother Mimi didn't like the way Digs spoke to her. She never joked or talked about her money or her livelihood, especially in front of company. "Now Mr. Digs, you can stop your nosing around to see if I got money hidden in this house. You know how I make my money and you know Vincent didn't leave me much. If you think I got money stashed all over this house, then you have my permission to look for it right now. Go ahead and help yourself. Besides, ain't you got some yeller gal sitting out there in that car of yours waitin' for you to take her shopping? The way you been looking lately 'taint' nothin' else you can do for her but take her shopping. I hear you been putting some of that smack up your nose."

The sly grin on Digs face faded. Sweat broke out on his forehead as he stood with his arms by his side and clinched fists.

He spoke with animosity in his voice, "Ain't no cause for you to go there, Mrs. Laurent. I be just joking 'bout your money. Ain't no cause for you to embarrass me in front of the cheerin neither, after all I do for you." Baby Boy, who never liked Digs, inched up the back porch steps and bit Digs on the ankle. Digs turned around and kicked at Baby Boy but missed him because he was too fast for the man. "You need to train that damn dog not to bite," he said, rubbing his ankle. The children nearly choked trying not to laugh.

Grinning, Grandmother Mimi sashayed past him and sat in the glider. She grabbed the spittoon from behind the chair next to the swing and spat out some dark tobacco juice. She took out her silver box and spoon and dipped more tobacco across her bottom gums. Digs and the children watched in disgust as she continued to rub her gums and hum to herself. Digs watched as she moved back and forth in the glider, humming to herself.

Wanting to dissolve the hostility that had suddenly risen between him and the old woman, Digs turned towards the children at the other end of the porch. Petey and Mimi were watching Jesse throw a small red ball to Baby Boy. The dog would run backwards until the ball touched ground and then grab it and bring it back to the boy. Jimmy and Danny sneaked off to find Lucky, ignoring their grandmother's warning.

"Hi ya'll doing? You cheerin doing okay?"

"Yes sir," they responded, still watching Baby Boy's odd way of not catching the ball Jesse threw at him.

"That's a big boy out there playing with Baby Boy. How old is he?

"Ten," Petey told Digs.

"He sho' is a big boy for his age. I bet he don't say no thank you to nothing edible." Digs laughed, slapping his leg.

No one laughed with him.

"Looka here, everybody. I got an idea." Digs turned to Grandmother Mimi.

Watermelon Road

"How 'bout me taking the cheerin to a baseball game up at Griffith Stadium tomorrow? They'd love riding in my caddy. You knows I'll show them a good time. We be eating hot dogs, drinking pop and such."

"I don't know 'bout that Digs. Their father plans to leave on Friday. Best you be getting his permission."

Petey, Mimi and Jesse held their breath. They were afraid to show excitement in case the Reverend said they couldn't go.

"Come on ya'll, let's go find your daddy," said Digs.

Jesse ran up the back steps and joined his two friends as they followed Digs down the hall to the library. The twins were still missing. Twice a cat cried out from another room.

It was a tight squeeze but they all crowded into the small library, surprising Reverend Beaumont who had dozed off while reading the morning newspaper.

Mimi shook her father awake. "Please daddy, please can we go to Griffith Park tomorrow with Mr. Digs?"

The Reverend, shaken from a restful nap, found a group of expectant faces staring down at him. The three children started shouting "ballpark, ballpark," in unison.

Reverend Beaumont banged his fist on the desk and yelled, "Stop this ruckus."

He turned to Digs and said, "Am I to understand that you want to take these children to Griffith Stadium for the day? Now you know that's a big undertaking. I have seven-year old twins and they aren't easy to control."

While the reverend was speaking, Mimi had backed away to stand near the doorway to give the twins more room as they entered to find out what was going on. They had heard the other children shouting "ballpark." Mimi gently took the cat away from Danny. Digs moved closer to her. They were wedged together in the doorway and Digs made no move to give Mimi more space. When he thought no one was watching, he ran his hand along the length of her ponytail and then down the back of her dress, caressing her behind. Mimi stiffened.

Petey saw this and watched them intently. Mimi moved further into the room. Digs did the same, brushing up against her behind. He placed his hands on her shoulders, massaging them.

Reverend Beaumont, blind to his daughter's distress, continued, "There is only one way I'm going let you take these children to Griffith Stadium."

"What way is that Reverend," Digs asked, smiling benignly.

"You got to take me too." Then Reverend Beaumont burst out laughing. Digs and the children laughed with him.

Mimi searched out Petey and their eyes met. He saw the one thing he thought he would never see in Mimi's eyes — fear.

Watermelon Road
Chapter II
Family Matters

Sheriff Richards arrested Jeremiah Lucas on suspicion of killing Suzy Fletcher the day the Reverend and the children left for Baltimore. Jeremiah was held in custody overnight and then let go. Mirabelle Lucas, eighteen and seven months pregnant went to the Bison police station to turn her father in. She told Sheriff Richards that her father had been raping her since she was twelve and that he had probably done the same to the little Fletcher girl. Sheriff Richards sent Deputy Rudy Cox to Horace Graves to pick up Mr. Lucas and bring him back to the station. Jeremiah was a raving drunk when Deputy Cox found him at a bar he frequented on the outskirts of town.

The Sheriff knew that little Suzy had not been raped but like others in the county, he had long suspected that Mirabelle had been sexually abused. Years ago, he had sent one of the churchwomen of his congregation to the Lucas' home to see what she could find out. The woman came back and said everything looked fine to her; that Jeremiah had two boys in the house and no way would those boys let their father carry on so. She also mentioned that Mirabelle said she was happy and that her daddy had never done anything bad to her. Now the Sheriff was sorry he had let it go at that and not followed up on his suspicions.

Two items were kept from the public regarding Suzy's murder and one was the fact that the murder had been committed with a short sharp instrument, not a butcher knife as was the rumor going around the county. The other fact was that Suzy had not been molested.

He could have held Jeremiah longer until some determination could be made about Mirabelle's allegations concerning her father's sexual abuse. But, he knew the bottom line would be just more gossip and the boys would never bear witness against their father. Besides, Mirabelle was on her way to becoming an unwed mother and the people in the county would have no sympathy for her due to her sexual exploits with wayward husbands.

Mirabelle and her father had argued the night before she turned him in as the murderer. He came home and found no dinner waiting for him. When he questioned his daughter about the missing dinner, she told him she was tired and was resting because her feet were swollen. He called her a beached whale and told

Watermelon Road

her to get her fat ass out of bed and fix him something to eat. She refused and he hit her upside her head. She started crying, but still refused to get out of bed. "I'm sick daddy. I feel bad in my stomach." Then she held her head over the side of the bed and vomited.

Jeremiah made her clean up the mess, and then fix him dinner. Mirabelle did as she was told. The next morning, while her father slept, she walked over to the general store and asked Mr. Batty to drive her to see Sheriff Richards. She wouldn't tell him the reason why she needed to see the Sheriff. Jonas Batty had a thing for Mirabelle, and took her to see the Sheriff. He was hoping she would return the favor by inviting him to dinner one night when she was home alone. Several hours later a drunken Jeremiah Lucas was picked up by Deputy Cox and brought to the Sheriff's office for questioning.

After spending a rough night at the County Jail, Jeremiah was a free man. He sat in his kitchen the next morning shifting through the stages of a hangover. His head throbbed as he downed two aspirin. His hands shook and his face was puffy with swollen lips. For breakfast, he poured himself a glass of straight bourbon.

Mirabelle sat across from her father. She rubbed her extended belly and smiled. With an evil sneer, she looked over at him and said, "I don't know who the father is, so it could even be a nigger baby. I'm going to parade it all around town when it's born. I'm going to shame you like you done me."

Jeremiah set the glass of bourbon down. He got up and took the hot coffee pot from the stove and threw it at Mirabelle's head. She didn't have time to duck and the scalding pot hit her square in the face, breaking her nose and dumping the hot liquid all over her front, down her dress and onto her legs. Caught off guard, Mirabelle screamed and fell backwards in her chair onto the kitchen floor.

Jeremiah ran to where Mirabelle was withering in pain on the hard floor. He knelt down and placed his huge hands around her throat. She tried to take his hands away, but he was too powerful. Her broken nose was gushing blood, the baby was kicking inside of her and the burning of the hot coffee was relentless.

"You stupid, filthy, whore bitch. You've been nothin' but an embarrassment to me ever since your ma died. You think you can blackmail me with a nigger baby now? Well go ahead and have your little pickininny. There ain't nothin' else you can do to me. Go on, tell your little dirty secrets if you want to. I don't give a damn no more."

Haley and Calvin walked through the backdoor and saw the carnage in the kitchen. Their eyes came to rest on their father and sister.

"Stop that daddy," Haley yelled.

Calvin, knowing his father was stronger than himself, grabbed one of the kitchen chairs and slammed it across his father's back. The chair legs broke and his father yelled out in pain and slumped to the floor. Mirabelle lay on the floor breathing heavily. Jeremiah was the one in tears now, rolling around the kitchen. Haley stood in the doorway, eyes bulging and said to Calvin, "What the hell did you do that for?"

"I had to stop him. You could see he done snapped. Mirabelle is pregnant and he got no cause hurting her like that."

Madeline L. Nowlin

Haley helped Mirabelle off the floor and sat her down in a kitchen chair. Calvin stood over his father, watching him cry like a baby. He suddenly realized the short stocky man he had feared for so long was just an old man. "What a pathetic piece of shit," he said out loud.

Between sniveling and trying to sit up, Jeremiah told his sons that as soon as he could stand he was going to get his shotgun and blow their heads off.

The boys had always known the time would come when they would have to leave home for good.

There was no time like the present. Jeremiah would kill them if they didn't go. Even if he didn't end up killing them, Horace Graves was getting too hot for them. People had been asking questions about who was lynching Negroes. A few white men had questioned them about the murders and Haley and Calvin denied that they knew anything. For now, they had been believed, but both knew the Sheriff would come for them in time.

Calvin ran to the back bedroom where his father slept and took the two shotguns that were kept in the closet. One of the shotguns had been used to beat Joel to death. He removed the two pillowcases from his father's bed and filled one with his own personal items. When he came back to the kitchen, he handed the other pillowcase to Haley and told him to go do the same. Jeremiah struggled to stand but Calvin pointed a shotgun at him and dared him to move.

Calvin told Haley to empty his father's pockets and take what money the old man had. Haley was afraid to approach Jeremiah, so Mirabelle did it. She gingerly stuck her fingers down into her father's pockets and came up with $45. She handed it to Calvin.

Mirabelle said "I got a few bucks in my room. You wait here and I'll get it." She came back with $108 she had been saving to buy baby clothes. She handed the money to Calvin.

"Where you get this kind of money?" Calvin asked.

"I have my ways of getting money. Mostly, I steal from daddy when he's passed out from drinking. I know I can depend on some church people in town to help me with what I need for the baby. Good luck to you," Mirabelle said. Calvin hugged his sister.

He walked over to Jeremiah and pointed the shotgun at his chest.

"Me and Haley stood by while you used our sister like she was our mama. We were young but we knew what them sounds were coming from Mirabelle's room and she no more than twelve or so. You leave her alone. You hear me daddy? If you don't, we will come back and finish you off old man."

"Haley, you grab the pillowcases, I'll carry the guns." Calvin looked at his father and sister for the last time. "Bye daddy. Bye Mirabelle."

The brothers jumped off the back porch and ran.

After they left, Mirabelle got a broom and started sweeping up the mess in the kitchen, her bruised body screaming in pain. Jeremiah got to his feet and went out the backdoor. He sat for a long time on the back steps, smoking and rubbing his back. At one point, she heard her father sobbing but she kept to her cleaning.

Watermelon Road
Chapter 12
Suzy Fletcher

"Look, Al, this thing with the Fletcher girl, I just don't get it." Deputy Rudy Cox stood near the coffee pot, readying his cup for his second cup of the morning. There hasn't been a child murder in our county since I can remember. People are acting crazy. I saw a couple of parents hanging around the schoolyard. One of them had a shotgun. We have to find a suspect soon. Although it won't be easy since the Negroes were all accounted for during the time frame of the murder and I can't see a white man doing it either. However, your checking out the town vagrants was a good idea."

The Sheriff looked up from the papers on his desk. He took out his handkerchief and wiped the sweat off his face. The heat in the office was oppressive. The fan on his desk was noisily circulating the hot air in the room.

Sheriff Richards looked at the back of his hands, noticing the liver spots. He was 45 but felt a lot older. He wasn't tall but he was tanned and muscled due to his work on his father's farm. He helped his aging father work his peanut farm outside the county whenever his job permitted "time off for good behavior," as he often joked with the Bison residents.

The Sheriff's piercing blue eyes looked over at his young deputy. He said, "You don't think this shit is tearing me apart? Every time I have to face that girl's mother and her grandfather, I get sick to my stomach. I don't like to feel this way. I've been at this job for 15 years and this crime has made me feel incompetent and ashamed. Tim West is on my back day and night. He has two grandsons but he doted on that ugly granddaughter of his. Lord, forgive me but that was a homely child. I've gone over everything. I've been to the site a hundred times but that three-day rain left me nothing. The fact that it took us two days to find her didn't help either. The autopsy gave little information except for the fact that she was stabbed to death with a sharp instrument. The doc said maybe a hunting knife, maybe not. She had puncture wounds in her chest area and in her neck. Every man, woman and child in Bison County has some type of sharp instrument, probably on their person every day."

"I can't get the sight of her small lifeless body out of my head. I'm glad you never mentioned to anybody that I burst into tears when you and I came upon her in the woods," Deputy Cox said, not looking at the Sheriff.

"It was the first time for both of us. I've seen children dead of sickness and accidents in my career as sheriff but never what we saw that day. Don't feel bad about having emotions, that's what keeps us human in this job."

"Maybe something will come up soon," said a hopeful Deputy Cox. He was the only deputy with permanent status in the Sheriff's department and a good friend to his boss. They could call on volunteers when needed but up until now, that had been rare. Sheriff Richards had enlisted the help of the town residents to search for Suzy when she was reported missing. Many came forward to help. He recently deputized a few more men just in case a suspect was found and things got out of hand. He was eager to wrap things up because the longer it took to do so, the worse it would be for him. He could pretty much count on not being re-elected.

"I've questioned Sissy Philips and the rest of the Philips brood. Their parents weren't home at the time I questioned them. I talked to Mrs. Bertie afterward. At the time I questioned them neither Mrs. Bertie nor the children knew the whereabouts of Mr. Philips. I let that go since he, according to the neighbors, comes and goes at any time. In any case, no one saw him in town the day Suzy was killed. Mrs. Bertie's two older children had quit school already and were accounted for at their respective places of employment.

The younger children, along with Sissy, swear that Suzy left their house by herself to walk home long before dark. Several people saw her walking alone near her school. No one saw her enter the wooded area for a short cut to her house."

He was a patient man, being Sheriff had taught him that much. Tim West was relentless and was driving him to distraction. He couldn't concentrate or relax when he went home to Katie and the girls at night. This damn case was robbing him of his appetite and his sleep.

Deputy Cox had no intention of hanging around Bison County too much longer. He planned to move to Montgomery and secure a position in law enforcement with a future as soon as one became available. He was content to learn from Sheriff Richards until he could make his move. He glanced in the mirror near his desk and thought, *Being tall, dark and handsome couldn't hurt my chances of moving on either.*

The Sheriff broke Rudy's self-absorption by saying one more time, "I'm tired of looking at Tim West every other day. If he don't come by, then his son, Bobby, is staring me down, trying to obtain information for that white supremacy group of his. Those two are persistent and I've given Tim more information about the crime than I should have."

"That's your fault. "If it were me, I'd tell him to stay the hell out of my office," thought Deputy Cox.

Unlike Sheriff Richards, Deputy Cox knew that the white supremacy group was not waiting patiently for them to find the killer. Rumors had been flying all over town that the group had a plan in place for action when the suspect was apprehended. Be the suspect Negro or white, they were going to take the prisoner, tie him to the back of a horse cart, hit that horse on its rump and send him

Watermelon Road

galloping down the middle of Main Street, right through town. This was the rumor. The real plan was to storm the jail if they had to, take the killer and string him up on a tree branch and set him on fire. This was their usual plan of action.

Deputy Cox knew this wasn't a rumor for sure because Bobby West had told him it wasn't. He wasn't a member of the group but he and Bobby were friends and he kept Bobby's secrets. He even told Bobby that he would help in anyway he could to make the turning over of the killer to the secret society go as smoothly as possible.

Tim West didn't know or care about his son's plans. He had one of his own and that involved using a rifle.

Watermelon Road
Chapter 13
Bison County

For centuries a large number of the Muskhogean tribe, along with some Choctaw, Koasati, Cherokee and Chickasaw settled in and around the territories of what is now Alabama and Georgia. They were a part of the Creek Nation of Native American Indians. The Choctaw, Cherokee and some of the other tribes eventually settled in the northern part of the United States. The Seminoles settled in Florida. The Muskhogean, a brave and strong tribe, battled the northern tribes, some of which were the Shawnee and Cherokee.

Sometime around 1813 the Creek War took place and they fought against the Americans. The Creeks lost and had to concede a large part of their lands to the United States. By the 1840's most of the eastern Native Americans had been rounded up and placed on Indian reservations in what became the Oklahoma Territory.

The land encompassing Bison County in Alabama was part of that concession. The county was a place unto itself. It was untouched by the First World War because most of the male residents in the three towns that made up the county were either too old or too young at the time the war began.

The area making up the county was mostly rural and many of the Negroes migrated north after World War I ended. However, the Jim Crow system was well in place and the Negroes that stayed definitely knew their place.

The three towns that made up Bison County had all been settled by the early 1900's.

The first town, Bison, was given that name by a settler of French decent named Bartholomew Brossette, called Bart by his friends and neighbors. He had originally come from Georgia, but decided to move his family further south where he could acquire cheap land for his growing family, which included a wife and eight children. He bought up several thousand acres in the middle of the territory that was now Alabama, moved his family into a makeshift house until a bigger place could be built for his large brood. He got the farm established quickly, planting peanuts, grains, melons and vegetables, unlike most of the other new settlers who planted cotton. His farm was one of the few farms that survived the boll weevil blight that took out most of the cotton farming by 1915.

Bart Brossette later decided to start a town on land he owned where he could

Watermelon Road

establish businesses and services he and other settlers required, including a school for his children's education. Because of the Indian history of that area, he decided to name the town Bison. He built small one-family houses, as well as boarding houses and hotels for workers employed in the recently established local coal, iron ore and limestone mines, as well as workers on the farms. Bart ensured that the town of Bison was a great place to raise a family.

One of Bart's sons, Horace, at the age of 17, started a fishing business on the banks of the Proud Rock River southwest of Bison. Horace decided to establish a hamlet and called it Horace Graves because it was built near an old Indian gravesite that he left undisturbed. The fishing business grew into a fishing industry and created jobs for the poor and Negroes in the area.

Bakerstown was established further south, much later than the other two towns by Aaron Baker. He was Jewish and had come from a city outside Berlin. He made his fortune in the lumber trade, including establishing a furniture manufacturing plant. Aaron was more liberal in hiring Negroes than either Bart or Horace. He never married but fathered several children with his mixed-blood housekeeper.

There were twice as many whites in each settlement as Negroes, and the whites were given the choice jobs. Negro men, women and the older children were used as day laborers on the farms. As the mines, fishing industry and lumber-related businesses thrived, Negro men were used for heavy labor because they were larger and healthier than the white men from the towns. The Negro women were employed as cooks or for raising children, and housework. Some of the Negro men were trained in certain skills needed in the mills, thus affording them some opportunities to improve their way of life.

By 1910 the elected officials of the three towns decided to form a township that constituted Bison County and established an official governing entity.

The inhabitants of this county considered themselves God-fearing people. They had lost loved ones to the Civil War, diseases and the First World War. They had suffered loses in their crops and their possessions but still clung to their faith in God and country.

In 1935, the only thing the natives of Bison County feared was polio until the murder of Suzy Fletcher.

Watermelon Road
Chapter 14
Tim West

Tim West sat in the trailer he used as an office when conducting business in the junkyard. He had a fifth of Jack Daniels about two-thirds empty on his desk. Tears rolled down his gaunt cheeks as he stared at the wall in front of him. "Oh my poor baby girl," he whispered and refilled his empty glass. Tim took the loss of his granddaughter, Suzy, harder even than her parents if that were possible. He was mostly angry that he had been singled out for such a tragedy. He hated to be pitied.

It was steaming hot in the trailer so he went outside on the short landing attached to the three steps leading to the ground. Taking out his handkerchief, he wiped his face, balding head and his neck. As he was wiping his head for the second time, his hand paused in mid-air. "What did Al say, sharp puncture wounds?" He thought about what he had heard in the Sheriff's office when he was there only that morning. "Wounds caused by a short sharp object, about four inches long" were the Sheriff's words when he discussed the murder weapon with Tim.

"Oh my God! I gave a pocket knife to Francis. I wonder what he did with it? Maybe he lost it and one of them vagrants that's been hanging around town found it and killed my grandbaby. I'll go see Francis right now."

Tim West arrived at the Hammond house at 8:00 that evening. Francis and Lily were sitting on the small front porch of the house. They watched his beat up old 1929 Ford pickup truck drive up to the front of the house. Tim got out and walked slowly up the paved walkway. He took off his hat and greeted Francis and Lily.

"Scorching day ain't it folks," he said as he neared the porch, wiping his face.

"Yes it is, sir. We thought it'd be cooler out here on the porch by evening, but it ain't," said Francis, puzzled as to why his employer had come by unannounced. Francis stood up.

"I need to talk to you for a minute, Francis. Ain't no cause to worry," Mr. West said with a smile. Francis looked down at Lily. He motioned for his employer to follow him down to the beginning of the lawn. They both walked

Watermelon Road

down and leaned on the old Ford.

"I've been thinking," Tim began. I heard that my granddaughter had multiple stab wounds from a short sharp object and that's what killed her. Now I remember giving you a pocket knife awhile back and I was wondering if you had it handy."

Francis froze. His heart was pounding so loud he could barely hear the words coming out of Mr. West's mouth as he continued to speak.

Before Francis could think, he blurted out "That little pocket knife? I gave that knife to my boy so he can learn how to carve wood with it. I don't know where he put it. I'll have to look for it. He could have taken it with him. Jesse is in Baltimore with the Beaumont children 'til the end of this week. They're coming back on Saturday. I can bring the knife to you then," said Francis, struggling to keep his voice down.

Then Francis grew angry and lost his temper. He said, "Why you want to look at that pocket knife you gave me? Ain't nobody else in town got a pocket knife? You know me, and you know my boy. As far as I know ain't neither one of us ever seen your granddaughter. I surely hope you ain't trying to pin her murder on me or my boy just 'cause we Negroes. A white man could have done it for all you know. If we had anything to do with it, don't you think some white person would have come forward and say they seen us with your granddaughter?" Francis was nearly screaming at Tim West by this time.

"Ain't no need in you getting all riled up 'bout this. I just wanted to look at the knife. In fact, I thought you had lost it and some vagrant might have found it and hurt my granddaughter. You acting like you got something to hide."

"I can't believe you would try and pin your granddaughter's murder on a small Negro child cause the Sheriff ain't found out who really done it. You know if word gets out that you gave me a pocket knife and I gave it to my boy, things will heat up in this town and all for nothing.

I know what you up to. You can't fool me. You ain't nothin' but a coward. You just want to accuse somebody, anybody so you can stop hurting. Let me tell you something, white man, you ain't never gonna stop hurting 'til you know the truth."

Hearing her husband speak harshly to Mr. West, Lily jumped up from the porch step and started walking towards the two men.

"I ain't accusing nobody of nothing, and you done lost your mind, nigger, talking to me like that. How was I supposed to know that you gave the pocket knife to your boy? You never told me that and you see me at the junkyard every day. I'm going to have a look at that knife whether you like it or not. If I don't hear from you before Saturday, the Sheriff will be waiting for your boy at the bus station in Birmingham."

"You can forget about coming back to work at the yard." With those last words, Tim West got into his pickup truck and drove away.

Lily stood tentatively behind her husband. "Francis," she whispered. "What is going on? What happened, baby?"

"You come on in the house, honey, we cain't talk out here in front of the

59

neighbors."

Francis took his wife's hand and walked her back to the house. They sat in the parlor while he told her about the conversation between him and Tim West. Before he got to the end of his account, Lily was sobbing. Her body, shaking with fear, slid off the settee onto the wood floor. "On Lord have mercy. Don't let them take my only chile," she said over and over again.

"Don't you worry, honey. Come tomorrow morning we gonna get us a ride over to Bakerstown and find us a telephone. People are too nosy here. We gonna call Baltimore and tell Mrs. Laurent and the Reverend what's about to happen here and they'll know what to do. The Lord will get us through this," he said, sitting next to his wife on the floor. He put his arm around her and they clung to each other until the sun came up the next morning.

Watermelon Road
Chapter 15
Digs

The library door was closed. No one heard the ominous ringing of the telephone. Petey was awake. He looked over at the clock on the night table between the twin beds. It was 7:00 a.m. He could hear Jesse snoring. A plan to save Mimi from Digs had formed in his head. His mind was clear, free of the hissing sound and bad thoughts. That frightened look in Mimi's eyes when Digs touched her was something he could not ignore. Her eyes pleaded with him for help. Petey couldn't understand why the Reverend had not noticed his daughter's uneasiness about Digs. *That man was so absorbed in the Lord's work that he couldn't see the evil around him*. Petey was disgusted with the Reverend's ignorance of his daughter's plight. He was different. The thing in his belly made him see everything, hear everything, know everything.

    He went down the hall to the bathroom, washed up, came back and got dressed. The day would be an exciting one for all of them. It would be the first time he and Jesse were in an actual baseball stadium and the first time they would see two national teams play. Today, June 5, the Washington Nationals would play the Boston Red Sox at Griffin Stadium. As grown folks say, "This will be something to tell his cheerin."

    Today, after the game, he would kill Digs.

    He worked it out. He would watch Grandmother Mimi's every move. He had to find out if she did have money hidden in the house. That was the only way he could get Digs' attention. He opened the bedroom door and tiptoed down the backstairs that led to the kitchen. The staircase in the vestibule didn't go to the third floor. He heard the faint ring of the telephone in the library when he reached the kitchen. The children were not allowed to answer the telephone so he let it ring. Petey went out the backdoor to the porch. The Baltimore weather was a little cool this morning and he wished he had put on a long sleeved shirt for now, but it would warm up in the afternoon. He reminded himself to bring a jacket for the trip just in case. The glider creaked as he moved slowly back and forth while smoking a cigarette.

    "If the old woman knew I was out here smoking I bet she'd beat the living shit out of me and send me home by myself," he said out loud, laughing as he imagined the look on Grandmother Mimi's face if she caught him. Although, deep down he knew that nothing could shock that old woman.

Petey put his head back on the high pillow covering the back of the glider and closed his eyes. He heard the telephone ring again, this time it stopped on the second ring. Althea, the housekeeper, must have come in and answered it. He put out his cigarette and went quietly into the house. Althea was on the second floor knocking on Grandmother Mimi's door. There was a lot of yelling back and forth through the closed door about the call that was for Grandmother.

Petey hid in the parlor across from the library with the door partially closed. This gave him a clear view of the hallway, stairs and the library door. Five minutes went by before Grandmother Mimi came down the stairs, wearing a long frilly yellow nightgown and matching robe.

"Fix me a big cup of coffee," he heard her yell to Althea and then she went into the library and closed the door. Althea hurried off to the kitchen. Grandmother Mimi got comfortable in the library chair, put the receiver to her ear and listened to Francis Hammond. Petey heard her say "Lawd Jesus," in a loud voice, but that was all he could hear. She didn't talk loud after that outburst. She did very little talking from what he could hear.

Satisfied that she might be occupied for awhile and that he would not be seen, he tiptoed upstairs to the second landing and went into her bedroom, closing the door. The first thing he saw was a large standing mahogany armoire with mirrored doors. The double doors opened in the center, so he pulled them apart and hid behind a collection of evening gowns and fur coats on the left side of the armoire. The right side contained hatboxes in all shapes and sizes. There was a wide shelf above the clothes that held boxes of shoes and hats. The enclosed space smelled of stale perfume and mothballs. He waited, breathing through his mouth because the smell made him nauseous. He opened the door a little so he could see out into the bedroom and also breathe a little better.

He could hear the other kids stirring above. The armoire was a good vantage point for viewing the entire bedroom. Meanwhile, Grandmother Mimi was still on the phone.

Since Theo left early that morning, Grandmother Mimi expected the call to be about something to do with the business. Maybe one of the gals had come up short, but Theo knew how to handle that by himself. "I hope it ain't no police trouble, I pays them well not to have no trouble," she thought to herself as she closed the library door and put the receiver to her ear.

Attempting to sound tough she said "Yeah, what you want? For a full minute all she heard was a man crying. She knew it was a man on the other end. She'd heard men cry before. She waited, her apprehension growing by leaps and bounds. She still did not recognize the voice. "Take your time," she whispered.

"Ma'am, you don't know me, but I'm Jesse's daddy. My name is Francis Hammond. Me and Jesse's mama, Lily, been sitting up all night crying and praying that God will let you help us. My wife cain't talk just yet. Jesse is our only child and she's too full up with fear to speak."

"Just tell me what happened. Pull yourself together and start talking,"

Watermelon Road

Grandmother said, using her command voice.

Francis did as he was told and related the whole situation back in Horace Graves. Grandmother Mimi sat back in her chair and put her hand to her mouth. She was breathing heavily by the end of the story Francis had imparted. He had told his story between bouts of crying himself and consoling his wife who was standing beside him.

The plump child that accompanied her grandchildren to Baltimore didn't look like he was capable of such a brutal act. She had raised two sons and had to deal with a lot of men in her business that thought they were wiser and tougher than her. She was good at judging a man's temperament and Jesse was a timid boy. She knew for certain that the ten-year old boy she had in her house was no murderer. This child was decent and respectful. Grandmother calmed Francis' anxiety by promising him that she would take care of everything from her end. She instructed him to convince the Sheriff, if it came to that, to meet the Reverend, Petey and Jesse at the bus station in Birmingham on Saturday, June 8. She told Francis to make sure the Sheriff understood that Jesse should not have to face a mob of angry white people if the Sheriff met them in Birmingham and then drove them home himself. Francis did not like this idea as it would still bring Jesse into Horace Graves where it could be dangerous for him.

"Mr. Hammond, you listen up real good. My son-in-law will let this Sheriff Richards know that Jesse took sick suddenly afore he left and had to be taken to a clinic up here. I know people working in a clinic downtown that will say your boy is there. You and your missus got to pull yourselves together 'cause your boy's life is on the line. You gonna have the Reverend telling lies for you and a whole lot of other peoples lying too, so you do your part. All you have to say is that you didn't know your boy took sick 'til you heard it from the Reverend when he came back to Horace Graves without Jesse. You don't say or do nothing else 'til you hear from me. I'll get word to you through my son-in-law. You got all that?"

"Yes. Thank you, I heard everything you said," was Francis' grateful reply to Grandmother Mimi's question. Lily reached in the phone booth and took the phone from her husband. "Thank you Mrs. Laurent and God bless you for looking after my baby," then she hung up the phone. Francis held Lily close as she stood next to him. "Honey, let's go get something to eat and then we'll hitch a ride back to Horace Graves. I'll tell you everything Mrs. Laurent told me once you get some food in you so you can stop crying and shaking so."

"Ain't that just like you," Lily teased. "Always thinking 'bout your stomach." They smiled at each other. Grandmother Mimi had brought them a little relief for the time being.

Petey could hear Grandmother's labored steps as she slowly climbed to the second landing. Holding his breath, he braced himself, praying that he would not be discovered when she entered her bedroom. God seemed to ignore his prayers because she went straight for the armoire. He made himself as small as possible behind the fur coats. She opened the right side of the huge closet and reached toward the back. He heard a latch click on that side. She pushed the gowns and fur coats further to the left, securing his hiding place. There must have been a secret compartment in the back because he heard the sound of a drawer being pulled open. He could hear her removing something from the hidden drawer, after which she closed the door to the armoire. Petey cracked the door a little on his side of the closet. He could see Grandmother Mimi standing in the sunlight flowing through her bedroom window. She was holding a small wooden box in her hands.

Grandmother walked over to her bed and sat down. He could hear her rummaging through the box. The sound of money being counted was familiar. In that moment he knew she was counting her hidden money. Petey was elated. He wanted to scream for joy. He placed one hand over his mouth, muffling any sounds he might make.

She took a portion of the bills from the box and put them on her night table. She then went back to the closet, replaced the box and closed the door.

He could hear her in the bathroom attached to her bedroom. She was singing while filling the bathtub with hot water. Petey found the latch to the secret place and pulled it. The box rested in the inner sanctum of the drawer. He took the box and hid it under his shirt. Baby Boy had been asleep on Grandmother's bed all this time. When he saw Petey come out of the armoire, he leaped off the bed, yapping at Petey as he headed for the door.

"Shut that damn noise up afore you wake up everybody," Grandmother yelled from the bathroom. Petey tiptoed to the door and looked out into the hallway. There was no one in sight. He closed the door in the dog's face and raced down the stairs, through the kitchen and out the backdoor.

Out back, he looked for a hiding place for the box and decided to hide the box behind the big shed at the end of the backyard near the gate to the alley. No one was likely to go behind the shed to look for anything or to clean back there.

Someone had let Baby Boy out of Grandmother's bedroom because he was at the backdoor, barking at Petey through the screen. Petey let Baby Boy out into the backyard so he could do his business. Back in the kitchen, Petey asked Althea to fix him a stack of pancakes and bacon while he waited for the other children to come down to breakfast. Baby Boy scratched on the screen door so he let the dog back in the house.

He played with the little dog while Althea made the pancakes and bacon. Baby Boy enjoyed the bits of bacon he fed him under the table. "I bet he likes me more than Jesse," he smiled as he considered the puzzled look on Jesse's face when he saw Baby Boy being friendly with him and not Jesse.

When Mimi, Jesse and the twins walked into the kitchen, they stopped when they saw Petey eating a stack of pancakes. He looked up and grinned at them. "Good morning," he said.

"I was wondering where you got to. I didn't see you in your bed when I got up. Where you been and how come you got dressed so early? Jesse asked as he pulled out a chair for Mimi to sit at the kitchen table. Petey and the twins burst out laughing at Jesse's gentlemanly gesture. Mimi cut them a mean look and that made them stop. Petey said, "Pancakes for everybody, it's on me." The children

Watermelon Road

talked over each other in excited voices as they ate their breakfast. Digs would be picking them up at 11:00 in the morning and it was already 10:00.

Reverend Beaumont joined them. He was as excited as the children. "I'm going to buy everyone a baseball cap," he said, watching the look of amazement on the faces around the table. After breakfast, the children went out to play with Baby Boy in the backyard. Lucky was in hiding as usual.

At 11:00 on the dot the doorbell rang and Althea went to answer it. Grandmother Mimi came downstairs dressed in one of her elaborate outfits. This time it was all one color — purple. She looked like a giant lilac bush. Even her jewelry was purple. She gave the children the once over. Her namesake was wearing a pretty dress. Little Mimi twirled around the vestibule in her ruffled white dress with a red belt at her tiny waist. She wore a white straw hat with a red, white and blue striped ribbon around the band. The twins were neat for a change in their red and white pullover shirts and brown cotton shorts with brown socks and sandals. The Reverend wore a yellow sports coat with white slacks and his best pair of black and white spats. Jesse and Petey wore new sneakers given to them by Uncle Sax. He surprised them with the shoes the night before they left for Baltimore.

Digs walked in, tipped his white straw hat and smiled at everyone. "Mrs. Laurent, Reverend Beaumont, cheerin." He was dressed in one of his usual flashy outfits. Light blue shirt, cream colored slacks with creases so sharp you could cut yourself on them. His red suspenders matched his red jacket.

"I guess I know who you all are routing for," Grandmother said. The children ran out the door yelling "Bye Grandma."

Digs looked at the old lady, "I'll bring them back safe."

You better, if you know what's good for you, she thought to herself as she waved goodbye. Mimi, Jesse, Danny and Jimmy piled into the back seat of the Cadillac convertible. Petey had pushed Mimi to the back seat and he sat up front between Digs and Reverend Beaumont. Mimi was relieved to sit in the back seat with the twins and Jesse.

Petey debated whether to tell the Reverend about Digs and how he used his hands on Mimi. However, he doubted that he would be believed. Besides, Mimi had not spoken a word to him about Digs so he didn't want to embarrass her. He wondered how long she had been afraid of Digs. Petey hoped it had not been for a long time.

Grandmother Mimi watched as the car pulled away from the curb. She closed the front door and went into the library and closed that door. She dialed a number.

"Hello, are you free to talk?"

"Yeah, we can talk," said the voice on the other end.

"I need a child's body," said Grandmother Mimi. There was a long pause.

"Five thousand," was the response.

"I got it," she said.

Watermelon Road
Chapter 16
The Quiet Before The Storm

The hour's ride to D.C. was anticipated just as much by the children, as going to the baseball stadium. They all felt envied when they rode along in Dig's 1935 dark maroon Cadillac convertible sedan. The numbers business was going well for him. Petey enjoyed watching Digs work the clutch and gears while he sat in the front seat between the two men. They breezed along the road cutting through the humid air, Mimi's ponytail whipping from side to side. Digs looked in the back seat from time to time to ask the children how they were doing and to wink at Mimi.

Griffith Stadium stood majestically on the corner of Georgia Avenue and W Street, N.W. in the District of Columbia. The children lined up outside the stadium behind Digs, with Reverend Beaumont bringing up the rear to make sure the twins didn't disappear. Led by Digs, they found their way to the Negro section at the right field pavilion after a good twenty minutes of bathroom trips. The Colored toilet was near their entrance but the Reverend didn't want the children going alone later, so they all went before the game started.

Digs sat at the beginning of the row so he could easily purchase snacks for the children. Petey managed to sit next to Digs so that Mimi wouldn't somehow end up in that space. Jesse sat next to Petey with Mimi next, then Danny and Jimmy and the Reverend at the end. Jesse wanted to sit next to Petey since this was the first time the two of them had been to a baseball game in a stadium.

Petey had been remote lately, as if he had other things on his mind and didn't want to be bothered. Twice Petey hugged him during the game as they laughed at the mascot's performance. Jesse hugged back and it felt like old times when Petey called him "Shade."

Mimi, unaware of Petey's intervention on her behalf, was happy to be sitting near him and not beside Digs. She wanted to tell her father that Digs made her uncomfortable but she didn't know how to broach the subject. It was too embarrassing to talk over with her father, and she was even more nervous about discussing her feelings with her mother or her grandmother. After all, Digs hadn't actually done anything bad to her. It was just a feeling that there was something wrong with the way he looked at her: some underlying sinful intention was at

Watermelon Road

work in his stare. She didn't know what to call it. Her instincts told her that if she did mention it to Grandmother Mimi the friendship between Grandmother and Digs would be gone forever and she was afraid of what would grow in its place.

Jesse was prepared to purchase his own snacks with the spending money his parents had given him. Digs would not hear of it. Throughout the game, he kept everyone supplied with popcorn, hotdogs, sodas, and roasted peanuts. The Reverend protested mildly but Digs refused to stop spending his money on the children. Nothing was too good for them.

"You are going to make them sick as dogs, Mr. Digs."

The children were in awe of the Nats as they watched the players on the field. The weather was perfect. It was a close game and at one point, the Nats and the Boston Red Sox were tied at 4 and 4 in the eighth.

Not long after the children left for the game, Mimi Laurent called a cab and went out. She returned home two hours later and $5,000 poorer than when she left. "I can always get more money," she told herself as she climbed the stairs to her bedroom to rest. Everything had been arranged and she was tired.

The children talked of nothing else but the game on the ride home. They waved their Washington baseball caps when Digs drove down Bottom Street. "The Nats won," they yelled from the car to neighbors and children on both sides of the street.

Althea met them at the door, smiling when she saw them all standing there wearing blue baseball caps with the big white "W" on them. "The Nats won 5-4 in the 10th inning," Danny and Jimmie yelled. Althea placed her index finger to her lips to quiet them before they entered the house.

"Be quiet, please. Your grandma is resting. You cheerin want something to eat?"

"No thank you. I'm sick in my stomach," said Danny. That's when Jimmy punched him in his upset stomach and Danny threw up all over himself and the shiny marble floor in the vestibule. The other children laughed and teased him and he began to cry.

The Reverend told Mimi to stop laughing and to take Danny up the backstairs to the third floor and clean him up. He told Jimmy to stay in his room for the rest of the day for hitting his brother. He ordered the others to go to their rooms for a rest before dinner and to wash up before they came downstairs again. "Don't come down until you are called for dinner," he said. "Oh, and don't forget to thank Mr. Owens for taking you to the game."

Before Jesse, Petey and Jimmy went to the kitchen to take the backstairs to the third floor, they thanked Digs again for taking them to the baseball game and for the snacks he bought them. Mimi had already taken Danny upstairs.

"Tain't nothin'," said Digs. "I'm glad you cheerin had fun." He shook hands with the Reverend and went out to his car. "I think I'll take a little nap myself," said the Reverend as he headed for the stairs.

On his way to the backstairs, Petey pretended to stop for a glass of water so

Jesse and Jimmy went up without him. After everyone had gone upstairs, Petey quickly ran outside and waved down Digs before he drove off. "Mr. Digs," he called out as he ran down the front steps.

Digs stopped in the middle of pulling away from the curb. "What you want boy," he asked somewhat irritated as his day with the children did not go as well as he had planned. He was miffed because he didn't get to sit beside Mimi. He had planned to put his hands all over her, brushing up against her as much as he could without her father knowing. He knew he could control her if he got her alone. He could do what he wanted to her and threaten to hurt her family to get her to keep her mouth shut. *Oh well, I got the whole summer and daddy won't be around.*

Petey opened the door and got in the car. Digs had a surprised look on his face at the boldness of the boy. "I got something to discuss with you," said Petey.

"Now what could that be, boy?"

"I want to make a deal with you. I see the way you look at Mimi. I see the way you touch her. I know she don't like the way you touch her all the time when you come to her Grandmother's house. Nobody else see it but me. Mimi won't say nothin' but I will, even if nobody believes me."

Without saying a word, Digs drove the two of them away from the house and down to the corner, turned right and drove to the end of the next block. Then he spoke, "You listen to me you fuckin' piece of country shit. I don't know what you talkin' 'bout but if you tell anyone what you done seen or what you think you done seen, I'm gonna slit your skinny little throat. You got that? I would never hurt Mimi or no chile."

"I found Grandmother Mimi's money," Petey said.

Digs looked confused for a moment.

"What money are you talkin 'bout?"

"The money you and Grandmother Mimi was arguing 'bout yesterday.

I hid in her bedroom this morning and watched her go to her hiding place. She had a secret drawer in her armoire with a wooden box in it filled with money. The box ain't even have a lock on it. I waited until she put the box back and I took the box after she went into her bathroom to take a bath." Petey knew he had Digs hooked.

"How much money are we talkin' about?" Digs asked slyly.

"I don't know since Grandmother took some out afore she put the box back and I didn't see what she did with it. All I knows is there's some left in the box if you want it. You got to promise to leave Mimi alone and I'll give you the money for sure. I'm a man of my word. Now you just told me you ain't gonna do nothing bad to Mimi so I guess you don't need the money." Petey opened the car door.

"Wait a minute. I ain't gonna do nothin' bad to Mimi but a man can always use a little extra money. I tell you what. You meet me at the end of the alley we just passed tonight, about 1:00 in the morning. Bring the money and we'll talk some more."

"I can meet you," Petey said. "I know how to get out of the house and won't nobody know I'm gone."

"I'm counting on that, my little man," said Digs. "Now you run on back to the house. I'll see you tonight"

Petey went back to the house and let himself in the unlocked front door. He went upstairs to the room he shared with Jesse. Jesse was fast asleep, worn out from all the excitement of the game and the food. Petey noticed the bulge in Jesse's back pocket where he kept the pocket knife. He would wait until Jesse went to bed that night and he'd take the knife for a little walk once again.

It puzzled him that he did not hear or feel the rumblings of the snake that often spoke to him, telling him to do something bad. All he felt was relief that he could save Mimi.

Althea served a light meal of crabmeat salad, corn on the cob, and creamy coleslaw at the kitchen table. After dinner, the adults and children went out to the back porch with Baby Boy close behind, his stomach full with under the table offerings from the children. Althea brought out a pitcher of sweet tea and glasses and placed them on the small glass topped table on the porch. She then went back in and brought out a tray weighted down with dessert bowls filled with homemade pineapple ice cream.

"If you don't need me for nothin' else, Mrs. Laurent, I'm gonna clean up the kitchen and go on home," said Althea.

Grandmother Mimi said, "You go on home as soon as you can. Thanks, sweetie, for all you been doing for the cheerin."

Grandmother Mimi looked over at the children and said, "I'm surprised you cheerin had any room left to eat anything after all that stuff you had at the game."

"I know what you mean Mother Mimi. Even Danny ate again after being sick." The Reverend had eaten his share of the food without complaint and was now enjoying the ice cream along with the children.

Jesse and the twins were sitting in the glider, slowly pushing it back and forth. It had been a warm day and it was still warm that night. Grandmother lit the two hanging porch lamps with a match. The screens surrounding the porch kept out most of the moths and gnats. Grandmother kept swatting at the bugs that got through the screens with her trusty fly swatter.

Petey and Mimi sat on the porch steps and watched the fireflies light up in the darkened backyard. Baby Boy lay peacefully in Jesse's lap. He was back to being friends with Jesse again since Petey had no more bacon for him.

The children went to bed a little after nine. Grandmother Mimi asked the Reverend to step into the library for a little talk before he headed off to bed. They went into the small library. Grandmother Mimi sat at the desk and the Reverend sat in the visitor's chair, the only other chair in the room. He turned the chair around to face her, sat down and clasped his hands in his lap. Grandmother Mimi lit a cigarette, smoked and thought out what she wanted to say. The Reverend, who didn't smoke, waited patiently for his mother-in-law to get her thoughts together. "The Lord only knew what was coming out her mouth next," he thought to himself as he waited for her to begin.

"I had to talk to you tonight, she began. I know you and the boys will be busy tomorrow packing up to leave on Friday."

By 9:45 p.m., Grandmother had concluded her talk with her son-in-law. She had told him everything she knew, beginning with the phone call from Jesse's parents that morning to the plan that she had already set in motion to keep Jesse safe.

Reverend Beaumont fell back in his chair, stunned by what he had just heard.

"I don't believe it," he said with conviction. "I don't believe that sweet child upstairs would do such a thing. I've heard rumors about the stabbing of the little girl but nothing about a pocket knife. I don't know what to say. However, I'm hoping you have a better solution than what you just told me. I don't want to be a part of anything as monstrous as what you may have planned. But I do know one thing, your solution will kill the boy's parents. You are taking a big gamble with their lives and the child's. I don't think they will ever forgive you."

"Well Reverend, you just sit there and analyze and pray. Meanwhile, I handed over the money and the deed will be done if it hasn't been done already. I can assure you that no one will be harmed. I promised his parents I would do whatever is necessary to save Jesse and I'm trying to do just that. All you have to do is play along and do your part when you get to Birmingham. You just say what I told you to say. Petey won't mess things up because he won't know the truth. Even so, all he can say is what he was told. In a month or so, all will be put right again."

Watermelon Road
Chapter 17
Fresh Kill

Petey didn't have a plan for disposing of Digs but he knew one would come to him. He got out of bed at midnight and took the pocket knife from Jesse's pants pocket while he slept.

He had pretended he was asleep when the Reverend looked in on him and Jesse at 10:00. At 12:30 a.m., Petey went down the backstairs in his pajamas and holding his slippers in his hand. He put on his slippers when he reached the kitchen and went out the backdoor and down the porch steps, leaving the backdoor closed but unlocked.

Petey walked toward the shed to retrieve the wooden box he hid behind it earlier in the day. Baby Boy suddenly appeared from under the porch. Petey was surprised to see the little dog still outside. Baby Boy started barking and jumping up and down on Petey. The terrier had his red ball in his mouth and wanted to play catch. To Petey's dismay, someone had forgotten to bring Baby Boy in for the night.

"I cain't believe Grandmother Mimi went to bed without Baby Boy in her room. She must have been really tired," he thought to himself as he reached down and picked up the dog.

Petey retrieved the box from behind the shed. He couldn't leave Baby Boy in the yard barking because someone would come for him and find the backdoor unlocked. They might get suspicious. He stepped out into the alley, holding the dog, and continued to the next block to keep his appointment with Digs. Baby Boy squirmed in his arms but Petey held on tight.

The streets were vacant and silent. No people walking, no cars coming or going. Not even the dogs were barking. Some light from the electric street lamps illuminated the alley. Petey and Baby Boy made it to the meeting place without being seen. In the alley, he noticed the residents had large galvanized trash cans stationed at their back gates. He searched some of the trash cans, looking for old newspapers or magazines. He found a stack of newspapers in one of the trash cans. He put the terrier down and took some of the newspapers from the trash can. He then put two of the large trash cans together and hid behind them. Baby Boy was busy sniffing the alleyway not far from where Petey was hiding. Petey took the money from the wooden box and put it in his pajama pocket. He tore the newspaper into strips and rubbed the strips between his hands to calm himself while he thought of a way to kill Digs. He had no prior experience in killing an adult, especially a streetwise and powerful man like Digs. Finding a way to catch Digs off guard would not be easy. He had to try something because there would never be another opportunity after tonight.

Baby Boy chewed on the strips of paper while Petey meditated. Petey rubbed his stomach, hoping that would make the snake come to life and tell him how to kill Digs.

"Help me snake," he pleaded, but the thing in his belly remained silent.

The alley was lit in places from the porch lanterns on the back of the houses bordering on the alley. After awhile, Petey took one of the large trash cans from in front of another back gate and placed it in the center of the alley where there was ample light for Digs to see it. This would cause Digs to stop his car. Unable to proceed, he would have to get out and investigate.

Petey placed Grandmother Mimi's empty cash box on top of the trash can lid and returned to his hiding place. Digs' headlights would shine on the trash can, and the box on top of the can's lid.

Baby Boy sniffed the trash can Petey had placed in the middle of the alley. Grandmother's scent must have been on the box. Petey called to him from his hiding place but the dog ignored him.

Digs pulled into the alley promptly at 1:00 a.m. The car's headlights illuminated the trash can in the middle of the alley. Digs came to a complete stop about five yards from the trash can. He still had the top down on the car. He sat in the car for a few minutes and listened to the sounds around him. He took a look around, turned off the engine and extinguished the headlights, leaving the keys in the ignition and got out. He held a flashlight in his right hand. Petey waited. He had removed his pajamas and slippers. He couldn't risk coming home with blood on his pajamas. He held the pocket knife, ready to attack.

Digs surveyed the alley again with the flashlight. He didn't see anything suspicious but wondered why Petey was not there. He walked towards the trash can, thinking that Petey would jump out of the large can and surprise him, playing some juvenile game. He felt stupid for showing up in the first place. He was now certain this was just a child's silly prank. As he got closer, he saw the box on the lid of the can. Baby Boy began to growl. Digs was surprised to see Baby Boy and wondered why he was there. He remembered that the dog did not like him and would bite if he got any closer. He spoke softly to the dog but the terrier, protecting his mistress' possession, starting barking at him.

With the opened pocket knife in hand, Petey came out from behind the trash cans and hid behind Digs' car. Digs kicked at the dog. This angered Baby Boy even more, so he jumped high and sunk his teeth into Dig's left thigh and held on. Digs, with his back to the car, dropped the flashlight and went down on one knee with his hands wrapped around Baby Boy's throat. Baby Boy was whining in pain but he wouldn't let go. Petey ran from behind the car and plunged the blade of the knife into the left side of Digs' neck, above the shoulder blade.

Watermelon Road

Petey knew this would not kill Digs, but would disable him enough for Petey to get the upper hand.

Digs fell forward, turned onto his back and looked up in shock at a naked Petey. He let go of Baby Boy and attempted to remove the knife from his neck. Petey picked up the flashlight and slammed it down on Dig's head. The blow didn't knock the man out but he was disoriented for a moment. At that point Baby Boy leaped into Digs' face and bit his nose. Digs was bleeding profusely from the wound in his neck. Petey pulled the knife out when Digs grabbed the dog to snatch him away from his nose. The dog was relentless and determined to hang on. Digs screamed from the pain in his neck and his nose. Petey ran to the car and got in and started the engine. Sitting in the front seat during the drive to Griffith Stadium earlier had given him the perfect opportunity to observe Digs' driving, and he was confident he knew how to maneuver the clutch and gears.

Still struggling with the dog, Digs sat up when he heard the car engine. Petey moved the clutch and gear shift into place and pressed on the gas pedal as hard as he could and the car leaped forward. He heard Digs scream. The noise of the trash can was deafening as it flew through the air, landing on other trash cans.

Digs and Baby Boy were pinned under the car. Petey had driven the car about 20 yards, dragging Digs and Baby Boy, before he came to a stop. Lights in all the homes backing the alley went on. Petey opened the car door and jumped out, still holding onto the pocket knife. He retrieved his pajamas and slippers and ran naked back to Grandmother Mimi's house. He never looked back.

Petey let himself into the kitchen and locked the backdoor. He took a dish towel from the pantry and used it to wash himself off in the water closet under the backstairs. He put his pajamas and slippers back on and wrung out the dish towel. He placed the towel under his bed to dry. When it was dry, it would be packed among his clothing in the sack to take with him. The plan was to discard the dish towel at one of the many places the bus stopped on the way back to Alabama. Althea had changed the beds yesterday morning and would not change them again until Friday, so there was no danger of her finding the dish towel under his bed.

He lay on his pillow, overcome with a feeling of contentment.

Mimi had nothing more to fear.

Watermelon Road
Chapter 18
Bad News

Reverend Beaumont sat at the breakfast table with his morning coffee. He read the daily newspaper's summary of the baseball game they attended the day before. The article related that on June 5, the Nats ended their losing streak by beating the Boston Red Sox 5-4 at Griffith Stadium.

When the children came down to breakfast, the Reverend read the section about the Nats aloud to them. He had been the first one up that morning and helped Althea prepare the huge breakfast they were all now enjoying. There was nothing in the paper about Digs' murder since it happened after the newspapers had been put to bed.

"Has anyone seen Baby Boy?" Grandmother Mimi asked as she entered the kitchen, still in her nightclothes. They all looked up from their plates when she spook. She was a vision in a pink and green satin lounging ensemble. Pink satin slippers adorned her feet.

"My door was closed when I went to bed last night, so one of you cheerin must have let him out to go to the bathroom." She turned to Jimmy and said, "Jimmy, you go look and see if he's out back."

"I'll go check," said Petey as he got up from the table and went out the back-door. He was hoping that Grandmother Mimi would remember that no one brought Baby Boy into the house last night; then she would eventually think that the dog squeezed through the back gate and ran away.

While Petey was out back pretending to look for Baby Boy, the doorbell rang and Althea went to answer it. Two white policemen stood on the front steps. One of them asked to speak to Mrs. Mimi Laurent. Althea invited the officers to come in and have a seat in the parlor while she went to get Grandmother Mimi. The officers remained standing in the parlor until Grandmother Mimi appeared. She came in with a frown on her face. She had no idea why the police were in her home at this hour, unless Theo had a problem with the business or he had somehow been injured or killed. Grandmother had to keep her cool in case they were there about her illegal activities. She had certainly paid off enough policemen to keep them out of her business and her home. She did not recognize these two men.

Watermelon Road

Althea stood listening outside the parlor door. Grandmother Mimi had not closed the door all the way.

Neither officer bothered to introduce himself. Grandmother Mimi was used to the disrespect of the "cops" as she called them. Like Althea, she offered them a seat but they remained standing.

"Do you know a man by the name of Cleveland Owens?"

"Yes, but I call him Digs for short. He's a friend of mine and I've known him for about 15 years now. Sometimes he comes to the house for dinner." She knew she was talking too much but she couldn't stop herself. "What about Cleveland?"

"He was found dead this morning in an alley about a block from here," said the taller of the two policemen.

Althea put her hand to her mouth. So it was true. Her girlfriend had stopped her on the way to work that morning and told her that Digs was dead. Neither she nor her girlfriend was surprised to hear that Digs had been killed, considering his lifestyle. Althea didn't expect the police to show up at Mrs. Laurent's door so soon, which is why she hadn't mentioned the news to her.

Rocked to the core, Grandmother Mimi said "Dead? Oh my God! How? Why? What happened?" Fear rose in her gut.

Hearing voices in the parlor, the Reverend walked past Althea in the hallway and stuck his head in the parlor. He was startled to see the policemen there.

"Is everything all right?" He asked his mother-in-law.

Grandmother Mimi was angered by his interruption and snapped. "This ain't nothing I cain't handle. You go on back to your meal."

Steve, the taller officer, continued to speak. "We got a call about a disturbance in the alley off of Finch Street. One of the neighbors put in the call. We arrived in the alley around 2:00 a.m. We found Mr. Owens dead. We questioned people in a two-block radius. Although the alley was dark, some of the residents had their back porch lights on. A few heard a commotion last night after 1:00 a.m. From their viewpoint, some said that they saw a man on the ground and another man standing over him. A few said they only saw a car without its headlights on. Then one or two thought they heard a dog barking near the car."

"I can't reveal exactly how he was killed but there was a dog lying beside him, a Jack Russell terrier which we found out belonged to you because of the dog collar he was wearing. This dog was also injured last night and is lying half dead on the back seat of our car."

"Oh no, Lord Jesus, please God no," Grandmother yelled and collapsed onto a settee nearby.

"Vick. Go get the dog." The shorter policeman went out to the police car.

Baby Boy was wrapped in a towel and Grandmother Mimi managed to stand up when the officer handed Baby Boy to her. She took him into her arms, crying all the while, making soothing noises to her baby. Baby Boy whined but did not move. His breathing was shallow.

Vick spoke up "Mr. Owens, ah, Digs, had a small empty wooden box with him. Do you know anything about that? We don't know what was in the box but it looks like Digs might have been killed for the contents of that box."

Grandmother Mimi stood still. "What did the box look like?" She asked.

"It's a small, cheap, wood grained box about eight inches long and four inches high. There's nothing special about it. What's left of it is down at the station if you want to come down and take a look at it. It was badly damaged. We doubt if we can get any fingerprints off the box. There must have been something valuable in it that the other man wanted. How your dog got in the mix is beyond us. We need some answers," said Officer Steve.

Grandmother Mimi wanted very much to rush Baby Boy to the animal hospital but she knew she had to remain calm and not lose her head. She didn't know how Digs could have done it but he must have gotten into the house and stolen the rest of her secret stash.

"I don't know nothin' bout no box. As you might have also heard from the neighbors, Digs was a loan shark and maybe kept his money in a box. Who knows? Maybe he was robbed and then killed. And, if you wonder why my dog was with him, sometimes I let him out at night in the backyard to do his business before I turn in. I might have left the back gate open." She made no mention of the children and the Reverend spending the day with Digs before he was murdered.

"I guess my dog ran out into the alley and followed it along to where Digs was meeting with somebody. Maybe he heard Digs' voice and recognized it. He never liked Digs and would try to bite him whenever he came around. The two cops gave each other the "look." They knew that the terrier had bitten Digs in several places on his body.

"We've questioned people in the neighborhood and no one seems to know how Digs spent his day yesterday. No one saw him or spoke to him. Don't you find that strange, Mrs. Laurent?" Steve was trying to be tricky.

"No sir, I don't find it strange. Digs was secretive and I'm sure no one knew his daily schedule but him."

Steve asked "Who else resides in this house with you?"

Grandmother Mimi answered truthfully, "My boyfriend, Theodore Cooke, who works as a baker downtown on Willow Street. Right now I have my son-in-law, three grandchildren and two of their friends. My son-in-law, Reverend Beaumont, brought my grandchildren up for the summer like he's been doing for years. He's leaving with the two friends on Friday. They reside in Horace Graves, Alabama."

"What are the ages of the children?" Vick was on a roll.

"The ages range from seven to twelve," she answered politely.

"I see no reason at the moment to question the Reverend and the children. We might have some more questions for you later. If we need you, we know where to find you. Thank you for your time, Mrs. Laurent."

"Officers, did anyone see who was driving the car?" Grandmother Mimi asked.

"No, and we fingerprinted the steering wheel but only got a lot of newspaper ink that was smeared all over it. Then we tried to fingerprint the rest of the car but it was clean as a whistle," Steve chimed in.

"Well that's not unusual," Grandmother Mimi said. "Digs did his loan shark

Watermelon Road

business in his car and was known to wipe it down after each meeting to protect himself and his clients."

While the officers were digesting this information, Althea came into the parlor, took Baby Boy from Grandmother Mimi and carried him out to the kitchen. The children watched with sad expressions while Baby Boy lay limp in Althea's arms. He raised his head once when he heard his name.

"What happened to him?" Jimmy was the first to speak.

"I think you need to ask your grandmother 'bout what happened. She's fixin' to take Baby Boy to the vet. She'll tell ya'll what happened when she comes back."

Danny asked, "How come them cops is here?

While the Reverend was trying to assist Grandmother Mimi in the parlor, Danny had sneaked up the backstairs and looked out their bedroom window facing the street. He saw the police car.

The Reverend ignored Danny's question and said. "You two boys finish your breakfast and go on out back and play. You better not hurt that cat if you find him out there. I sure hope you two didn't have anything to do with Baby Boy getting hurt because if you did, I'm going to whip your behinds. Then I'm going to turn you over to those cops."

Being handed over to the cops was the number one fear on the twins' list of scary things. They hit the backdoor without looking back. The Reverend, Althea, Jesse and Mimi laughed. Petey kept silent. He didn't look at the dog nor did he make any comments about the situation. Jesse and Mimi noticed that Petey had had little to say all morning.

Looking around the parlor, Officer Steve said, "This is certainly a nice house, Ma'am."

"My husband left it to me when he passed away several years ago. Before then, it had been in his family for a long time, so I come into it by marriage." Grandmother Mimi did not look the officer in the eye when she spoke, but retied her robe and checked the comb in her hair.

"Can I get you officers something to eat or some coffee maybe?"

"No thanks," said Steve, also speaking for Vick.

Officer Vick, trying to show some authority said, "Please stick around town in case we need you to come down to the station."

"I will be happy to do that, officers. I'll wait to hear from you. Meanwhile, I'm going to rush my dog to the animal hospital." She paused and said, "Can you please tell me now how Digs died and how my dog got hurt?"

The two policemen looked at each other. Steve nodded and Vick said, "Mr. Cleveland was run over by his own car in the alley and he was holding your dog at the time. I guess whoever was driving the car didn't care if the dog got hurt as long as they got Mr. Cleveland."

After the officers left, Grandmother Mimi went up to her bedroom and opened the armoire. The secret door was closed. She opened it and the compartment was empty. The wooden box was gone. She tried to imagine what had happened. Somehow Digs or someone he hired had gotten into the house and found the money. How the thief got into the house without anyone knowing was a mystery to her. In fact it was damn unbelievable. Digs was out all day yesterday with the children and could not have come back and searched her room while everyone else was still at the game in DC.

She could not and would not believe that anyone staying in the house helped Digs steal the money, so help had to have come from someone outside. Some desperate junkie had come in and did the dirty work for him. She had only been out of the house for a few hours yesterday to run an errand. Baby Boy was in the backyard. She dreaded to have to question Althea about the comings and goings of yesterday. Grandmother Mimi hoped Althea wouldn't get upset if she asked her questions.

I'm glad you're dead. I hope whoever killed your dumb ass gets away with it even though they stole my money after you stole it and hurt Baby Boy. Except I'm going to kill the mother fucker myself if I find out who done hurt my dog and left him to die in the street.

She dressed quickly and had Althea call a cab. While she waited with Baby Boy, Grandmother Mimi asked Althea if she had heard Digs was dead. Althea admitted that her girlfriend had told her earlier that morning and that she had planned to tell Grandmother Mimi but the police beat her to it.

"Althea, while I was out yesterday, and everyone else was in D.C., did you happen to hear any strange noises coming from my bedroom? Where was Baby Boy while I was gone?"

"I ain't seen Baby Boy."

"I was in the kitchen cooking. I did some cleaning down on the first floor and a little dusting on your floor. I changed the beds on the third floor after the Reverend and the children left. Yesterday was washday so I didn't stay upstairs long."

"When you came in this morning, did you notice anything strange in the house? I mean like did you find a door or window already open?" Grandmother Mimi tried not to imply that she was accusing Althea of any wrongdoing.

"I ain't see nothin' different. Everything looked all right when I come in."

"I was just wondering if someone was trying to get at us, too, since Digs got killed. I'm going to take Baby Boy to the animal hospital and I want you to keep an eye on the children. Thank you, Althea."

"Ain't no trouble Mrs. Laurent."

After Grandmother Mimi left, Althea started cleaning up the kitchen now that breakfast was over. Reverend Beaumont continued to read the newspaper. He looked up at one point and asked Althea "Do you know why the police were here this morning?"

Althea looked over at Petey, Jesse and Mimi still sitting at the kitchen table.

"Yes sir, I knows something 'bout it, but Mrs. Laurent ain't the one that told me."

Reverend Beaumont took the hint and told the three children to go outside and keep an eye on the twins.

Outside in the backyard, Petey told Jesse and Mimi that he was going for a walk and started out the back gate. Mimi was incredulous "You don't want to hear what they are talking 'bout in the kitchen? There's a window open above the kitchen sink where Althea is standing. We can hide under the window box there and listen.

Come on Jesse, let Petey miss everything and don't you tell him what happened either since he wants to go walking."

Petey took his hand off the gate. "Okay, I'll go listen. Come on show us where the window is. This better be good."

"It's gotta be good," said Jesse. "It's always good stuff when grown ups tell you to leave the room."

Mimi led the boys around to the side of the house and made them sit on the ground under the huge flower box that was hanging overhead.

They sat under the flower box with Mimi in the middle. Jesse said "I bet them twins is hiding in their bedroom closet, thinking them police is gonna come and get them." The two boys started laughing. "Shush!" Mimi put her finger to her lips and then pointed up.

"Well, I'm waiting," they heard the Reverend say to Althea.

"I got this friend that works around the corner on Finch Street. She told me on the way to work this morning that Mr. Digs was killed last night in the alley off of Finch Street. Now get this, Reverend, she say he was run over by his own car. He had been stabbed a couple of times too. There weren't nothin' in the papers this morning 'bout Digs, so I don't know what the truth is. All I know is that somehow Baby Boy got run over in that alley too and Mrs. Laurent done took him to the vet. That's all I knows. None of it makes sense to me."

"Lord have mercy! Digs got himself murdered? How could this be? We just spent the whole day with him yesterday. I know he was a man of secrets but for someone to kill him, that's unbelievable. We were with him all day yesterday. I can't believe it. And Baby Boy got hurt too? What in the name of Jesus was Digs doing with Baby Boy? I hope that dog lives 'cause it will kill my mother-in-law if he doesn't."

"Ain't that somethin'," Althea said, looking every bit the proud bearer of bad news.

Outside the window, Mimi reached over and held and squeezed each boy's hand when she heard Digs had been killed. Mimi cried softly and Jesse was upset because he didn't have a hanky to hand her like the men in the picture shows. Petey squeezed Mimi's hand and bent over and kissed her cheek. He knew and only he knew that she was crying from relief.

"That ain't all, Reverend." Althea continued. "My friend, Ruthie, say the peoples she works for heard noises in the alley and a dog barking and then a car gunning its engine. I hear it was a mess in that alley. That car was on top of Digs and Baby Boy. Digs bleeding from his neck and trash cans scattered every which way. Mr. Jones, the man Ruthie works for, said he found strips of paper, some in little balls, and some scrunched up, behind two trash cans standing together. He thinks the killer was hiding behind the trash cans and that he gave the dog the newspapers to chew on to keep it quiet. He said the killer threw the dog on Digs when Digs come into the alley.

Ruthie and me laughed 'cause that ain't got nothin' to do with the murder. That Mr. Jones thinks he's some kind of detective. Maybe he can tell us why Baby Boy was there since he's Mr. Detective."

Mimi let go of Petey's hand. She still held tight to Jesse's. She turned to Petey and said "Petey, were you there last night? Did you see Digs get killed?" Jesse was too afraid to say what he was thinking. He kept quiet.

Petey looked into Mimi's eyes and said "No, I wasn't there. I was home in bed like ya'll. Jesse knows I was in that bed across from him. If I'd been there, do you think I'd let Mr. Digs and Baby Boy get hurt?"

"You could help the police if you were there and saw what happened, and more so if you saw who did it," Mimi tried to reason with him.

"Like I said, I wasn't there. I was sleep. Ain't that right Jesse?"

Jesse crawled away from the window and went to the back gate. They followed him.

He turned to Petey and said "I was sleep too, so you could have sneaked out if you wanted to. All I know is you stole my pocket knife and I want it back."

"What knife? Mimi questioned. "You talkin' 'bout that pocket knife you showed us at the church picnic?" Petey looked away. He didn't like what he saw in her eyes. He tried to explain. "I jest borrowed the knife. Jesse knows I borrowed that knife sometimes so's I can whittle something." He moved towards Mimi and she backed away.

"What's the matter with you Mimi? Are you stupid or something? Why you acting like you afraid of me? If you think I killed Digs with that little pocket knife, why don't you say why I did it? Huh? What's the matter? Did you like the way Digs put his hands all over you, up and down your back and your ass all the time whispering in your ear? Did I kill your boyfriend?"

Mimi was rooted to the ground. She was frightened and humiliated by Petey's outburst.

Jesse got in between Petey and Mimi. "What's wrong with you, Petey? You steal my knife and say you didn't, now you is scaring Mimi. She ain't done none of those things with Digs. I don't know what you talkin' bout. You ain't got no cause to call Mimi names. She ain't say you done nothin' to Digs. She jest asked if you see something."

"You listen Mr. Fatback Blackjack, you ain't got no cause to accuse me of nothin' and if you keep running your mouth 'bout me borrowing your knife I'm gonna kick your big black ass right out here in front of your little hussy." Petey stood in front of Jesse with clinched fists.

Jesse stood his ground. "Go ahead you crazy nigger. Why don't you take out my knife and stab me with it like you did Digs and that Suzy girl." Petey took the pocket knife from his pocket and started to open it. Mimi screamed and ran towards the back porch.

Reverend Beaumont heard her scream and came running from the kitchen. Petey put the knife back in his pocket, turned and ran into the alley. He kept on running in spite of the calls from the Reverend for him to come back.

Watermelon Road

"What in the name of Jesus is going on out here?" Jesse looked at Mimi who had gotten herself under control and was sitting on the back steps. Jesse said, "Me and Petey were arguing about who Mimi liked the best. Mimi thought we were going to fight so she started screaming."

"Is that what happened baby?" Mimi nodded "yes" without looking at her father. "Look at you," he said laughing. "You got boys fighting over you already and you ain't but twelve years old. I see I'm going to have a hard time when you get a little older."

"Don't you two worry about Petey. I'm sure we'll see him when it's time to eat," the Reverend added. With that being said, he playfully pulled Mimi's ponytail on his way up the steps and back into the house.

Mimi followed him. Jesse sat in the glider, swinging slowly as strange thoughts ran through his mind. Petey had changed. He was different somehow. He didn't joke or want to play or wrestle any more. He seemed sad all the time. Mostly he was quiet. Jesse had thought the two of them would have the best time of their lives in Baltimore. He had envisioned them sitting in the secret hole back home talking for hours about the time they had in Baltimore.

He only accused Petey of stabbing Digs and Suzy Fletcher because Petey had taken the knife again and would not return it when he asked for it. He just wanted to hurt Petey like he had hurt him by ignoring him all the time. Petey called him Fatback Blackjack like all the other children back home. That really hurt. Then he felt ashamed for the way he was thinking.

There's no way Petey could have killed Digs. Digs was a grown man. No child could kill a grown-up, especially with a little pocket knife. Jesse decided to talk to Petey when they returned to Horace Graves. Besides, he wanted to know why Petey said those things about Mimi and Digs. He couldn't ask Mimi about Digs and get her upset again.

Later on, everyone was in the kitchen eating lunch, except for Petey. He had not returned. The children heard the faint ring of the telephone in the library. Reverend Beaumont went to answer it. He returned to the kitchen looking downcast as he reported the bad news.

"I just heard from your Grandmother. Baby Boy died in her arms a little while after she got to the hospital. The vet told her the dog was much worse off than she thought. His back was broken.

When she gets home, I don't want any of you saying one word or asking one question about Baby Boy. Do you hear me?"

The children nodded in unison. Mimi couldn't trust herself to speak. This had been the worst day ever for her and she wouldn't want to live it over again for anything in the world. Jimmy and Danny started crying and yelling that they didn't do anything to Baby Boy. The Reverend told them that he knew it wasn't their fault and they stopped crying.

Suddenly, the Reverend became cheery, clapped his hands and said "Got some good news, though. Jesse, your parents have decided to take a vacation and they are leaving on Sunday to ride the bus up here for a visit. You won't be leaving for home tomorrow with Petey and me." Jesse was shocked. He couldn't believe what the Reverend had just told him. But then, that was the Reverend's first lie towards saving Jesse's life.

"I can't believe this," he said out loud. "My folks never go any place 'cause they have no money. Now, they are coming here?"

Mimi felt relieved. At least Jesse didn't have to take that long ride back to Horace Graves with Petey.

Petey came back at dinner time. No one asked him where he had been. He had only wandered several blocks from the house where he found a public park and that's where he stayed most of the day. The twins told him the good news about Jesse's parents coming up and that Jesse would stay on for a few more days. Petey was surprised and just as relieved as Mimi. He didn't want to take the long ride back to Alabama with Jesse. He decided not to return the pocket knife. As far as he was concerned, it was his.

The next morning a silent Petey got into the taxi with Reverend Beaumont and headed for the bus station. Petey wouldn't look at the children waving at him from the front steps. Jesse refused to ask for the knife again. *Let him have it if he wants it so bad.* Jesse had tried to have a conversation with Petey that morning but his best friend had ignored him while packing for the trip home.

Reverend Beaumont said goodbye to Grandmother Mimi earlier that morning. She sat in a chair by the window in her bedroom. The Reverend knocked on her door to let her know they were leaving. Dressed all in black, she let him in. She shuffled across the bedroom floor and sat back in the chair by the window again.

"Mother Laurent, I can't tell you how much you made us feel welcomed these past few days. I'm leaving my children here in hopes that they will cheer you up and make you smile again. I know it's hard to lose a loved one and you just take all the time you need to grieve. Mimi can look after the twins 'til you feel like yourself again."

He looked up when Petey entered the room. He motioned for Petey to go to Grandmother Mimi. Petey went over to her.

"Thank you for letting me come here and stay for awhile and for all that good food we had. You is a nice lady." Grandmother Mimi held out her arms and Petey went into them and was hugged and squeezed for the second time during his visit. He stepped back and the Reverend hugged his mother-in-law. "I'll be praying for you," he said.

She looked at both of them with swollen red eyes and nodded her head. She put a hanky to her lips, unable to speak, fending off a fresh flow of tears. The man and the boy backed out of the room and closed the door softly behind them.

Watermelon Road
Chapter 19
Birmingham

Reverend Beaumont and Petey arrived at the Travel Light bus station in Birmingham early Saturday morning. They were met by Sheriff Al Richards and Deputy Rudy Cox and taken inside of the station for questioning. Petey was mostly quiet, shaking his head or nodding in response to the Sheriff's questions about Jesse and their stay in Baltimore. The Sheriff also asked a lot of questions about the Fletcher girl. They asked Reverend Beaumont and Petey about the pocket knife, but both denied having seen Jesse with a knife of any kind.

Petey was afraid the Sheriff would search him and find the pocket knife, but no such thing happened. After all, he wasn't a suspect. He felt relieved that, before they reached Birmingham, he was able to discard the towel he used to wash himself off with after killing Digs. He told the Reverend he had to go pee. After he was out of sight, he stuffed the towel in a trash can in back of a diner at a rest stop.

The Reverend had explained to Petey on the bus to Birmingham, what had taken place in Horace Graves while they had been away. Petey was told that Jesse might be accused of killing the Fletcher girl and that Jesse's parents were going to Baltimore to get Jesse and take him to a safe place. He told Petey to say that Jesse had taken sick and was rushed to a nearby clinic, and that was why they came back without him. They couldn't wait for Jesse to get well because they couldn't miss the bus. The Reverend had to get back to his church in Alabama.

"I hate to have you lie," said the Reverend, "but we have to protect one of our own and Jesse is one of us. Everything seems to hang on something about a knife that was given to Jesse. Do you know anything about that?"

"No sir, I don't," said Petey.

Petey was sorry about Jesse's dilemma, but he was heading home with the pocket knife and Grandmother Mimi's money and had no regrets. He finally had an opportunity to count the money he had stolen from the armoire. It amounted to $5,000.00.

He knew that Jesse and his parents could convince everyone that Jesse did not kill the Fletcher girl. The police wouldn't find the pocket knife on Jesse so he should be safe. Jesse would never tell anyone that Petey had the pocket knife.

Mimi was another matter, however. She might talk to save Jesse. He would have to have a talk with Mimi when she came home.

Sheriff Richards was not satisfied with the answers given to him by Reverend Beaumont or Petey. He had his Deputy call the Baltimore Police Department and check out the story. The next day he got a call from the Captain at police headquarters in Baltimore. The Captain told him that they had called the clinic where Jesse was hospitalized and the clinic confirmed that Jesse was there. He had been treated for a stomach virus and was resting comfortably.

Jesse was never at the clinic. Oblivious to the storm around him, he was happily packing his beach clothes and shoes because Grandmother Mimi had promised the children a picnic at the beach on Sunday morning.

Watermelon Road
Chapter 20
Grief

By the following Monday night, it was all over town that Jesse had drowned in the Chesapeake Bay on Sunday while at the beach with the Beaumont children and their Grandmother. Grandmother Mimi had a telegram delivered to Sheriff Richards three hours after the tragic incident. The telegram said for the Sheriff to call her because it was a matter of life and death. She had her telephone number on the telegram.

The Sheriff called Grandmother Mimi. She related the circumstances surrounding Jesse's drowning. The Sheriff wanted to know how she knew for sure that the boy had drowned in the Chesapeake Bay because it usually takes days, sometimes weeks for a body to wash up on shore.

Grandmother Mimi said that the child's body did wash ashore three hours later further down the Bay from where he must have gone into the water. She said she had already identified the body for the Baltimore police. That satisfied the Sheriff.

Grandmother Mimi suggested to Sheriff Richards that he should take her son-in-law, Reverend Beaumont, with him when he went to the Hammonds to give them the bad news. She also suggested that a doctor be present.

The Sheriff could not get hold of a doctor but he did stop by the church and ask Reverend Beaumont to go with him to the Hammonds.

Reverend Beaumont accompanied the Sheriff to Francis and Lily's house to inform them of Jesse's tragic death. Lily fainted and had to be hospitalized for a few days. When she recovered, she refused to be comforted and kept to her bed where she oscillated between periods of consciousness and incoherence. Her doctor prescribed heavy sedatives for her depression.

Francis was by her side the whole time and neither could attend Jesse's funeral, which was held in Baltimore. The funeral was held on Thursday, June 13, 1935. The service was made even sadder by the children's tears.

Jesse's casket was closed, no viewing allowed. There wasn't enough time for his parents to send a picture of him to be placed on top of the closed casket. Grandmother Mimi and the three grandchildren were the only mourners to attend the funeral service. The service was held in a small room at the funeral home, and officiated by a Baptist minister associated with the funeral home. Althea was unable to come to the funeral because she felt her heart would surely break when she looked upon the casket of the little boy who had come to visit and never went home again.

Grandmother Mimi did not force the children to go to the gravesite. She knew it would be too much if they saw the open grave. It would have been much easier and safer for her to have had the body cremated, but Jesse's parents indicated that cremation was against their basic religious beliefs. Jesse's parents wanted their child's body to rest in peace intact so that when Christ came again, he would not have to put pieces of Jesse that were scattered over the earth back together again. That was the explanation Grandmother Mimi got from the boy's parents.

"All right, now." Grandmother Mimi thought to herself. "If there is any trouble down the road, I can easily have the body dug up and cremated."

Mimi and the twins were devastated. The last time they saw Jesse was on the sand near the water's edge. Jesse had announced he was going to look for a place to pee. He never came back. The children were so depressed that they wanted to leave Baltimore immediately after the funeral. Grandmother Mimi called Olivia's Diner and told Olivia to have Reverend Beaumont call her. Olivia told Grandmother Mimi that the church had recently put in a telephone at the parish house and gave her the Reverend's number. Grandmother Mimi let the children call their father to let him know that they wanted to come home. Reverend Beaumont told them that they had to stay in Baltimore until the first of August before he could come back to get them.

Back home, Lily was often despondent and would not accept visitors to the house. She hated Grandmother Mimi because she didn't honor her promise to keep her child safe. Jesse was not a good swimmer and had no business at the beach. Jesse's sudden death and the accusations that he was somehow involved in the murder of Suzy Fletcher were more than she and Francis could bear. Francis had to be the strong one, but with each waking moment he felt as if his heart would burst. It hurt even more that they were unable to attend their only child's funeral.

Petey didn't know what to think. This was as bad as Joel's death. He couldn't believe Jesse was gone and he never got to say goodbye or tell him the truth about the snake inside of him. He hid the pocket knife and the money in the shed in his backyard and left it there untouched for awhile. Jesse was gone. He went often to their secret place where the memories of his best friend would overtake him and he would burst into tears, leaning against the old cypress tree. He had lost Mimi's friendship as well but he believed he could fix that. He wrote to her often while she was in Baltimore, confessing to everything, including Suzy Fletcher's murder. Mimi never wrote back.

Watermelon Road
Chapter 21
I Died Young

"Stop that crying, you a big boy. You sure is a big boy for 10." I jerked my body off of the cot. I had the sensation of ascending like a bucket of water from a deep dark well. I stood in front of her, weaving back and forth, trying not to fall down. The high heels she wore made her appear a lot taller than me. She could have been sixteen or seventeen years old but looked older because of the heavy make-up. There was the look of lost innocence in her eyes. Looking back on my life, I can truly say that Strawberry was the most fascinating character, next to Grandmother Mimi, I had ever encountered.

"Here. I brought you something to eat. Ain't much but I know you must be hungry and scared. I come to keep you company. I'm Strawberry."

She gave me a hug. She was thin but soft. I hadn't noticed the breasts of the young girls I knew back in Alabama. Well, I noticed them but I had not experienced the urge to see them in their naked form as yet. I noticed Strawberry's right away. They were in my face and felt like two firm pillows. She noticed me eyeing her breasts. "This is why they call me Strawberry," she said. She pulled up her tiny shirt and pointed to a birthmark over her uncovered right breast that looked like a red strawberry. I couldn't look away. The look on my face made her laugh out loud. "Ain't you seen tits before? You sho' 'nuff is a funny little boy."

When I was older, I understood that Strawberry had afforded me an opportunity to experience the unguarded and sometimes liberating qualities of a person who is truly at home in their own skin.

She was dressed to look younger, around Mimi's age, but that was because she had to look that age on that day. Her hair was long, black and shinny. It was parted in the middle and made into a ponytail on each side of her head with a large ribbon on each ponytail to keep the hair in place. The pancake makeup and the rouge spot on each cheek reminded me of a porcelain doll I had seen in Mr. Batty's General Store one Christmas. Strawberry's eyes were heavily made up with mascara and long false eyelashes.

She had on a short sweater that showed her midriff, a very short skirt and patent leather shoes. She was playing the part of some pervert's fantasy above the basement where Grandmother Mimi's girls worked. At ten, I didn't have any fantasies except to spend time with my best friend, who I suddenly remembered might well be a crazy murderer. It was coming back to me now. I was a little groggy and disoriented before.

I remembered that we were all at the beach. Grandmother Mimi had taken us children there for a Sunday picnic. I was so happy. My parents were coming to get me on Monday, and we were to go off on our first vacation together. We were at one of the Chesapeake Bay beaches and I had left the group to find a place to relieve myself near the water's edge. That was the last thing I remembered until I woke up to see Strawberry staring down at me.

My legs felt weak, so I sat back down on the cot. Strawberry pulled up a small stool from the corner of the tiny dank room.

She handed me a souse sandwich and a bottle of milk. That was the beginning of my weight loss. I definitely have Strawberry to thank for that.

"You be all right. I hear Mrs. Laurent put you here to save you from the police cause they think you kill somebody back where you live."

I broke my silence. "What you mean I kill somebody? I ain't killed nobody. Grandmother Mimi told me that my parents were coming to Baltimore for a visit. I was going back with them and that's why I couldn't go back with the Reverend Beaumont and Petey. Grandmother Mimi took Mimi, the twins and me to the beach while we was waiting for my parents to come up. At the beach, I went to find a spot to pee and I cain't remember nothin' after that 'cept I woke up in this little room."

Strawberry said, "I don't know none of them other people you talkin' bout, I only knows from what I hear the other girls say. They say some little girl was stabbed with a pocket knife and that you had a pocket knife like the one that killed her and that the police want you to come home but Mrs. Laurent done made it so you dead."

When I heard this I stood up and backed away from her and hit the wall of my cell-like hole. I was shaking. She giggled and helped me back to the cot. "You jest hiding out like peoples in them picture shows. You a gangster."

After she left, I lay on the cot most of that day trying to make some sense of everything. I didn't know what was going to happen to me. No one told me the plan and I feared I would live out my life in hiding in that cold, dark place.

"What place is this?" I asked Strawberry when she returned with my dinner of watery chicken soup and a slice of white bread.

"You is in the basement of Madam Laurent's Whorehouse. Ain't nobody gonna look for you here. You have to remember one thing while you here, don't ever try to come upstairs. You got that?"

I nodded my head, still not comprehending the full impact of my dilemma.

When she left, I lay on the cot and tried to remember the chain of events that led to my present circumstances.

After we suspected Petey of killing Digs and possibly Suzy Fletcher, Mimi and I avoided Petey as much as possible the day before he and I were to leave. I didn't find out about my parents coming until Reverend Beaumont made the announcement at lunch in Grandmother Mimi's kitchen the day before the

Watermelon Road

Reverend, Petey and I were to leave for Horace Graves.

    I had been overjoyed the next morning to see Petey and the Reverend sitting in the back seat of the taxi as it pulled away from the curb in front of the house on Bottom Street. Mimi, Danny and Jimmy stood on the front steps and waved goodbye to their father. I stayed inside and looked out the parlor window. The tension between Petey and I was palpable and we could not look each other in the eye. I had no proof that he had done anything wrong but I was still afraid of him. He was not the same person inside. He still had not returned my knife and I refused to ask for it back. If my father asked me about it, I had made up my mind to tell him the truth that Petey had stolen it.

    My parents were not coming for me. Grandmother Mimi and the Reverend had lied to all of us. I bet my parents didn't even know they were coming up for a visit. Grandmother Mimi was a horrible woman even if she was trying to save me from being lynched back in Alabama. I didn't know what to think of Reverend Beaumont's part in this. I couldn't think of one person I knew that would believe that I was the one who stabbed Suzy Fletcher. I still found it hard to believe that Petey might have done it. I kept thinking that he wanted to keep my knife because he coveted it.

    Mimi was afraid of Petey. He was so strange after Digs' death. Those things he said about Mimi and Digs confused me. It was a long time before I fully understood Petey's motive for killing Digs and then I wholeheartedly agreed with his actions on that point.

    After about a week in my cell-like room, Strawberry let me out into the other part of the basement. It was windowless and dark like my room. The air was musty with an underlying smell of something ancient. The dust made me sneeze. There were large boxes in one part of the room filled with old clothes, all women's things: hats, dresses, stockings, shoes, that sort of paraphernalia. Another section of the basement had stacked canned goods on shelves against the wall. Old mattresses, blankets and a lot of cleaning supplies were in a corner. There was also a huge locked liquor cabinet packed with filled liquor bottles under the basement stairs.

    From one end of the room to the other were hanging clotheslines loaded down with women's unmentionables, as my mother used call them. Washing clothes and hanging them up to dry was another one of Strawberry's chores. She did the washing upstairs but brought the wet clothes to the basement to dry if the weather was bad outside. At some point, I started helping her hang the clothing. I used to find myself thinking that, if they hung some of the items I saw hanging in the basement on the outside clotheslines, they must have been the talk of the neighborhood.

    Strawberry would let me come out of my room and walk around, like she was letting out her dog to do its business. Doing my business was another embarrassment, besides her making me strip from time to time so she could wash my clothes and hang them on the line next to the unmentionables. I tried to cover my lower body parts with my hands after I handed her my dirty underpants.

    She would giggle and say, "What you hiding yourself for? I seen lots of penises and you ain't got one yet." After those remarks, I made a promise to myself that if I ever got out of that basement, I would never undress in front of a woman again. Years later, I forgot all about that stupid promise.

One day, Strawberry showed up with two changes of outer clothing and underwear. They were all new and very much appreciated. I kept wondering why Grandmother Mimi didn't send my clothes to the whorehouse that I brought with me when I came to visit her. I guess she must have thrown my old clothes away after I supposedly died.

There was a chamber pot in the little room for me to use. I tried to hold it for as long as possible because I never knew when I'd see Strawberry. I didn't want to have that smell in the room for days until she showed up. I never got used to the embarrassment of this assigned chore of hers and she made sure I felt embarrassed by making fun of me. No matter how well we were getting along, when the time came to empty the pot and bring it back, she would act stupid and make nasty comments. Sometimes I wouldn't see her for two days. By then I'd be so hungry and thirsty and the room would reek of urine and excrement because I could not delay my bodily functions any longer. That's when she'd open the door and say, "Lawd, it smells like shit in here."

I spent most days on the cot, looking up at the ceiling. Sometimes I'd doze off and dream of our secret place and the fun times Petey and I had before he turned bad. I even missed Old Man Miller coming up Watermelon Road, our name for Fisherman's Lane. I wouldn't let myself think about Mimi, it hurt too much.

I lost track of time while I was in the basement. With no sun, moon or stars, one day ran into the next and sometimes I would have to ask Strawberry, "What day is this?" when she came down to the basement.

I cursed Petey for getting me into trouble. I wished him dead when Strawberry told me that they thought I had killed that Suzy Fletcher girl. I couldn't imagine why anybody would accuse me. I was only ten years old at the time and didn't know how to go about such a thing as murder. I prayed daily that they would find the real murderer even if it was Petey, so I could go home. I knew my parents were worried sick about me, especially my mother. I kept remembering her words about me being her only child and how she didn't want anything to happen to me. Thinking I was dead could have killed her for all I knew.

About two weeks into my stay at the "Whorehouse Hotel" as I came to call it, Strawberry brought me a *Popeye* comic book. It had been well read, probably by her. "Here," she said. "This might be something for you to do. Some of them pages are missing but you can read most of it. You can read, cain't you?" I nodded and thanked her for the gift. She was, in spite of her profession, a very kind person. I never had contact with anyone else while I was in that place. I began to regard her as my best friend since Petey had turned against me.

I must have read that comic book until I could recite each comic square by heart. I complained about the basement being so dark even though Strawberry had placed a kerosene lamp in the room with me, along with a box of matches. I was afraid of the lamp catching fire while I was locked in that room so I only lit it to read the comic book when my door was opened.

Watermelon Road

After I told her of my fear of a fire in the basement, she found a flashlight upstairs and gave it to me so that I wouldn't have to light the lamp if I didn't have to.

There used to be a light bulb in the ceiling of the main part of the basement but it had not been replaced. Sometimes the women in the house brought kerosene lamps down with them to illuminate the basement so that they could find what they needed on the clotheslines. Strawberry always locked my door before they came. I could hear them laughing and whispering about me, the little fat gangster boy.

Strawberry came down one morning and said she had to go away for three days. I panicked when she told me this. I started screaming that I would die before she came back. She told me that she was going to leave me enough food and water for two days. She said the food would last three days if I stretched it, so that made me feel better.

The day before she left, she changed my bed and brought me a basin of fresh water so I could wash myself and brush my teeth.

Strawberry did return in three days but never said why she had to go away. I asked her but she ignored me.

Sometimes she brought me something really good to eat like fried chicken and chocolate cake. The food definitely got better, but I still lost 15 pounds during the length of my stay in that house.

I always knew when she was coming because I could hear her jingling the set of keys she carried with her. There was a key to the main basement door and one to my room. Fourteen steps in the basement led up to the entrance to the rest of the house.

One day she got distracted and left the door to my room unlocked. I was out in the larger part of the room when someone opened the main door and called down to her.

"Strawberry, get your ass up here, girl. Mr. Smith is here early. You got to get yourself ready."

She went flying up those steps without her set of keys. I guess she had to hurry and get into costume.

The keys lay on top of a box. I stood looking at them. A plan formed in my head. If she didn't come back for them that night, I could walk out of this place and find my way back home. I didn't really need the keys since she had not locked the door above the stairs but I didn't know if I had to unlock any other doors to get out of the house. I went into my room and took the pillowcase off the pillow and started packing it with my other clothes. I had no money but I thought I could beg someone outside to help me get word to my parents that I was alive. I had no intention of trying to find the police for fear they would arrest me and send me back to Horace Graves for killing Suzy Fletcher.

I gathered up the pillowcase and the keys and got halfway up the basement steps. The door opened. Strawberry stood at the top of the steps. She had not changed her clothes. She came down to one step above mine and stood in front of me. She was frowning. The next thing I knew, she pulled back her hand and slapped me so hard I fell down the remaining steps with the pillowcase landing on top of me. She stepped over me and bent down and picked up the keys that had fallen out of my hand during the fall. My face stung for a long time. We never spoke of that incident and I never tried to escape again.

I was always confused by my feelings about her and surprised by our friendship. She was a child and a grownup at the same time. We played checkers and other games and even played hide and seek in the basement. Down there with me she was a playmate but when she went upstairs, she was a grown-up, fulfilling the sexual passions of men who probably had daughters her own age. She never spoke about what she did upstairs and I never asked. Sometimes she would come down in her costume and makeup so I could see her. I always told her she looked nice whether I meant it or not. I didn't want to take any chances on getting slapped again.

Only now do I think of how strange her life was. How paradoxical one's life can be. Looking back at her situation made me understand Petey better. His home life had been nothing like my own. I had a living father and mother who loved me and each other. His father had died and his mother was an alcoholic and a violent person.

The next time I was free to roam the basement, I took the kerosene lamp from my room and cranked it up so that the light shone so brightly in the basement that I could see into the dark recesses of the room. This was much better than the limited light from the flashlight.

I saw a trunk behind some boxes that I hadn't noticed before. I dragged it out and opened it easily because it was not locked. Inside were novels, books on human anatomy, etiquette, foreign languages, and other items. There was even a book about voodoo. I had hit a gold mine!

I had not been a great reader before finding the trunk. Now, I was happy to read anything other than the Popeye comic book. I, of course, took the book out on the human anatomy first because of the pictures. Those pictures were a little confusing so I decided to look at the rest of the pictures later. Then I looked at the pictures in the voodoo book and got scared so I left that one alone. I reached in again and pulled out a novel entitled "The Great Gatsby" by F. Scott Fitzgerald, published back in 1925. I thought it was a book about a great warrior or a famous magician, but I was wrong. I tried to read the book anyway, but the story line was unfamiliar to me and I didn't understand the subtle significance of the writing. I put that one away after a day.

While I was searching in the trunk for something interesting on another day, I found several blank notebooks at the bottom of the trunk along with a few dull pencils. I took out one of the notebooks and a pencil.

"What you doing, writing a letter to your parents?" I was sitting on my cot with the notebook open, thinking hard about what to write. I looked up to see Strawberry staring at me. I didn't hear her come in.

"I can read a little but I ain't good on writin' nothin'." She was not afraid to admit to her limitations.

"My parents made me do my school lessons so I can read real good and write good too," was my response.

Watermelon Road

"Ain't no use in writin' no letter to nobody 'cause I can't take it to them or mail it for you," she declared. "Maybe you should write about this place so you won't forget why you was here." As an afterthought she turned to me and said, "Write about me and how pretty I is." She smiled sweetly as she left the room, locking the door.

The next morning I took out the pencil and the notebook and put my name at the top of the page and the day and date. I thought about what Strawberry had said about writing something down so I wouldn't forget. And, I didn't know how long I would be in that place. I wanted to keep up my reading and writing so I wouldn't fall behind if I got the chance to go back to school.

I thought for a long time about the things I didn't want to forget. I lit the kerosene lamp, opened the notebook and licked the point of my pencil. Then I wrote:

"Petey and me hid in the bushes by the dirt road. The road is Fisherman's Lane but we call it Watermelon Road 'cause that's the way the melon man come when he sell his fruit. He name Mr. Miller. Them words on the sides of his cart say "Miller's Melons." We laugh hard every time we see them words. We call him "Old Melon Head Miller." He got melons and cantaloupes and them big green things that taste so sweet you wanna hold that juice in your mouth and never swallow. I think they's called honeydews."

Strawberry asked me to read to her what I had written. I told her it was a secret. I didn't want to share Petey with anyone. I didn't want her to know he called me "Nightshade" and that I loved him even though I had come to realize that he was not always lovable. I knew she would look for the notebook the next time she came down so I hid it in different places in the basement so she couldn't find it.

By the time my parents came for me, I had filled three of the notebooks, both front and back of the lined pages with the telling of my story. From then on, I was never without a notebook and a pencil.

Watermelon Road
Chapter 22
Gone Fishing

Petey and Peewee hung over the side of the small boat and watched the fish snap at their fishing hooks loaded with worm bait.

"Sit up afore you tip this boat over," Sax yelled at the two boys.

"We can jest pick up them fish with our hands," said Peewee.

"That's 'cause your worms are falling off your hook into the water and the fish are coming to the top to eat them. You boys put your worms on the hook wrong. I told you to put them worms on tight. You ain't afraid to touch them worms are you?" The two children said "No."

Petey and Peewee sat up straight in the boat and started piercing the bait on the hook. Neither of the two boys liked touching the worms or the fish for that matter but they would never have admitted that in front of Sax. They both hated fishing but enjoyed the rare quiet moments the three of them spent together.

Sax set down the battered bean can filled with worms in front of Petey. The boy gingerly took one out, holding it between his thumb and index finger. He couldn't let Sax think he was scared so he closed his eyes and baited the hook at the end of his line. He got the worm completely around the curve in the hook and placed it in the water. "Do me," Peewee demanded.

Sax laughed under his breath at the two children. At least they were having a good time for a change.

He looked over at the two boys in the boat.

"I brought you boys here to spend some time with you so's you'd remember a good day when things ain't so good. I'm going away for a little while to find work as a musician. I'm tired of working in the mill and I loves to blow my saxophone. You know that. I'm heading for either Atlanta or some other place like that to try my luck in the clubs. I might be gone two months or more. I know I'm leaving you boys at a bad time but you have to grow up and do things on your own and help your mother. I can't be with Esther now. I got to get out and make some money and think about what I need to do for the future. Esther got to help herself get back on her feet less she gonna die. I know you boys don't want your mother to die.

Petey, you got to be the man of the house when I'm gone. Your mother's

Watermelon Road

been depending on me to keep things going but I need to go. I got to hold onto what money I got left to keep myself fed, and a place to sleep 'til I get a job.

Petey, you are old enough to find work. You'll be 13 by the end of the summer. You and Esther need to find something to keep things going at the house. Esther has got to pull herself together. I'm not gonna tell Esther when I'm leaving. I'm jest gonna leave. I may be back, I may not." Sax looked from one child to the other as he told them his plans.

Petey thought about what Sax had said. "I can find me a job. I'm gonna try and get mama to stop what she doing to herself."

"That's all any man can do is try," Sax said, encouraging Petey.

Peewee didn't say anything. He needed his mother but he didn't want to be called a big baby. He had stopped wetting the bed. Ever since he had befriended Danny and Jimmy, he wanted to emulate them. They were fun to play with and never boring. Peewee trusted Petey. Petey would take care of him and mama.

"Uncle Sax, why do our mama act like this?" Peewee asked.

Sax thought for a moment and said, "I think it might have something to do with the rough time she had when she was little. She grew up thinking no one loved her 'til she met your father. Besides, she has lost two loved ones and people handle grief differently. Your mother feels better when she drinks.

Anyway, she run off with your daddy when she was about 16 and your daddy was 20. I don't know for sure but I heard your daddy wasn't no angel either. When your parents got married, they both decided to use the name of Creek as their last name. Esther didn't know her parents but the missionaries who raised her named her Esther Creek. Your daddy was running from somebody or the law from where he came from. He changed his name to Creek too. Esther never told me what your daddy's other name was.

Amos was into panning for gold along the riverbeds in this region. He panned enough to rent the house you live in now from Mr. Batty and to support Esther and you three boys. That was long before Joel passed.

You boys know how your daddy died. Then I come along 'bout three years later. Your mother did good for a couple of years before I come around. She worked hard cleaning houses to put food on the table and to pay the rent. Joel was a big help to her.

I tried to get Esther to tell me about her past, but she said there was nothin' to tell. She said it was hard but she got through it. Sometimes I'd find her up in the bedroom or out on the porch in the rocking chair, crying and rocking to beat all. She'd say to me, 'Poor Amos, he died so bad and he had it bad already. He was a strong and loving man. I don't know why God took my husband so soon.' That was before your brother was murdered. Esther got worst after Joel passed."

The boys were silent for awhile. They sat in the boat and watched the kingfishers swoop down and catch the croakers in the lake. They had started fishing early and by ten o'clock that morning the boys were hungry and ate the packed lunch Sax had made for them.

Petey took Sax by surprise when he asked "Is you gonna marry Miss Patty?"

"Where you hear 'bout me and Miss Patty?"

"Oh, no place in particular. People been talking 'bout you staying at their farm sometimes."

"Well it ain't none of people's business and it ain't yours neither. Me and Miss Patty is jest friends."

"Okay," said Petey. "I was jest thinking that's why mama so sad lately."

Out of the blue Peewee asked Sax "How come Jesse died?" This took Sax and Petey by surprise. Sax thought for a long time, not wanting to say the wrong thing.

"I don't know nothin 'bout God stuff and religion. My people are from Mississippi and they didn't know how to read and write. I learned to do both from a circuit preacher that come by our little patch of a dirt road from time to time. I can't remember a thing that preacher said cause I wasn't really listening. I jest wanted to learn to read and write so's I could get out of that piece of shithole where I lived. I got out too, but, to give you a reason for dying, the hell if I know. I'm still working on why we were born in the first place.

I look at them fish and I know that if I take one of them out of the water and put it in the boat, he would live for a few minutes then he'd die. He'd flop around for a short while and that's his lifetime in the boat. If we put him back in the water afore he dies, he'll swim off. So, maybe we was taken from some place and we jest flopping around here for a short time 'til we die. That short time is what our lifetime is. Some of us can flop around awhile longer than others.

Don't you believe nothin' bad you hear 'bout Jesse. He was a good boy. He didn't drown on purpose, neither. The way I figure it he went swimming and it was an accident. That's all it was."

Petey, who didn't want to let on that he was listening, wiped away a tear.

Peewee got a bite. He was whooping and hollering to beat the band. It was a foot long croaker. Sax added it to the four he had caught and they went home to fry the fish.

When they returned home, Petey pulled Sax aside and asked him about the promise he had made two years ago. "How come you know about that?" Sax was taken aback by Petey's knowledge of the promise he made with Junior Rocket and Earl two years before.

"I was listening that night on the stairs. I hear you say you was going to kill the Lucas family for Joel's revenge. You ain't gonna leave before you do that, is you?"

"I wish I'd known you were listening but that don't matter now. Don't be worrying 'bout my plan for revenge. I got me a plan and it's gonna start any time now, especially while I'm away. See, I don't want to be in town when things start to happen. You know what I'm talking 'bout?"

Petey said "Oh yeah, I know what you saying, Uncle Sax. I jest want to help you."

"You listen to me. Ain't no cause for you to get involved. You jest stay out

Watermelon Road

of trouble and take care of your mama and Peewee while I'm gone. That's all you got to do. You want your mother to find another son beaten to death or hanging from some tree? You know that would kill her and Peewee would be left all alone. Keep your mouth shut and stay low."

    Later that day the three of them went over to the church grounds for a Fourth of July celebration. Reverend Beaumont told everyone he was glad they all came out in spite of the oppressive heat. It must have been 110 in the shade that day. Esther didn't come with them, as she was not feeling well. Everyone understood.

Watermelon Road
Chapter 23
Uncle Sax Moves On

A pall hung over the Hammond household, eventually engulfing the whole town.

Esther had taken a plate of fried chicken over to Lily but had been turned away by her sad husband. "We just ain't got no appetite. People been leaving stuff and it's just too much. I had to throw it out or take it to Mrs. Bertie's house for her cheerin. I thank you very much, Esther, but Lily ain't up to eating nothin' right now." Francis closed the door and went back to sit by his wife's bedside. Esther had not been put out because Francis did not invite her in. She knew better than anyone what Lily was going through.

Lily's sorrow seeped into the very fabric of Horace Graves. Everyone felt her unhappiness. The Negroes greeted each other with solemn faces and tight lips. First they heard rumors that Jesse was suspected of killing the Fletcher girl that left everyone in a state of disbelief. Then they heard of his tragic death. Some believed that Jesse knew what would happen to him if he came back home, so he must have taken his own life. People did not believe that his death was an accident. They all felt helpless when it came to doing something for Lily and Francis.

Horace Graves' residents were made even sadder to learn that Francis and Lily had packed up and moved to Baltimore the day after the Fourth of July celebration. Francis told everyone that Lily wanted to be near Jesse's resting place so they were moving to Baltimore. The Hammonds were gone. Things happened so fast. Jesse died and his heart-broken parents left town. Tim West kept a low profile around town after Jesse's death. Good thing too because Francis might have lost his composure and killed him on sight.

Sax left town about a week after the Hammonds. He had made plans to move on because he had a promise to fulfill. Esther's increasing dependence on alcohol and her violent behavior made it easy for him to leave.

Esther's drinking had escalated to the point where Sax and the boys had been staying away from home each day for as long as they could. She had ceased keeping up the house and cooking their meals. Now she was letting herself go. Her long hair would go unwashed for days and she would not bathe regularly. Sax was coming home later and later in the day. Some nights he didn't come

Watermelon Road

home at all. Esther would rile at him and strike out at him, throwing things and cursing, when he finally did show up. The boys stayed out of sight because they knew they would receive some of her anger if they got in her way. Peewee found refuge in the summer program at the church. Other times he would take his paper and crayons and go to a quiet place and draw.

Petey went to the secret place in the woods and more often than not cried himself to sleep there in the place he and Jesse loved most. He no longer went "dark" as Jesse used to call it. He spent most of the time talking to the snake in his belly but the snake never answered.

Sometime before Sax left town, he started spending time at the farm with Desiree and Patty. First he would come for a visit for an hour or so, bringing fresh caught fish for them and the children. Desiree and Patty would sit in the kitchen and regale him with stories about the visitors to their farm from Horace Graves and other parts of the county to sample their corn liquor and gin. No one in the county had paid any attention to Prohibition and even the authorities looked the other way.

The three of them would drink the corn liquor and Sax would pass out sometime during the night and sleep on a cot in the kitchen. Not long after his visits, he and Patty began to dance and she would tell him things about Joel and he'd hold her close while she cried. One hot night in late June, Patty took his hand and led him to her bedroom. Desiree sent the kids upstairs to bed.

He didn't love Patty but they needed each other to help them through their endless nights of discontent.

On July 11, Sax left Esther and the boys. He walked down the road with his suitcase in one hand and his saxophone case in the other hand. He stopped once and looked back at the house. Petey and Peewee had come out and were sitting on the front steps, watching. Sax put down his suitcase and waved at the children. They waved back.

Watermelon Road
Chapter 24
Growing Up

After Sax had been gone for few days, Esther flew into a drunken rage and demanded that Junior Rocket drive her out to the Jackson's farm. She had heard the rumors. Junior Rocket and Earl showed up at the house the next morning and did as she asked. They tried to talk her out of it since Sax had told them his plans and they knew he wasn't at the farm.

Junior Rocket and Earl knew they were doing wrong when they came to pick up Esther in a borrowed car, but neither could resist the anticipation of the two women going at each other. Esther sat in the back seat looking straight ahead and not speaking. Junior Rocket and Earl were in the front seat, exchanging glances and grinning at each other. When they arrived at the farm, Esther jumped out of the car while Earl was parking. She ran up the front steps and into the house, slamming the screen door behind her.

Patty was in the kitchen cooking breakfast. Desiree was out in the cornfield. Esther ran through the house screaming Sax's name. She looked into the small rooms downstairs and did not see him. She ran past Patty and up the backstairs to the loft where the children slept and woke them up with her shouting. When Desiree heard the ruckus she ran for the house. By that time Esther had come downstairs and had Patty down on the kitchen floor, pulling her hair and scratching at her face. The women were wearing summer dresses that revealed their underwear in the scuffle. Junior Rocket and Earl stood watching the fight and enjoying themselves. When Desiree entered the kitchen, the two pretended to pull the women apart.

There was a pan of lukewarm water sitting on the side of the stove and Desiree grabbed the pan by the handle and threw the water on Esther, then she wacked Esther in the head with the empty pan. Esther felt the warm water and thought she was burnt. She let go of Patty and ran out the backdoor to the water pump and pumped cold water over her body to keep from blistering. Desiree, Junior Rocket and Earl stood on the screened-in back porch, laughing at Esther.

Desiree opened the porch door and screamed at Esther. "The damn water wasn't even hot. If you weren't acting so evil, you'd know I wouldn't throw no scalding water on you, Esther. Even so, you know better than to come in here acting like a fool and trying to hurt my sister. I don't know what's gotten into you. If you had treated Sax right, he wouldn't be sniffing round here in the first place. He told everybody he was leaving town so I don't know why you think he's here."

Desiree slammed the door closed after scolding Esther. She went around the kitchen straightening up and mopping up water.

Junior Rocket and Earl started wiping up water with rags Desiree gave them. The two men kept trying to hold back their laughter and ended up giggling most of the time.

Esther came in and sat on the floor in a corner of the kitchen, her head in her hands, sobbing her heart out.

"What the hell did you go and hit Esther in the head for?" Junior Rocket asked Desiree. "Wasn't no cause for you to go and do that."

"We had everything under control," said Earl.

"Well it looked to me like the two of you were sure taking your good time 'bout helping my sister."

The six children were standing in the kitchen, some of them crying. "Shush your mouth. Your mama ain't dying. Get your butts back upstairs 'til I call you for breakfast." Desiree commanded and the children obeyed.

Desiree handed Esther a towel to dry herself. Esther took the towel and placed it around her shoulders. She sat silently, dripping on the wood floor.

Everyone talked and moved around the kitchen ignoring Esther. They acted as if she were invisible. The men helped the sisters put things right in the kitchen. Patty went into her bedroom and inspected her face in the mirror. The scratches from Esther were mostly superficial. She applied salve to the scratches.

Desiree finished cooking breakfast. She called the children down to eat. They bounded down the backstairs making a lot of noise. Everyone but Esther sat at the table. From time to time the children would glance over at Esther sitting quietly in the corner of the kitchen. Desiree got up and fixed a plate of homemade sausages, bacon, biscuits with creamed gravy, scrambled eggs with cheese, and fried apples. She placed the plate on the floor beside Esther, then got her a cup of strong black coffee and set it near the plate. Esther picked up the plate after awhile and ate some of the food. It was good so she ate it all.

Harry, Desiree's youngest, at three years old, kept pointing a finger at Esther and saying "seeeee" in his high-pitched child's voice. This made every one at the table laugh. Even Esther had to smile. One of the other children would put little Harry's finger down but he'd put it up again, pointing at Esther. After the children finished eating, they left the table, losing interest in Esther. The adults continued to ignore her and talked of Jesse's death, the Hammonds' move to Baltimore and other news around Horace Graves.

Esther got up and went out to the car.

That night she lay in bed smoking a cigarette. Petey knocked on her bedroom door. She told him to come in. "Mama, I'm gonna look for a job tomorrow. I been thinking of asking Mr. Batty if I can help out in his store. For now

I can work all day, and maybe he'll let me work there after school starts too. I could work after school and all day on weekends. If he don't let me work for him, I can work over at Miss Olivia's doing clean up and washing dishes. What you think?"

Esther put out her cigarette. She looked at Petey. For the first time she noticed how grown up he looked and she was proud of him for taking on the responsibility of wanting to help support the family. "I think that's a good idea. I don't know if Sax is coming back so we got to look after ourselves."

"Petey, you are the man of the house, now. I've got to find me some work too. It's time I took care of you boys and stopped depending on men to help me out. I think that when Desiree hit me in the head with that pan, she knocked some sense into me." She started laughing and put out her arms for Petey to come hug her. He laughed too as he felt his mother's arms around him.

Watermelon Road
Chapter 25
Joel's Revenge

Petey looked around at the General Store's wooden floor. He picked up a broom, went to the barrel of sawdust and sprinkled a handful over a small area in front of the broom. He swept in small circles so that the dust would not fly up or settle in other places around the store. He knew Mr. Batty was watching him. The old man was simultaneously cruel and kind with his constant backhanded compliments. "You remind me of your brother, Joel. You do good work for a Negro boy." Petey was happy to be compared to Joel even if the compliment often prefaced an insult.

Early on a Saturday morning around the middle of July, Petey went and asked Mr. Batty for a job. He wanted to help out at home and he needed something to occupy his mind. He felt friendless now that Jesse was gone. There was nothing inside of him but the fat snake. The snake was eating his insides, trying to make him forget what he had done to Jesse. He let people go on thinking that Jesse could have murdered Suzy Fletcher. He was a coward. He didn't have the nerve to clear his friend's name because that would mean putting himself in harm's way. Sometimes Petey liked to think that he would have come forward and confessed had Jesse been in danger of being lynched if he had returned to Horace Graves. It was a dilemma, but one he dodged by rationalizing that it was the snake that made him do bad things so that whatever happened was not his fault. He let out a sigh and continued sweeping, ignoring the ramblings of Mr. Batty who had given him a job the very day he went to ask for work.

"You missed a spot boy." Petey had been working at the General Store for only a few days and Mr. Batty was already on his back about everything he did.

Tim West showed up at Batty's store one morning. Mr. Batty retrieved two sodas out of the cooler and the two men went out the backdoor to the porch and sat on the steps. Petey could hear them talking through the screen door. They were laughing and telling lies about fishing trips. The two men had a lot in common and enjoyed each other's company. They grew up together in Horace Graves and married their high school sweethearts. Tim West's wife, Barbara, had passed away several years ago. Mr. Batty's wife, Abigail, was an invalid, suffering with complications from diabetes. Both her legs had been removed due to peripheral vascular disease. He arranged for her to have in-home nursing care around the clock. She didn't want for anything, except for her husband to spend some time with her. Mr. Batty found solace elsewhere.

While the two men were on the back porch, Petey let his mind wander. He noticed the stack of funny books near the front of the store. He loved being in the store because he found something new or different each day that took his mind off his troubles.

Batty's General Store was filled to the rafters with everything a person needed from the beginning of their life to the very end of their days. Mr. Batty even had one or two caskets in the back room. He could have a pine box or a handmade crib delivered to the store on order in no time at all. Baby clothes and supplies needed to raise a child were housed in the children's section among bassinets, wooden cribs, baby bottles and nappies.

The store was huge and took up a large section on the west side of Main Street. It looked like a house from the front with a long wide porch, and three steps leading up to the massive double doors. The back porch was just as long and wide as the front but was mostly used for storage of supplies and items that had not, as yet, been picked up.

While the two men were occupied, Petey moseyed over to the candy counter. He liked the assorted candy even more than the funny books. The homemade fudge was his favorite. There were small pieces of fudge on a platter in the display case that Mr. Batty offered as tasting samples to his customers. He went behind the counter, reached in and took several of the broken pieces of chocolate fudge with nuts. He crammed his mouth with fudge and went back to sweeping the floor.

Once the sweeping was done, he started straightening up the sundry items displayed in the store's front window. He looked up and saw Mirabelle waddling towards the store from across the street. She was coming from Olivia's Diner. She was eight months pregnant and huge. People remarked on how swollen she looked and wondered if she had been seeing a doctor during her pregnancy. The only women Mirabelle would talk to were two or three women from "Grace Hope Baptist Church. The same church that Mr. Batty and his wife belonged to.

Mirabelle entered the store. "Hey there big boy. Have you been waiting for me?" She walked over to Petey and put a finger under his chin. He refused to look at her. "You are a lot cuter than your dead brother. I could go for you in a big way. Is you still a virgin?" Petey looked up at her then. Mirabelle looked ten years older than 18. All that fat she was carrying made her look matronly. She had on the biggest dress Petey had ever seen on a woman. It was swishing around her whenever she walked. Maybe it had been her mother's. Her face was puffy, her hair was stringy and she smelled of sweat and something else he couldn't identify.

Lookin' like a hippo and still flirting, is what Petey was thinking when Mirabelle approached him. He stepped away from her.

"You want to rub my belly?" She grabbed his hand and put it on her stomach and then she moved it up to her breast. He jerked away and went to the other side of the store. "Okay, you want to be unfriendly. After I drop this load, we'll see how unfriendly you want to be then, you uppity nigger."

Presently, the two men came in from the back porch. Mr. West tipped his hat to Mirabelle and walked past her out the door. She disgusted him.

Mr. Batty did not share that sentiment. "Hey pretty lady. You out for a walk?"

"I got tired of hanging around the house. I thought I'd take my big self over to Olivia's and get me something to eat. After that, I wanted a big ice cold soda pop from your cooler, so I stopped in." Mirabelle knew old Batty had a thing for her and she was always teasing him. Sometimes she would deliberately brush against him. *Just to give him a thrill,* she told herself. Petey thought it funny the way Mr. Batty drooled over Mirabelle as if her fat ass and big stomach were attractive. But on the other hand, Mr. Batty wasn't a great catch either.

Mr. Batty reached into the cooler to get her a cold soda pop. She brushed her hand across his backside while he was bending over. He pretended he didn't feel it and handed over the free soda. She started to giggle and walked towards the door. "You boys stay cool now. Bye."

It was early and the heat was already in the 90's. The fans were blowing all around the store but only hot air was being circulated. All of a sudden, Mr. Batty told Petey that he had to close the store for a few hours and for him to come back later in the afternoon. Petey didn't know what to think of this. He needed a full day's pay. Granted it was hot but this was not a holiday. Mr. Batty took off his apron and threw it on the counter.

"Here's a dollar. Get yourself some lunch and come back around two o'clock. I just remembered I got something important to do," Mr. Batty said. He ushered Petey towards the door.

Petey took the money and left the store. He went across the street, stood in an alleyway and lit up a Camel. Mr. Batty came out and locked the double doors. He went down the street and made a right turn at the next block. Petey followed him at a safe distance so that the man wouldn't spot him. He had an idea where he was going.

He was a little surprised because he thought Mirabelle was only teasing the old man, but there might be something going on between them. He followed him because he wanted to be sure his suspicions were right. He watched from a distance as Mr. Batty knocked on the Lucas' backdoor. Petey eased up to the side of the house and watched through the kitchen window. He could see Mirabelle as she shuffled to the door. Even she had a surprised look on her face when she saw Mr. Batty standing there. She opened the door wide for him to enter.

Petey looked around to make sure no one was watching or coming to the house while he continued to look and listen at the kitchen window. He overheard bits of their conversation through the open window. Mr. Batty was going on about wanting to make some kind of arrangement with Mirabelle after the baby was born.

"You know I got money and if you were to service me, I'd take good care of you and that little one on the way. You know you been after me for some time.

Madeline L. Nowlin

I didn't want to start anything with my wife sick, but a man has needs." Old man Batty was pleading his case.

Petey heard Mirabelle laugh. That was a fatal mistake. She was laughing and pointing at Mr. Batty who had sat down at the kitchen table. He jumped up from the table and went over to her. He pinned her against the stove and started kissing her on the mouth.

"Ewwwe. You nasty son of a bitch. Get your stinking mouth off of me. Your breath smells like cow shit. You old mother fucker."

Batty looked stunned. He slapped her hard in the face, causing her to stumble sideways and hit the kitchen wall. He raised his hand to hit her again but she ran through the kitchen doorway and down the hall into her bedroom and locked the door. She was screaming more obscenities at him through the door. Mr. Batty ran after her. When he found the door was locked, he pushed and hit it with his body until he broke it down. The door fell inward onto her bed where she was lying down. He picked the door off the bed and threw it out into the hallway. That's when Petey entered the house.

The Lucas house was in a wooded area a half mile away from their nearest neighbor. No one heard Mirabelle screaming for help. Petey got on his hands and knees and crawled down the hallway, following the voices. "You think I'm an old fart, huh? I'll show you who's old. You ain't nothing but a heifer and I'm gonna treat you like one, pregnant or not".

Still on his hands and knees, Petey peeked into Mirabelle's bedroom. Mr. Batty had Mirabelle pinned down on the bed. He had his left arm across her throat. She was twisting, hitting at him, and trying to breathe. Mr. Batty hit her with his right fist hard in the face, like he was fighting a man. Mirabelle kept struggling so he hit her again. She held up her hands and said, "Please don't hit me no more. I'll do whatever you want, just don't hurt the baby."

"Now you talking like you got some sense, gal." He opened his trousers and took them off and laid them across the back of a chair near the bed. Mirabelle tried to sit up. Petey could see that her nose was bleeding and one of her eyes was swollen. Blood was running from her nose into her mouth. Mr. Batty pulled up her big dress and pulled down her panties. When he had turned away from her to take off his drawers, with his back to the door, Petey crawled into the room and slid under the bed. He heard Mirabelle say "No, Mr. Batty, don't do that, you'll hurt me."

"I can do whatever I want. Your belly is too big, turn over on your stomach and get up on your knees. You better do as I say or I'll beat this little bastard right out of you." She did as she was told and took the thrusting pain until Mr. Batty was satisfied. When he was done with her, he got dressed and quickly left the house without any regard to Mirabelle's condition. Petey lay still under the bed. He was glad when it was over because the creaking of the bed was driving him crazy. He could hear sniffling and moaning. The moaning became increasingly loud.

"Oh shit, ouch, ouch. What's happening to me? Why does it hurt so bad? These cramps are really bad. Ohhhhh. Jesus, it hurts." Petey heard a loud fart.

Watermelon Road

"Oh that feels better," he heard Mirabelle say.

She tried to sit up but the cramps hit her again. She fell backwards on the bed with her legs spread apart. "That stinking bastard, raping me when I'm eight months pregnant. Just wait 'til I tell my daddy. He's gonna kill that old bastard. Ooowww, somebody help me, please God, please help me."

Her cervix had dilated. Mirabelle was in the first stage of rapid labor. She had not seen a doctor during her entire pregnancy. She thought she had time to line up a midwife in town. The pain was overwhelming.

"Oh, mama, this hurts so bad. I wish you were here. I need you now."

Holding her stomach, Mirabelle bolted up from the bed. She cried out in pain when she tried to make it to the bucket in the closet. Blood and water squirted down her legs. The contractions were coming fast, and she was getting breathless. Holding onto the doorframe, she had an involuntary bowel movement, which made her cry out in shame. Petey watched this from under the bed. He lifted up the frilly bed coverlet to see better. The smell was horrific and he put his hand over his nose and mouth. Mirabelle stepped in her own feces when she tried to make it down the hall to the kitchen. There was no indoor plumbing, but a pail of fresh water was always kept in the sink.

She went down on her hands and knees and started to crawl. She was determined to clean herself off. She wanted to get the smell of Mr. Batty off her as well as the stench of her bodily fluids. She made it to the kitchen and pulled herself up to the dry sink. The movement made her vomit. She bent over into the sink but a lot of the vomit got on her dress. When the spasms ended, she took the cup sitting near the pail and drank some water. She took off her dress, removed the tablecloth from the kitchen table and dipped that into the bucket of water and proceeded to clean her naked body. The contractions became so severe that Mirabelle dropped to the floor again and crawled back to her bed without finishing her bathing. Somehow she managed to get herself back into bed. Mirabelle lay back on the pillows, her knees up, feet flat on the bed, hands gripping the bed covers.

She put her hand down between her legs and felt the sticky blood. "Oh no, I think the baby is coming." She felt strong urges to push but didn't. Once she raised herself up and gripped the headboard, panting and grunting. The contractions came on and off for another half hour. Petey lay quietly, listening to Mirabelle screaming in pain.

He crawled out from under the bed when he heard her yell again that the baby was coming. He stood where she could see him.

"Petey, where did you come from?" She asked in a weak voice. "Help me. You gotta run and get help. I think I'm having the baby now and it's a month early. This hurts so bad. You run along and get me some help now." Petey did not move. "I can help. I saw my little brother be born. My mama didn't know I was hiding in the closet and I saw everything that midwife did. I knows how to do it. You jest keep yo legs up and keep pushing and something will happen." He pulled her legs apart to see if he could see the baby's head.

"I don't see no head yet, but I knows it's gonna show."

Madeline L. Nowlin

Mirabelle yelled. "You dumb fuckin' nigger. I told you to go get help."

"I see something. I see a head coming through," Petey declared excitedly. "You gotta push some more 'til it's all done come through your cunt." Mirabelle pushed. There was a big gush of blood and the baby shot out onto the bed. Petey picked up the baby and shook it and the little boy started to cry. "Let me see it," she said.

"Here, you hold him and I'll go get something to cut the cord with," Petey told her. Mirabelle held the screaming baby to her breast and kissed the top of his head. Petey ran to the kitchen and found a pair of scissors. He came back and cut the umbilical cord exactly like he had seen the midwife do it the night Peewee was born. While cutting the umbilical cord, he noticed that the baby looked white but had Negro features. The coloring of the baby's earlobes and the skin around his cuticles was a darker color. His nose was cute but wider than a white baby's and his lips were fuller. The boy also had brown eyes and tight black curly hair. The child reminded him of someone he had seen before, but Petey couldn't remember at the moment. He took the baby from Mirabelle and used a small blanket he found on her dresser to clean the baby and then he handed the baby boy back to her.

Mirabelle was bleeding profusely from her uterus and getting weaker. Her lips were turning blue. She tried to nurse the baby but didn't have the strength. The little thing was crying and waving his arms in the air. Petey took one of her breasts and put it in the baby's mouth. It started to suck. Mirabelle's eyes were closed. Petey thought she was so tired that she had fallen asleep. He called her name several times but she didn't move. Then he shook her and she opened her eyes a little but didn't focus on anything. He sat in the chair by the bed listening to the baby suckle. Five minutes went by and the baby started to cry again. Petey put his head to Mirabelle's chest to listen to her heart but he couldn't hear anything, and she wasn't breathing. He looked at all the blood on the bed and the floor and knew Mirabelle was dead.

The baby was crying because the flow of milk had stopped. Petey picked up the baby and wrapped him in some towels he found. He checked Mirabelle one more time but nothing had changed. His concern was now for the little boy. He would take the little boy to someone who would know what to do. The child was mixed and Mirabelle's father would kill it.

Petey stuck his finger in a pool of blood on the bed. He wrote the word "Batty" on the wall above her headboard. He slipped out the backdoor with the baby and kept to the wooded area behind the house. The baby was quiet due to the walking motion. Petey headed for Reverend Beaumont's house. The Reverend would know what to do.

Watermelon Road
Chapter 26
The New Born Son

Petey knocked several times on the backdoor of the parish house. Reverend Beaumont opened the door and stood there staring at him in surprise.

"Petey, come in, come in. What have you got there?" Petey handed him the bundle and pulled back the towel so the Reverend could get a look at the baby's face. Reverend Beaumont looked as if he had taken a forceful blow to the stomach. He stood transfixed as he looked down at the little boy. Just then Lydia came in and saw Reverend Beaumont holding the baby. She came over to him and looked down at the infant. She looked her husband in the eye and with a sad voice said, "Xavier, not again."

Before the Reverend could respond, Petey said "That baby come out of Mirabelle 'bout an hour ago. Her dead. I checked."

They both stared at Petey as if he were speaking a foreign language.

"What do you mean this baby came out of Mirabelle?" Lydia asked.

Petey moved over to the kitchen table and sat down. He told them everything that had happened at the Lucas house that afternoon. Petey told them about Mr. Batty raping Mirabelle. He added that he thought that was what made the baby come out so soon. He smiled when he told them how he birthed the little boy and cut the cord. They asked how he knew how to do all this and he told them about the night Peewee was born. He left out the part about the bloody writing of Batty's name on Mirabelle's bedroom wall.

The Reverend and Mrs. Beaumont listened in silence until Petey was done with his narrative. "Did anyone see you go in or come out of that house?" The Reverend asked Petey. "Are you sure no one followed you here?" Petey assured them that no one saw him. The baby was squirming and started to cry. Reverend Beaumont gave the baby back to Petey and said he was going across the street to borrow the neighbor's car. Lydia left the kitchen right after her husband.

While Petey was alone with the baby, he thought of Mimi and the twins still spending the last of the summer months with Grandmother Mimi in Baltimore. He wished Mimi were there now so he could show her how he had grown up while she was away.

The baby in his arms reminded him of Reverend Beaumont's twins. He looked like an early photo of Danny and Jimmy that was sitting on Mrs. Beaumont's desk at the school. But then again, all babies looked like somebody familiar. He thought no more about it; although it did bother him when Mrs. Beaumont looked at the baby and said something about "not again." Maybe people were always bringing babies to the church or to the parish house.

The Reverend sat in front of the parish house in the neighbor's car. He blew the horn for Petey to come out with the baby. Mrs. Beaumont was nowhere to be found. Petey went out to the car and got in the front seat beside the Reverend.

"We're going to find this child a good home before somebody finds out that Mirabelle had her baby and start looking for him. I guess you can tell his daddy isn't white so I'm getting involved because I don't want him to get hurt or even killed. You understand, don't you Petey?"

"Yes sir. That's why I brung him to you. I know you know somebody that can hide him and keep him safe. I bet people leave babies at the church all the time." Reverend Beaumont looked over at Petey but made no comment.

Petey had no idea where the Reverend was taking the baby but he knew he could trust him to find the child a safe place to live. No one would ever know that this was Mirabelle's baby. He shared an important secret with the Reverend and his wife. The happenings of the day made him feel old and weary. *This is what it must feel like to be a grown up,* he thought.

Before they drove away Mrs. Beaumont came to the backdoor and called to them. "Wait," she yelled. A few minutes passed then she came to Petey's side of the car. Lydia handed him a coke bottle with a rubber baby bottle nipple stretched over the top of it like real baby bottles have. The bottle was filled with warm milk. Petey thanked her and placed the nipple in the baby's mouth. Lydia stood there a moment looking down at the baby. She placed her hand gently on his head. Holding back tears, she looked over at her husband. The Reverend turned away. She went back to the house. The baby made sucking noises and Petey held him and played with his tiny hands, talking baby talk to the infant. "You'd make a good father," said the Reverend.

"I feel like I raised Peewee so maybe I am a good father already," Petey remarked.

They drove away from the parish house. "We have about twenty or so miles to go." Petey continued to feed the baby as the Reverend drove down through back roads to avoid being seen. The baby sucked nosily on the nipple, holding his little fists close to the bottle. Petey smiled down at him.

"Where are we taking him?" Petey wanted to know in case he decided to sneak back and see how the baby was getting along in its new home.

"You'll see when we get there," was the Reverend's short reply.

Half way to their destination the Reverend started to whistle. "Ain't Nobody's Biz-ness If I Do," was the name of the tune. When he heard Joel and Mirabelle's favorite song, Petey turned his face to the window and a tear rolled down his cheek.

It was nearing sunset but Petey could see the cornfields on the horizon. They pulled into an opening between the fields and started down a long winding dirt road that ended in front of a large farmhouse. Petey saw a kerosene lamp burning on the porch. The screen door opened and a woman stepped out onto the wooden porch. She was tall and thin with coarse hair brushed back into a ball at the back of her head. The hair was streaked with strands of premature gray. "Is that you Reverend?" She asked.

"Yes, Desiree, it's me and I brought some friends along."

"Come into the house and bring your friends," she offered, never one to turn away visitors. The Reverend went in first then Petey with the baby. The baby, full from his bottle, had fallen asleep.

"What's that you got there, boy." Patty had come into the parlor. Petey stared at her without blinking or turning away. She looked exactly as she did the day she come by the house with her sister to comfort his mother after Joel's funeral. Later, he had overheard his mother say to Uncle Sax that Patty was the love of Joel's life.

"I got a little baby that needs a home," he told her.

"Well bring him here chile and let me have a look at him. You ain't scared of me, are you?" She teased. "No Ma'am." Petey handed the tiny bundle over to Patty as she held out her arms to hold him. Patty took the baby into the warm kitchen where there were more lamps burning. There was a loud noise of shouting and laughing as the sisters' six children bounded down the backstairs into the kitchen. They were falling over each other and three of them ended up on the floor. "Stop this ruckus," yelled Desiree. "We heard somebody come in," said 12-year old Tom.

"That don't give you no cause to come falling down here into the kitchen," his mother replied.

"What's that mama's holding?" This time one of Patty's children was inquiring. "It's a tiny baby boy. Look like he ain't but four pounds at the most. Here look at him." Patty let the six children take turns looking at the baby. Then they all stared at Petey and the Reverend. Petey had heard about Patty's and Desiree's children but he had never seen them. They all looked so different from each other. One even had red hair and freckles. They all appeared to be healthy and happy.

Desiree said to her oldest child "Tom, come get your new brother and put him in the center of my bed. I'll be out there soon. Tomorrow, we'll give him a name. Now, all of you go back to your books. I'll be up soon to listen to your lessons." The children were used to new babies being in the house so they obeyed and went back to their studies.

Petey noticed that the Revered was staring at Tom the whole time he was in the kitchen. Tom took no notice of the Reverend, he was busy looking at the baby.

Reverend Beaumont kissed Desiree on the cheek and said "Thank you. I'll send something as soon as I can." Desiree nodded and led them to the door.

"We miss you coming by, Reverend. The children are always asking after you. It would be nice if you could find the time for a visit. Tom said he wanted to be just like you when he grows up. Ain't that something? He wants to be a reverend too. I'm going to have to bring him to your church one Sunday, so he can see what you do. We don't get to church too often out here."

The Reverend mumbled something in response while standing on the front porch. Desiree knew that Reverend Beaumont would tell her the story of the baby boy when he was ready. She accepted the child with no questions asked.

"I'll be coming back here as often as I can. I'll want to check up on the baby. I know I can trust you not to say a word about this."

As they drove past Desiree standing on the front steps, the Reverend told Petey to roll his window down. He leaned across Petey and yelled out the window, "Call him Charles or Charley. That's my father's name."

Watermelon Road
Chapter 27
Two Birds with Two Guns

Jeremiah Lucas came home from hunting rabbits late in the evening. He had caught three in his traps. He took his shotgun along just in case a deer trotted across his path, even though it wasn't deer hunting season. *Nothing like venison stew like my Mary used to make,* he thought to himself.

He opened the back screen door and saw the mess in the kitchen. "Mirabelle, you lazy bitch. You better get your ass in here and clean this shit up for I take a broom to you. Pregnant or no pregnant, I'll take my strap to you. You know I don't hold for no mess in the kitchen. What's this shit on the floor? You done upchuck and left it here? Gal, you have lost your damn mind."

"Mirabelle, get your fat ass in here!"

Jeremiah stopped yelling. He noticed the house was unusually quiet. Mirabelle always had the radio going day and night. He started back to her bedroom. He noticed her broken bedroom door lying in the hallway. Jeremiah stepped over the door and into his daughter's bedroom. It took him almost a full minute to register the scene in the bedroom. After the initial shock, he put his hand over his mouth to muffle his sobs and to keep out the smell. Jeremiah staggered over to the bed. He put two fingers to his daughter's neck and, feeling nothing, put his hand on her wrist to see if she had a pulse. Her naked body was cold to the touch. There was dried blood everywhere. Her face was bloodied and bruised. One eye was black and blue. Her legs were wide open, but in his state of shock and grief, he had forgotten for a moment that she had been eight months pregnant. He sat in the chair that Batty had folded his pants over a few hours before. Jeremiah stared at his dead child for a long time and then he wept some more. The weeping stopped when he realized he did not see or hear a baby crying. He could see that she had given birth. He searched the bed, the bedroom and the rest of the house for his newborn grandchild. He looked for it as if it had gotten up from the bed and simply walked away.

After Jeremiah did a thorough search of the house, he went back to Mirabelle's bedroom, that's when he saw the writing on the wall above her bed. That one word, "Batty," filled him with rage.

Looking down at his dead daughter he said "That son of a bitch! I knew he was after my girl. She told me he kept flirting with her every time she went to the store. Ever since Mirabelle turned 13, that no good dirty old Batty's been trying to get into her pants. Well he done finally gone and done it. He killed my baby girl and took my grandbaby. I know I ain't done right by her but I ain't never hurt her like this. I wouldn't leave a dog looking like this. Poor child, died alone, while he ripped that baby out of her belly. I bet that child was his and that's why he took it. Well, mister high and mighty storeowner, I got something for you. I took Mary from you years ago and married her. Now you done took my daughter and grandchild from me. I swear on my wife's and my daughter's dead bodies I'll get you and I'll get my grandchild back."

Jeremiah went back into the kitchen and opened a drawer. He took out his special box of slugs, loaded his shotgun and slammed out the backdoor.

Two hours later, Sheriff Richards and Deputy Cox stood in the middle of the floor at Batty's General Store, surveying the bloodshed. There was a hole in the backdoor from a shotgun fired from inside the store. Another hole was in the same door from a shotgun being fired from the outside into the store. It was obvious that Jonas Batty had been expecting Jeremiah and shot through the backdoor hitting Jeremiah in the chest. Before Jeremiah Lucas died, he had managed to shoot through the door and hit Jonas Batty in the chest. Both men bled to death.

It appeared that Jonas Batty had been waiting beside the backdoor inside his store. There was a chair near the door and a bottle of whiskey on the floor by the chair. He knew Mirabelle would tell her daddy what happened and Jeremiah would come after him. He was going to get the first shot in.

Sheriff Richards turned to Deputy Cox and said, "Will we ever know what the fight was about? They had to be awful mad at each other to shoot each other." The only report he got from witnesses was that they had heard shots and came running but nothing could be done for the dying men.

He told Deputy Cox to go over to the Lucas house and tell Mirabelle that her daddy's gone. Deputy Cox left the store. He returned a half hour later and told the Sheriff what he had found over at the Lucas house.

Ten minutes later, Sheriff Richards sat in the chair in Mirabelle's bedroom and shook his head. He looked tired. He was tired. He still had not as yet closed the Suzy Fletcher murder case since he had no real proof that Jesse Hammond had actually murdered the girl.

The word "Batty" written above Mirabelle's bed explained a lot. It was a foregone conclusion that Jonas Batty had done something to cause Mirabelle's death and the premature birth of her child. The Sheriff would have to let the coroner clear this one up. The coroner might be able to tell if Batty had sex with Mirabelle before she went into labor. The coroner would need the baby and some of Mr. Batty's blood to prove the baby was his. In any case, Jeremiah came home and saw the mess and went for Batty. It was also obvious that Batty knew he was coming and waited for him. Batty probably gave the baby away so Jeremiah wouldn't know where it was or what it was.

"That Batty was an evil man," the Sheriff said to his Deputy.

Watermelon Road

The Sheriff told Deputy Cox to stay at the house in case Calvin and Haley showed up, which he doubted. The brothers had not been seen around town for over a month.

Sheriff Richards went over to Jonas Batty's house. Their maid, Josephine, let him in. The house was dark and quiet and they spoke in whispers as if they were in a funeral home.

Sheriff Richards told Josephine briefly why he was there. He did not mention Mirabelle and what he found at her house.

"Apparently, Mr. Batty and Mr. Lucas got into an argument and ended up shooting each other to death," was the only information he gave to the maid regarding the double murder. Then he asked to speak with Mrs. Batty.

"Oh, Jesus! God in heaven, what is Miss Abigail gonna do?"

Josephine was talking much louder now. "I can't believe something like this happened. Those two men been good friends forever."

Again the Sheriff asked to speak with Mrs. Batty.

"You can't wake her up right now and tell her Mr. Batty's dead. It would kill her," Josephine said.

"Where's the nurse?" He asked. "I can speak to her and maybe she can relay the message to Mrs. Batty. Then I can come back later and speak with Mrs. Batty when she's up to it."

"Mrs. Tillman went on an errand. She'll be back shortly."

"Come on back to the kitchen, Sheriff, and I'll give you a nice tall glass of my lemonade."

The Sheriff followed her to the kitchen and sat down at the kitchen table while Josephine served him that ice-cold glass of lemonade she promised. The Sheriff took a big gulp. It was delicious, the best lemonade he had ever tasted.

"My secret is a little honey," she said, smiling.

"How long have you been with the Battys?"

"I've been working here a long time. I come here a few years after they married. That's been over twenty years now. Mr. Batty is real good to Miss Abigail, she never want for nothing."

"Exactly what is Mrs. Batty's condition?" The Sheriff asked.

"She come down with sugar years ago and her body's been breaking down little by little. They took both legs two years ago and now her kidneys ain't doing so well."

"Well, I won't disturb her then. Do they have any children or close relatives I should notify?"

"No, no cheerin. Miss Abigail was too sick to worry 'bout having babies. As far as I know, Mr. Batty had a brother that lived in Georgia but they had a falling out years ago and then he died before they could make up. Miss Abigail was an only child and her parents been dead awhile now."

The Sheriff sat quietly, sipping on his lemonade.

"Can I get you another glass, Sheriff?"

"Yes, please."

Josephine handed him another tall glass of her tasty drink.

"I thank you," he said.

"There ain't nothin' to thank me for. I love to see folks enjoy my lemonade."

"Does anyone ever come to visit the Battys?"

"No one comes 'cept them church people over at Grace Hope Baptist on Fairview Avenue. Sometimes some members of a women's organization from that church come by for a visit. When they come, Mrs. Tillman and me get a nice rest for a few hours.

They give Miss Abigail a sponge bath and talk to her while I go shopping for groceries or clean the house. They both belonged to that church. Sometimes their pastor comes by to serve Miss Abigail Holy Communion."

Sheriff Richards wondered who would be making the funeral arrangements for Mr. Batty's remains. He didn't have to wonder long.

Josephine sighed and said "I guess Mrs. Tillman will have to get in touch with the Battys' lawyer over in Bison to make funeral arrangements."

"Do you know who that might be?"

"No sir. But, I do know Mr. Batty keeps all his important papers like that in his office in the back of the house. I'll show you."

He followed her to the tiny office in the back of the house off the kitchen. Josephine left him alone in the office.

The Sheriff searched through Mr. Batty's desk drawers and file cabinets. Most of the papers he found related to the running of the general store. After a few more searches, he came across the name of the lawyer that represented the family. He wrote the name down on a pad he found on the desk, tore off the piece of paper and placed it in his pocket. He waned to know as much as possible about the Battys. This information might give him some idea as to who took the baby.

He went back to the kitchen. The nurse had still not returned. He did not want to wait any longer so he told Josephine to tell Mrs. Tillman to give him a call when she returned."

"Please don't say anything regarding Mr. Batty's death until I've talked to the nurse," he said to Josephine before he left the Battys' residence.

"Yes sir, I won't say nothin' to nobody."

"Too late for that," he thought. He knew the news about the deaths was probably legend in the county by now.

While standing outside of Jonas Batty's house, Sheriff Richards threw his hands in the air and brought them down, slapping his thighs. Talking out loud to no one, he said, "What the hell do I do now? Huh? Who would take a baby? I don't even know where to start looking. I'll put the word out around the county that a newborn has gone missing, but we don't know whether it's a boy or a girl or even what race it is, knowing Mirabelle's love of male company. If that baby shows up, somebody is sure to tell us who has it. Either way, the Sheriff's Department ain't looking too smart right now."

The Sheriff called the Battys' lawyer as soon as he got back to his office. The information he received was useless in helping him find the baby. The

Watermelon Road

lawyer didn't have a clue as to who Mr. Batty would give an infant to. Mr. Batty might have gone elsewhere for his pleasures but he must have been very discreet. He wasn't too optimistic about having a talk with the nurse either, so he decided to put it off until later. There was something about the Batty house that made him feel creepy, as if discontent had taken form and was guarding the house against any attainment of happiness.

Watermelon Road
Chapter 28
Petey

It was an early Saturday morning near the end of August and the heat was already climbing. Petey got up early to go to Olivia's Diner. He had been working there for a couple of weeks. Today was the day Olivia had promised to start his cooking lessons. Petey was looking to move up from his busboy position to cook's assistant. That would give him a little more money. Olivia still wouldn't let him wait on tables but he was allowed to clear them and wash the dirty dishes. She gave the waiter position to his mother. Esther needed all the money she could get to keep up the rent on the house.

Tim West let Petey go after he bought Batty's General Store from Abigail Batty. Mrs. Batty was in poor health. She wanted to liquidate her assets and leave her small fortune to her church after she died. Tim West convinced Mrs. Batty to sell the general store and all of Mr. Batty's rental properties to him. Her lawyer advised her that she was selling short but she didn't want to hear it. She wanted to get rid of everything that reminded her of her husband.

She had been unloved and untouched by her husband for many years. She knew her days were numbered and she wanted everything taken care of before she passed away.

If Esther was late on the rent, Tim West charged a hefty penalty. It was as if he were punishing them for what he believed Jesse had done because he had been Petey's friend. He had become uncivil to the colored people in town. They no longer shopped at his store but went further out to obtain what they needed.

Esther worked at the diner Monday through Saturday. Mrs. Bertie, Olivia's sister, worked sporadic hours during the week to complement her day job of cleaning houses.

Bumpy had been gone for almost two months and Mrs. Bertie was concerned. Although Bumpy wandered off from time to time to follow a traveling poker game or two, he had never been away this long. He always called Olivia at the diner to tell her to let Bertie know he was all right and when he would be home. Mrs. Bertie had no word from him as yet.

Esther had received a letter from Sax. He had taken a gig in Atlanta. He was performing in a jazz quartet at a club in the city. Sax indicated in the let-

Watermelon Road

ter that he would not receive any money until the quartet made enough to cover their overhead expenses. He advised Esther to find work until he could send money. Bertie and Olivia had worked on Esther until she curtailed her drinking and got up on her feet. She was much stronger now.

When Petey arrived at Olivia's Diner around 6:30 a.m., he knew right away that Olivia had gotten there before him. She was in the kitchen humming and kneading dough for the morning's dish of biscuits and gravy. After that, she had to make the honey butter biscuits. The smell of coffee permeated the diner and made Petey crave a cup.

He got out the broom and started sweeping behind the lunch counter. He'd done that the night before but he needed something to do until Olivia was ready for him in the kitchen. He made a few half-hearted sweeps of the floor and laid the broom against the counter.

"Miss Olivia, can I pour me a cup of coffee?"

"Sho' boy. Go on and help your self."

Petey reached for a large cup on a shelf behind the counter and poured a cup of strong black coffee from the big urn sitting on the counter. He leaned his elbows on the counter and breathed in the heavenly scent of freshly ground coffee beans. He loved coffee and his smokes. He felt calmer these days. After Jesse died, Petey couldn't stop rubbing paper between his hands. It would go on for hours. But now, he hardly ever felt the need anymore to rub things with his hands to calm down.

"Ain't nothing like that first cup of morning coffee," he said out loud. Olivia kept on kneading dough and humming to herself.

After he drank his coffee, he started sweeping again. It was almost 7:00 and the place would be open soon for breakfast. Benny, the chief cook, came in and told Petey to fill up two large pots of water from the utility sink in the back room and place them on the stove. He was pleased to do that and glad that Olivia had indoor plumbing. There was even a water closet beyond the kitchen where customers could go but only in an emergency. Olivia cleaned that water closet herself. After he filled the pots and placed them on the big burners on the huge gas stove, Benny got down a sack of beans to stew and told Petey to peel potatoes for boiling. Petey got a paring knife and started peeling potatoes. After he peeled them, he rinsed the potatoes and put them in the lukewarm water of one of the pots. He then donned an apron and started plucking the two fresh chickens Benny brought with him that morning and had laid out on the kitchen counter for chicken stock.

While Petey sat in the kitchen plucking the birds, Jesse's face flashed before his eyes and his heart sank. He missed his friend so much. He still couldn't believe he was dead. Jesse had left him all alone. He had no one to share his pain. No one else seemed to feel his pain.

Peewee spent most of his time that summer drawing pictures on anything he could find. "Upon This Rock Baptist Church" had Vacation Bible School for the month of July. Petey had gotten up early every day during that month and made sure Peewee attended Bible School. The day classes were established mainly to keep the children out of trouble, and to educate and entertain them. Breakfast and lunch was included in the daily program. The classes were free and the parents were relieved to be rid of the children for a few hours, especially since the houses had no air-conditioning.

Peewee didn't understand the depth of the pain and loss that Petey experienced. Petey couldn't talk to his little brother. Esther kept her thoughts to herself about what had happened to Jesse. She had a lot on her mind these days and only spoke to Petey about work. She even stopped mentioning Sax.

Mimi, Danny and Jimmy returned home the first week of August. Mimi still would have nothing to do with Petey. He started sending her letters after she returned home. She had read each letter with dread. They were like the letters he sent her while she was in Baltimore. Petey held nothing back, even telling her about the snake and how it made him kill Suzy Fletcher. He also confessed to the murder of Digs and told her why. She burned the letters after she read them. Every night she prayed that God would change Petey and save him. Her parents never asked her what the letters were about. The envelopes did not have a return address and Mimi told them they were from a friend back in Baltimore. Luckily, her parents never bothered to look at the stamped postage on the envelopes.

Mimi avoided Petey and made sure he did not have any contact with the Danny and Jimmy. She no longer trusted him and believed that he was evil. She encouraged Peewee to continue his friendship with the twins so that he might be safe. It was the same situation as it was with Digs. She couldn't tell anyone about Digs and his behavior and now she couldn't tell anyone about Petey. The two of them could never be friends again, and she would never tell what she knew.

It was unfortunate that they could not share their pain of losing their best friend. Her silence hurt him almost as much as losing Jesse. In a way, the two children felt as if they had each lost two best friends.

Petey kept going over and over in his head about the things that had transpired. The timing of everything had been off. If he had known before he and the Reverend left Baltimore that Jesse was suspected of the murder, he would have confessed right on the spot. At least that's the way he looked at it now. One thing he knew for sure, he would have told Jesse about the snake.

The snake tried to rear its ugly head again and again. Whenever he saw a little white girl that he felt was unattractive, he fought back the snake and the urge to kill. Even the death of Mirabelle did not appease that thing in him. The curdling would start in his stomach, move up into his chest, then his ears would hear the hissing of the evil coiling reptile. Most times he could keep it under control. Other times he went to the secret spot in the woods and waited until the hissing subsided. Sometimes he would run around the clearing, screaming and waving his hands to stop the hissing of the snake in his head.

He still had the pocket knife, which in a strange way brought him a little comfort. It was well hidden in their shed along with the $5,000 he took from Grandmother Mimi's moneybox. It was so well hidden, he believed no one could find it.

Watermelon Road

His thoughts came back to the chickens he was plucking. Petey finished plucking and cleaning the chickens. He asked Olivia and Benny if there was anything else he could do. They both told him they would let him know when he was needed. He went out to the dining area and sat at one of the tables facing the big picture window. He watched Main Street come to life as the sun blazed down over the rooftops of the stores. It was nearly 8:00 a.m. Mr. Wong's Cleaners was just opening. Miss Sally, next door to the right of Olivia's, was sweeping the front stoop of Sally's Bakery and Tea Shop. Smithy's Hardware was at the southernmost end of the street. He could see Lulu, Smithy's wife, dragging something in a big box into the hardware store. It looked heavy. He wondered why Smithy wasn't dragging that box. *Fat lazy bastard,* he thought and smiled.

On the left side of Olivia's Diner was Marie's Dress Shop. Marie was one of those starched and prim white ladies that smiled at you all the time without showing any teeth. She always wore white gloves, a hat and pumps on her tiny feet. She owned every color of pumps ever made. She always wore the same type of empire dress with matching accessories. Everyone was shocked when she went away for a month one summer and came back with a husband. *Lawd, did the townsfolk talk about that,* Petey shook his head, laughing out loud.

While looking out the big picture window, Petey watched the latest model Chrysler pull up in front of Marie's Dress Shop. A well-dressed white lady got out on the driver's side. The woman, who could have passed for Marie's sister because of her appearance, went around to the front passenger side of the car and opened the door. Out jumped a little girl about 8 years old. Petey watched the little girl, wearing a frilly dress, bounce and skip around her mother as they entered the dress shop. She reminded him of someone. Then he remembered. She had the same coloring as Mirabelle Lucas. Only this child looked a lot healthier than Mirabelle ever did. Especially the last time he saw her. At a quick glance, the little girl had that white blond hair just like Mirabelle's. She also had pretty rosy cheeks. He couldn't see the color of her eyes but if they were brown or blue, she would be a looker when she grew up. He remembered Mirabelle had brown eyes. With her mother watching over her, he knew this little girl wouldn't end up like the girl that got his brother killed.

Lewis's old 1930 Ford stopped in front of the diner. Freaky Joe was in the passenger seat. The two men waved at Petey when they saw him sitting at the table in front of the window. Petey waved back and watched them enter the diner. Olivia heard the bell ring above the front door and came out from the kitchen, wiping her hands on her apron. She smiled at her two regular customers and told them to have a seat while she got their coffee. Petey joined them at the counter.

"Where ya'll on your way to? He asked.

Freaky Joe said "It's our day off so we's going over to the Jackson farm. We thought we'd hang out there today and see if the ladies need help. We like playing with the cheerin. Maybe do some fishing in the Proud Rock River and bring some red snapper back to the women and let them fry it up. It'd be a good treat for them cheerin. I hear they's got seven kids now 'cause one of them gals musta gone and dropped another one. You know there's gonna be eight cause one can't have more than the other. The sisters might give us a bushel of corn to bring home if the corn is ready to be picked."

Lewis sat quietly, studying the menu.

At that moment, Esther came bustling through the front door. "How do, everybody? I'm running a little late but I can knock out them breakfast orders as soon as I get my apron on." She hurried by the lunch counter and went through the swinging doors to the kitchen.

Five minutes later, Esther came out of the kitchen, tying an apron around her middle. She asked the two men if they wanted the usual. They said they did. Petey asked her for a donut and got up and fixed himself another cup of coffee. He also poured cups of coffee for the two men because Olivia had forgotten to do that.

Lewis said, "It seems so strange with them gone. We were used to having Joel and your little friend, Jesse, around." Lewis surprised Petey with his remarks.

"I got up this morning thinking the same thing," Petey admitted.

"This town will never be the same," added Freaky Joe.

Petey handed them their coffee and sat back down at the counter.

Twenty minutes later, Esther hurried out of the kitchen with a tray loaded down with steaming plates of thick sliced ham, eggs over easy, cheesy grits and biscuits. Freaky Joe and Lewis moved condiments around on the counter to make room for their breakfast.

"Petey, you can go back in the kitchen and grab another donut. We got plenty. I can't believe that's all you're eating. Boy, you been working here a good while and you ain't hardly touched any of Olivia's good dishes. You better start eating some real food. You look like you done lost weight and you don't have none to lose. Look at him, Lewis, he's nothin' but skin and bones."

Esther looked at Petey and then at Joel's friends as she rambled on about Petey not eating. "I know you don't think I'm cooking anything at the house after I been on my feet in here all day. My other boy, Peewee, eats whatever Petey brings home or fixes for him. Peewee ain't no trouble at all. He's home drawing all day and all night. I can't tell if he got any talent or not. Them pictures look like he traced them from the funnies to me."

Freaky Joe and Lewis nodded their heads in agreement each time Esther looked their way. To them, Petey did look a little sickly but he'd been grieving for Jesse. He was only a boy, after all.

Mrs. Bertie came in with three of her youngest children and sat at one of the tables. "I'm just here for a cup of coffee," she called out to Esther.

"We sure got us some nice weather today," Bertie said when Esther brought her a cup of coffee. On the tray with the coffee were four donuts and three glasses of milk.

Bertie looked at the food and said, "Lawd, chile, you know I cain't pay for this here food."

Watermelon Road

"Don't worry about it. Olivia put it on the tray." Esther patted Mrs. Bertie's shoulder.

Everyone knew Bumpy had disappeared, and Mrs. Bertie had fallen on hard times. Bumpy still hadn't sent any money. Working at her sister's place, cleaning houses and babysitting was barely enough to make the rent and keep the children fed. The older children had found odd jobs around town and that was helping the family to get by. Times were hard for everyone so Mrs. Bertie never complained. Esther kept an eye on the children after she got off work if Mrs. Bertie needed a sitter until she came home later. The two women were waiting to hear from their men and hoped the men would come home soon. Sax had been gone since early July. Bumpy had been gone a little longer.

After Freaky Joe and Lewis left, Petey cleaned off the diner's wooden counter and went into the kitchen to start washing up the breakfast dishes. Elbow grease was necessary for the fry pans. He had to really scrub them. As Mrs. Bertie was leaving, customers were piling in.

The diner was getting busy again. Mrs. Bertie took her children home, left them with her oldest child and came back to help with the morning rush. Petey kept the tables clean and the condiments handy. He also took care of pouring the beverages into solid thick drinking glasses, filling them with sweet tea, lemonade, soda pop or ice water. Either Esther or Mrs. Bertie would carry the tray of beverages to the waiting customers at the tables.

The diner was full and noisy. Petey was busy cleaning a table near the front entrance when the bell over the door rang. He glanced around to see who was coming in. He needed to clear a table so the new arrivals would have a place to sit. He recognized the well-dressed white lady and the little girl that had gone into Marie's that morning when they entered the diner. The little girl looked like one of those baby angels he had seen in the church pamphlets Peewee often brought home. Peewee called the little angels "cherubs."

The little girl looked up at Petey. She had blue eyes. He looked back at her for a moment and turned to finish clearing the table. Esther came over and spoke with the mother. She assured her that a table would be ready soon.

His mother brought the two customers over to the table he was clearing. Petey lifted the tray full of dirty dishes and turned towards the kitchen. As he did so, his nostrils caught the scent of the little girl. It was a fragrance he had smelled often. The fresh, strong bouquet of baby powder wafted up his nostrils, making his fingers and toes tingle. The scent traveled downward through his lungs, stomach and into his groin. There in his groin, his most private place something began to stir. The feeling was unexpected and unfamiliar. Petey became dizzy and his legs began to tremble. He dropped the tray. Glass and pottery flew in every direction. The noise was deafening. Then he fainted. He fell forward and hit his head. Some of the customers rushed over to see what was happening. The lady and the little girl quickly left the diner. The sight of so many Negroes in a state of confusion had frightened the mother.

Esther stood dumbfounded in the middle of the floor looking down at Petey and the big mess he had made. Two men left their table and came over, picked

Madeline L. Nowlin

Petey up off the floor and sat him in one of the chairs at the empty table. One of the female customers started fanning him with a menu. Although Petey looked unwell, Esther was too angry with him to speak. Olivia and Benny ran out of the kitchen to see what caused the disturbance. Petey swooned and came to when Mrs. Bertie sprinkled water in his face. Olivia handed him a glass of water laced with a little whiskey, which he drank down.

"He don't eat nothin', that's why he can't stand up. He don't have enough strength in him to lift a tray of dishes. I don't know what to do with this chile," Esther shouted out in desperation.

No one responded to her outburst. She threw her hands up in the air and went to find a broom. Benny started picking up large pieces of stoneware, broken dishes and drinking glasses. Some of the customers helped with the clean up. When his legs felt steady enough, Petey went through the kitchen and out the backdoor. He sat on the back steps and smoked a cigarette. He began to feel like himself again. He was still confused about what had happened to him. *Did the snake come out? Did people see what was inside of him when he fainted? No one let on that he looked any different so he must have looked like himself while he was passed out on the floor. His body was betraying him more and more. He was losing control.* His thoughts frightened him.

He closed his eyes and the face of the little girl came floating into focus. The scent of baby powder was overpowering in his nostrils, as if the little blond girl were standing right in front of him. Petey was afraid. He knew he had killed Suzy Fletcher because he hated and pitied her. To him, she represented all that was bad about Mirabelle. Yet, the child he saw today possessed all the beauty of Mirabelle and he liked it.

Am I acting like Joel? I never even felt this way 'bout Mimi. I'm going to have to see this chile again and see what happens. I cain't be like Joel. I won't be like Joel!

Esther was in deep thought as she swept the floor of the diner. She knew she hadn't been much of a mother since the children's father had passed away years ago. Then she lost Joel, which made her withdraw even more into herself. Now, Sax had left her to fend for herself.

Petey's reaction to Jesse's sudden death was as she had expected. They were very close. Jesse accepted and understood Petey. Yet, even before Jesse's death, Petey had become a stranger to her. Now that his best friend was gone, he was moody and would not speak for days on end. He disappeared for hours only to return home to sleep for hours. Sometimes she heard him talking to himself.

Her heart went out to Jesse's parents. Esther felt Lily's pain. She knew the depths of hopelessness in losing a child. Nothing brought comfort and never would. She envied the Hammonds for leaving Alabama. She would love to live in a big city like Baltimore. Maybe she could save enough money to move out of Horace Graves where there were so many bad memories for her. *Yes, that would be a good thing to plan for*, she sometimes thought to herself. *Let old Sax come back here and find me gone. Then he can spend his precious time wondering about me for a change.*

Watermelon Road

She had finally got on her feet. She had accepted full responsibility for her two boys. It was time to fix whatever was wrong with Petey.

Peewee hardly noticed Sax was gone. He was spending his waking moments with the Beaumont twins. He had practically moved in with them. It didn't bother her none. Lydia got Peewee to stop wetting the bed. Esther was happy to let Lydia become a second mother to Peewee. It was one less person to worry about.

Esther thought about the first time she noticed a change in Petey. It was not long after Joel was killed. She didn't want to deal with his problems. She had her own demons. Everybody told her to take Petey to a doctor right after he started rubbing things between his hands and experiencing blackouts. She didn't have money for a doctor. *What if Petey needed an operation on his head or something?* She had asked Sax to have a talk with Petey about what was bothering him but Sax never got around to it.

Sax was gone and it was her turn to clean up the messes. Petey fainted for no apparent reason she could see. Esther decided to have a talk with her son right after she cleaned up the mess in the diner. If having a talk with Petey didn't reveal much, she would make him have a talk with Reverend Beaumont.

Olivia came out of the kitchen and looked around the diner. Esther had put things right again. "You go take your boy home, Things are slowing up here. He's out back smoking. He thinks I don't know about that," said Olivia. "You take the rest of the day off. You both look like you could use a good night's sleep. I'll see you tomorrow. "

Esther went out back and told Petey to go home. She followed him, walking at a slower pace, gathering her thoughts together. Petey needed the assurance that she loved him. He wanted love but he wouldn't give it. He was nothing like his daddy or his brother, Joel. They had had a deep capacity for love and showered it on everyone. Esther knew that Petey thought she blamed him for Joel's death because he watched Joel die without trying to save him. Petey was right, she had blamed him, but that time had passed. Sax yelled at her once that she was stupid because if Petey had revealed himself to the Lucas brothers she would have lost two sons that night. She knew Sax was right.

Esther felt that Petey also blamed himself for Jesse's death even though he wasn't even there when it happened. *Poor boy, my poor baby boy, I've got to make him say what's on his mind, otherwise, I cain't help him.*

By the time Esther reached home, Petey had already gone up to his room to lie down. She called up to him that she'd bring up an aspirin later in case he had a headache from his fainting spell. Petey had a small bump on his forehead.

A half hour later, she went upstairs with a bowl of soup and two aspirins. Petey ate the soup in silence and shook his head when she offered him the aspirin.

Peewee came home about that time. He asked if he could eat dinner with the Beaumonts. "They's having my favorite, fried chicken and rice and gravy." She gave her permission and watched his back as he ran to his second home.

Esther sat in her favorite chair on the front porch. She leaned back, wrapping her arms around herself. *I could really use some corn liquor right now,* she thought. The idea was just a thought because she would not go down that road again. She wanted Sax to see a different Esther if and when he came back to her.

Watermelon Road
Chapter 29
Peewee

Peewee had searched his mother's bedroom and now he was searching Petey's bed for loose change to buy crayons and coloring books. Sometimes Petey would leave change lying around. He'd never miss it. Peewee went through the pockets of a dirty pair of Petey's pants lying on the floor near his bed. He found two nickels. This was enough for a new box of crayons and a large coloring book.

Peewee heard children's voices in the backyard. He went over to the window. The children were running through his yard on their way to play ball on the church grounds. They were friends of his. He raised the window and called out to them but they didn't hear him. Then his eyes fell on the shed.

He had noticed that Petey had gone out to the shed a lot lately but never brought anything out. Once he had asked him what he was doing in there and the answer was, "None of your damn business." He knew better than to pressure Petey about his secrets and he knew enough to never follow him into the shed. He could end up hurt bad because Petey would beat the living shit out of him if he thought Peewee was trying to find out what he was doing when he was alone.

He decided to take his chances and search the shed to see if Petey had been hiding the money he got from working at Miss Olivia's in there. Esther and Petey would not be home for awhile.

Peewee went out to the shed and tried the door, and found it unlocked. It was dark in there. He left the door slightly ajar so light could come in. There was a small window at the back but it had a towel thrown across it, keeping out the light. With the door open, he was able to see two flashlights lying on the floor inside. He picked up one and turned it on. There was enough light from the flashlight to see inside, so he closed the shed door all the way.

The shed was filled with old furniture, clothing, and other discarded items. He used to come in here when he was little and look for buried treasure.

Treasure huntin' might be a good game to play with the twins one day, was his first thought while he moved things around to make room to walk. It was a good-sized outbuilding. His father had built it before he died. Peewee walked along kicking the wooden floorboards near the walls to see if anything was loose.

Madeline L. Nowlin

He didn't like being in there because he knew there were rats hiding in there too. Petey told him that he saw rats scurrying around whenever he went into the shed. The rats dug holes under the shed and came up through the shed floor.

Esther bought cans of rat poison and sprinkled it around the shed inside and outside. She kept some in the house too, under the sink and was always telling the two boys not to touch it. Peewee knew he would drop dead on the spot if he saw a rat in the house.

He was so busy looking for rats, he slipped and fell forward, coming down hard, using his hands to break the fall. He lay there with his chin on the floorboards breathing heavily. The dropped flashlight was shinning on a loose board behind an old metal bucket that Uncle Sax had used to carry wood back to the house. With nimble fingers, Peewee pushed the bucket aside and pulled the loose floorboard up just a little. He peeked in and saw something green. Peewee raised it a little more and his eyes grew big. He raised the floorboard all the way out of its grove and was stunned to see so many $20 bills. He picked up the money to count it and that's when he saw the pocket knife lying there under the money. He knew he couldn't take any of the money because people would question him about how he got it. Even just one $20 bill would bring suspicious looks from everyone. And, Petey would kill him. He reached in and picked up the pocket knife with the snake handle. The glass eyes looked as if they glowed in the dark. He pulled the knife open and touched the blade. It felt cool against his fingers.

Peewee decided to take the pocket knife since Petey wasn't using it anyway. He would show it to the twins. They would keep it a secret, knowing what Petey would do to them if he found out the three of them had the knife.

The next morning Peewee walked down the front porch steps past Petey who was sitting there openly smoking.

"Ain't you scared mama will catch you smoking?" Peewee asked his brother.

"I ain't scared of nothing no more," was the answer Peewee received from his brother.

"Oh yeah, there is something I am scared of," Petey said grinning. "I gets the shakes and trimbles every time I see them pictures you draw."

"You wouldn't be shaking if you seed the ones I drew of you and your sweetheart. Petey and Mimi sittin' in a tree, k-i-s-s-i-n-g."

"Where them pictures at?" Petey asked. "You better not show them to nobody."

"They upstairs under my bed if you wants to look at them. I did a good one of Miss Mimi by herself too."

Petey stood up and ground his cigarette into the dirt. "Where you on your way to?" He asked Peewee.

"I'm going to play with Jimmy and Danny. Mrs. Beaumont say I can come over and have breakfast. She say I can spend the night if I wants to."

"Ain't you scared of peeing in the bed and them laughing at you?" Petey asked.

Watermelon Road

"Nah. I don't pee in the bed when I'm sleeping over there. Besides, they don't call me Peewee no more, either. They call me Simon 'cause that's my real name. I like that a lot. Maybe you and mama can call me Simon now since I don't pee in the bed no more."

Petey didn't say anything.

"Well, I gotta go. Mrs. Beaumont is fixin' pancakes. They ain't as good as the ones mama used to make afore she had to take her medicine so much. Mimi is making spaghetti for us for dinner tonight. Want me to bring you some?"

"No, don't do that. I get enough food at work."

"I see ya later," said Peewee.

"Well, I don't know 'bout that seeing as how you a traveling man now. Too bad you gotta run. I was going to tell you 'bout how I fainted in Miss Olivia's yesterday and broke a whole tray of glasses and dishes. This is a good story to tell the twins."

"You fainted? Like a girl?" Peewee asked, getting excited. "Is that why you have that bump on your forehead?"

"Yeah, want to touch it?" Petey leaned forward so his brother could touch the bump. When his brother came close, Petey grabbed him and shook him playfully. "I ain't no girl," he said laughing.

Peewee touched the small bump. He then stood back and looked at Petey in a strange way.

"What you thinking?" Petey asked.

"Oh, nothin'. I was thinking 'bout drawing a picture of you. I was thinking I should draw a picture of you and mama sitting together."

"Why don't you do that and put yourself in the picture too so we can be a family like the Beaumonts."

Peewee laughed at Petey's sarcasm. He ran out of the front yard and never looked back. He didn't want to be around when Petey discovered his knife was missing.

Petey ran upstairs as soon as Peewee left the front yard. He searched for the pictures his brother had drawn.

He found the pictures under Peewee's bed just like he said. There was one of Petey. He was standing outside the Upon This Rock Baptist Church, smoking a cigarette. He made a mental note to slap Peewee upside the head for drawing him smoking. Under that was the picture of Mimi. Petey caught his breath when he saw it. Mimi was sitting on the blanket she had brought to the church picnic. She was leaning against the tree with her legs tucked under her. Only her shoes and lace stockings were showing from under her dress. The dress was drawn so beautifully. It was the dress she had worn with the white daisies all over it. He was amazed at her face. Peewee drew her features so true that it looked as if a light was shining under her skin. Peewee got the coloring right. She was holding a bouquet of daisies.

He then looked at the picture Peewee had drawn of him and Mimi together on the blanket. Petey was kneeling and was in the process of handing her the bouquet of daisies. She was looking up at him and smiling that brilliant smile.

Madeline L. Nowlin

There was no doubt in Petey's mind that his little brother was an artist. He put the pictures back under Peewee's bed. Maybe later he would tell Peewee to show them to their mother.

That night, while lying in bed, Petey's mind wandered back to the little blond girl. He made a promise to himself to find that little white girl again. He had to see her again so he could find out why he had fainted when he smelled the baby powder on her.

Watermelon Road
Chapter 30
Mimi Beaumont

Mimi turned 13 in August after she and the twins had returned from Baltimore. Her parents gave her a surprise birthday party at the parish house. Her friends from school and many of the church members were there. Lydia gave her an invitation to give to Petey to attend her birthday party. Mimi tore the invitation up and threw it in the trash as soon as she was alone. She didn't give it a moment's thought. Although her actual birthday was August 15, a Tuesday that year, the party was held on Saturday, August 12.

Mimi had started her period while she was in Baltimore and Grandmother Mimi had a talk with her about becoming a young woman. Aside from the cramping and messiness, it did make her feel womanly. When she returned home, Lydia had "the talk" with her, embarrassing them both. She handed Mimi a booklet to read in case she needed further information. The older girls at school had already told her everything. It was a good thing, too, because her mother had left out a lot.

The three children had been glad to leave their Grandmother's house. The house in Baltimore had been filled with sadness. Even Danny and Jimmy were depressed. The deaths of Jesse and Baby Boy were on everyone's mind.

Grandmother stayed in her room most days, Uncle Theo was gone a lot, and Althea had little to say. The adults left it up to Mimi to entertain the boys.

One good thing happened. Althea taught her how to sew during the time she was at her Grandmother's. She took to it right away and Althea said she was a natural at it. They found remnants of material around her Grandmother's house. When Mimi asked her Grandmother if she could have the pieces of material she found, Grandmother Mimi always said yes, not really looking at what was in Mimi's hand. Althea brought yards of cloth to the house that she had received from her friends. Soon Mimi was making dresses for herself. She had even made shirts for the twins. It was good that she had learned to sew now that the Hammonds had moved to Baltimore to be near Jesse's gravesite. Mrs. Hammond would no longer be available to make the pretty dresses she loved to wear. If she wanted a special dress, she could always go to Marie's Dress Shop and pick something out. Otherwise, she enjoyed sewing her own clothes Lydia was delighted with Mimi's new talent and encouraged her to continue so that she would always have something to fall back on to support herself.

Mimi did not see Petey until school opened on September 3. He sat behind her in class. No one else, not even her mother seemed to notice the change in him. At least they didn't acknowledge what they saw. Petey was taller, and thinner with a shadow of a mustache above his upper lip. He looked older to her even though he had not turned thirteen yet. His birthday was the following Saturday. There was no presence in his eyes when he looked at her.

He waited for her outside of school one day and begged her to talk to him.

"You're my only friend now Jesse dead."

She ignored him and kept walking until she reached her house. Standing on her front step, she turned to him and said:

"You are the reason you don't have any friends. You are the reason you have lost my friendship. You killed Jesse as sure as you put your hands on him. You set him up with that pocket knife. You ain't nothin' but a coward. I hate you. If you don't stop following me I'm going to show your letters to my daddy and he will take them to Sheriff Richards and then the white people will beat you, like they did Joel, or hang you from a tree. You deserve it but Joel didn't. Don't you talk to me no more. I ain't your friend." With that being said, she ran up the steps and into her house.

Petey stood there with his hands on each side of his face. He held the sides of his face together so no one could see the reptile features he surely must have had. His face felt like fire. He couldn't believe that Mimi had said such things to him. He had risked his life for her. He had saved her from Digs.

Petey stayed home from school for two days. Mimi was relieved. She prayed that he had dropped out and that she wouldn't have to look at him again. He returned to school at the end of the week, telling Mrs. Beaumont that he had not been feeling well. He never spoke to Mimi again. Mimi had a new boy in her 7th grade class that she liked and he liked her right away. They kept making eyes at each other during class. Petey noticed but would not let himself feel anything. If he got angry, he would lose control and the snake would take over his thoughts. He didn't want to hurt Mimi or the new boy.

The two days Petey was absent from school, he spent the time sleeping in the woods at the secret place where he and Jesse had been happy. He dreamed that Jesse was still with him. He was glad he had told Jesse about Uncle Sax's promise to revenge Joel. Two of the Lucas family members were now gone and two more to go. He was the one who got rid of Mirabelle and her father, not Uncle Sax.

Watermelon Road
Chapter 31
Ain't No Cause to Worry

Now that school had started Mrs. Bertie's house cleaning jobs had picked up. White folks wanted their houses cleaned while the children were at school. Mrs. Bertie was so busy and Viola, who worked for the Worthy family, had asked Mrs. Bertie to help out while she attended her mother's funeral in Birmingham. Mrs. Bertie asked Petey to go with her to the Worthy house after he got out of school so he could help her clean and get her work done faster. Esther had said it was all right.

    He met Mrs. Bertie at her house at 3:30 that Friday afternoon and they set out walking to the Worthy house, which was a mile west of Main Street. Mrs. Bertie walked slowly, carrying all her cleaning paraphernalia as Petey followed behind with extra buckets and rags. They stopped at the corner of McKenzie Street and Rockford Pass. At the corner where those two streets came together was the Worthy house. It was huge — more than twice the size of Grandmother Mimi's house. Although he was in awe of the size of the house, Petey grumbled to himself because Mrs. Bertie had three sons and two daughters out of her eight children, who could have helped her with the cleaning but they were lazy and knew she wouldn't pay them if they helped. She had promised Petey $2.50 if he did a good job. That was good pay but not enough to clean this big house. He had to think about how to approach Mrs. Bertie and ask her for more money. After all, he was doing this to help his mother out.

    The house was quiet when they entered it. The family wasn't home at the time but the backdoor was left unlocked for Mrs. Bertie to come in and clean the kitchen and the four bathrooms. She moved quickly through the house, gathering more cleaning supplies from the kitchen pantry and handed Petey a bucket to fill with water from the kitchen sink. Petey did as he was told. Mrs. Bertie couldn't find the new sea sponges Viola told her about. She and Viola liked using the sea sponges because they were good for cleaning bathrooms and kitchens. They were a rarity in Horace Graves. Viola told Mrs. Bertie that she would find the sea sponges in the cleaning pantry, but they were not there when she looked for them.

Mrs. Bertie sent Petey to look for the sea sponges in the two upstairs bathrooms and linen closets. He walked through the front parlor to get to the stairs instead of using the hallway. He stopped and looked around the parlor, noticing the heavy, expensive furnishings and rugs. There was a beautiful portrait of the Worthy family over the fireplace. Petey stared at the painting for a long time. In the painting the young blond girl he saw at the diner, was sitting on a settee next to her mother. Her father and her older brothers stood behind the settee.

Petey noticed a grand piano positioned in front of the parlor windows. The top of the piano was down and a white lace cloth covered it. Framed family photographs were lined up along the top of the magnificent instrument. Petey went over to look at them. All the frames were made of silver. His breath caught in his throat when he saw the little blond girl in some of the photos. Her beautiful face seemed to rise up from the frame and stare at him. With shaking hands, he picked up a few more of her photos and looked at them for a moment.

Mrs. Bertie's loud voice erupted from the kitchen, piercing his thoughts. "Boy, what's taking you so damn long?"

He put the photos down and ran upstairs and retrieved two sea sponges from the bathtub of one of the upstairs bathrooms. While on the second floor, he decided to look around and peeked in each bedroom along the hallway. He came to a pretty room at the end of the hall. It had a half circle of bay windows with a soft window seat the length of the windows. There were frilly pillows thrown around the window seat, matching the pillows on the canopy bed in the center of the bedroom.

The dressing table and mirror against one of the walls had satin material covering the bottom of the dresser. It was a pretty pink color with little bows sewed around the edge of the dresser and on the bottom part of the satin material near the floor. The canopy bed had a pink and white lace top that matched the bed coverings. Stuffed animals of all shapes and sizes littered the bed. There was a bureau on another wall and on top of that were photos and bottles of lotion, perfume and baby powder. Petey sniffed the baby powder. He sniffed it several times but it did not have the same effect as when he smelled it on the little girl.

He noticed opened windows on each side of the canopy bed. He went over and looked through the screen of the left window. It gave a clear view of the backyard that held an elaborate swing set and a playhouse, almost as large as his shed. Outside the other window was a large oak tree with branches close to the house. The branches started low and came up the tree, almost like a stairway to the window and beyond. A thought formed in his head as to how he could get back into the house.

He took the sea sponges down to Mrs. Bertie and she was happy to see that he had found two of them.

While working in the kitchen with Mrs. Bertie, Petey mentioned how he had never seen such beautiful picture frames when he passed through the parlor. He also said that the family was very nice looking, especially the little girl and that he had seen the mother and the girl in the diner the day he fainted.

Watermelon Road

"I hope I didn't scare them so bad that they won't come back to Miss Olivia's."

Mrs. Bertie told him that Mrs. Worthy and little Bonnie understood what happened that day. She said that Miss Olivia told Miss Marie, next door, to tell Mrs. Worthy that, "Petey ain't had no food for a whole day and was hungry and dizzy." Mrs. Bertie told this to Petey, mimicking her sister's proper speaking voice and they both laughed.

Mrs. Bertie went on to say that "Mrs. Worthy come back in Olivia's a couple of days later and bought a big dinner to take home to her family. Ain't no cause to worry 'bout your fainting spell scaring nobody."

Watermelon Road
Chapter 32
Bumpy

Bumpy sat at the end of the bar in a jazz club in Atlanta. Every now and then he'd look at the small stage where Sax was performing in the jazz quartet. Moving his head to the beat of the music, he reached for the beer the bartender handed him. Sax was hot tonight. The two and four beats spoke to him. He felt the wail of the saxophone down deep. He wanted to laugh and cry at the same time. He kept his emotions in check. Bumpy once asked Sax why he didn't do the New Orleans scene and Sax said he wouldn't be unique in that town. Bumpy understood.

Bumpy knew and only he knew the real story of how Sax came to play the saxophone. Once while they were fishing together on the Proud Rock River, he had asked Sax how he learned to play such a daunting instrument so well. Sax told him that the saxophone was the only thing in his life that he truly had a passion for. "When you have a passion for something you know is a good thing, you try to make that thing your lighthouse. You want what you can do well to show people the way."

On a calm river while the fish were jumping, Sax told him his story.

I've had a hard life, I ain't gonna lie 'bout that. It was so hard it made me ashamed of myself and of my beginnings. I ran away from home in Mississippi when I was 14. I ran from a mother who thought breeding babies made her smart and I ran from a daddy who thought making babies was all a man had to do. So I left my 13 brothers and sisters, and all them people who didn't know nothin', but still was proud of it. I come to know that there were people out in the world that know a little more than what I came from. Oh, I don't blame my parents 'cause that was all they knew. That's where their beginnings were and I guess they were so beaten down they didn't know it, and the passion to move on to something better just was not in them. I'm glad I was different. My grandfather was a runaway slave, so maybe I'm like him.

Playing the saxophone was easy for me. After leaving home, I did the usual begging and stealing to survive. I made it all the way to New Orleans by the time I was 17 and spent a lot of time listening to the kind of music in that city that made people want to get up and shake their butts. I got work in a nip joint and started hanging around the musicians. One of them, Dewey, the sax player, started teaching me the notes on his horn. That's when I realized I had a passion for that horn. I practiced whenever Dewey let me. Dewey got drunk one night and strangled one of his women to death, and went off to prison. Before they took him away, he gives me his saxophone and told me to take care of it 'til he came back. I took that saxophone and ran from that town and I've been running ever since. I been looking behind me to see if Dewey was catching up on me but that ain't never happen. That's one of the reasons why I stay out of New Orleans 'cause he might still be there looking for me. But, I think that after all this time, he probably dead.

 The joint was hopping and the ladies were looking good in their summer dresses. There was something graceful about the women in their soft cotton dresses, swaying as they danced around the floor. Someone had left the door wide open to the joint so that the warm summer breezes would blow through the place.

 It didn't matter to Bumpy what age the women were, he loved the way the thin-strapped, low cut, back out, dresses made them look younger and full of life. He tapped his feet to the music while he watched the dancers glide across the dance floor, hips shaking, hair waving, hands clapping. He and Bertie used to cut a rug like that. That was awhile ago, but now that he was in the process of making a little money, he might take Bertie dancing when he got back to Horace Graves.

 He and Sax had been exchanging letters through Sax's friend Earl. They sent letters to Earl, letting him know where they could be reached. Earl would then forward information back to Bumpy and Sax. Earl also wrote to them about the death of Mirabelle, her father and Mr. Batty. That news made Sax even more anxious to fulfill the rest of the promise.

 Bumpy was missing Bertie and the children. He couldn't contact them yet. Letting them know where he was could be dangerous even though it had been a couple of months since they had heard from him. If he did write to Bertie, someone might put two and two together and figure out Sax's plan. Bertie, with her big mouth, would tell somebody where he was and that could hurt him and Sax. He was on a mission and it was almost finished. He had finally tracked down Calvin and Haley Lucas.

 Although no one at home knew it, the friendship between Sax and Bumpy went way back to their school days. They often went fishing together but were seldom seen together. Sax had loaned Bumpy money plenty of times to buy whiskey or to put food on the table for his family. Sax knew how hard it was for a colored man with a drinking problem and no skills to find work. Bumpy would do anything for Sax and he would soon prove it.

 Finding the Lucas brothers gave him a sense of satisfaction and accomplishment. He had been given an assignment and he had completed it. He began his search the first week of July and now it was early September. It had been a long journey through back streets and small towns, treading railroad tracks, and trespassing in wooded areas to rest and sleep until it was time to hunt again. He remained invisible until he had to show himself to gain information. While hitching rides and sometimes walking for miles, Bumpy had tracked the brothers through Alabama, Mississippi, Tennessee and parts of Georgia before he caught up with them in Atlanta. In Atlanta he almost came face to face with one of them.

Once while he was following Haley, Haley made a U-turn and came walking back toward him on a busy street in Macon, Georgia. Bumpy quickly dropped to one knee and pretended to tie his shoe. He thought for sure he had been spotted, but Haley walked right by him.

Calvin and Haley Lucas skipped around a lot, doing odd jobs, stealing when they had an opportunity, and even killing when they found it necessary. He just had to keep track of them until the time was right for Sax to make his move. He and Sax had to take both men out at the same time.

Sax and Bumpy thought the brothers had gotten wind of something coming down on them in Horace Graves concerning the bodies of the Negro men found hanging in trees near the churches in town. The beginning of 1935 brought more talk and more suspicion upon the Lucas boys concerning Joel's murder back in 1933. That was the reason why they thought the Lucas brothers had left town.

As far as Horace Graves' residents knew, some time in June of 1935, Calvin and Haley suddenly disappeared. Jeremiah and Mirabelle never spoke of them unless pressed for information. Inquiries about the two men elicited the same response from the father and daughter, "They went elsewhere to look for work. We hear from them from time to time."

Near the end of June, not long after Bumpy had returned from a floating poker game in Georgia, he overheard Jeremiah Lucas tell Jonas Batty that he had gotten a letter from his boys. Bumpy was cleaning tables at Rolly's Bar and Grill at the time. The two men didn't notice him clearing a table next to theirs. He heard Mr. Lucas tell Mr. Batty that his sons were in jail in Tupelo, Mississippi for stealing rabbits from a cage in someone's backyard.

"They getting' what they deserve," said Jeremiah. Then both men burst out laughing.

"That's hell of a price to pay for a couple of rabbits," added Mr. Batty.

Bumpy told Sax the next day about the letter Jeremiah received from his sons. Right then, Sax pulled out two hundred dollars from his money belt and asked Bumpy to go to Tupelo and see if he could find the brothers' whereabouts in that city. If they were there, Sax said he would come to Tupelo and find a way to kill the Lucas brothers for what they had done to Joel. Bumpy understood and told Sax he wanted to be included in the kill.

He reminded Sax that it was normal for him to be gone for long periods of time, mostly following floating poker games. Bertie never complained as long as he sent her money and let her know that he was all right. She was glad he had been out of town during the time Suzy Fletcher was murdered.

When he got to Mississippi, the boys were gone. They were let out of jail on good behavior.

A colored man could not be seen asking after two white men, so it was hard to pick up their trail again. He got a job cleaning toilets at the prison where the

Watermelon Road

Lucas brothers had been incarcerated. After a week on the job he got a chance to have lunch outside the prison with one of the prison guards. He worked the Lucas brothers into the conversation while the two of them were having rabbit stew for lunch. This made the prison guard laugh at the reason Calvin and Haley were there for a short time. "I wonder where them two dummies are now?" Bumpy cautiously asked the guard. The guard said that he had heard through the prison grapevine that the two of them had headed toward Arkansas. Later, Bumpy had heard over the radio that two men in Arkansas had been robbing small town banks and getting away with a fair amount of money. Bumpy wrote Sax that he was heading for Little Rock.

By the time he reached that city, the brothers had moved on to Tennessee and after that to Macon, Georgia. It was a large city and he had no idea how to track down Calvin and Haley. Dressed in his bib overalls and a small straw hat on his head, he kept up the white man's image of the "dumb nigger," so no one looked at him twice. He looked for work in the bars in Macon that were patronized by whites but was unable to find work.

His luck ran out after a few weeks. He had trouble getting a lead on where the brothers were because he had to find a job and a place to sleep. Bumpy sent a letter asking for more money to keep going. Sax sent another $200.00 he made from music gigs and this kept Bumpy supplied with food, housing and transportation until he could find work. He found a job at a bank, cleaning, and kept his eyes and ears open. As far as he knew, Calvin and Haley had not spotted him and they never got wind of him tracking them.

Lady Luck blessed him again when he read in the newspapers that two unidentified white men had robbed a bank on the other side of town. The article indicated that the suspects had escaped the police. Macon police had reports of two men spending large sums of money in the towns strung out between Macon and Atlanta. The two men were reported to be in their early 20's, had strong Southern accents and were heavily armed. They were seen handing out large tips at restaurants and hotels. When the cops got close to them in Macon, they escaped by stealing a delivery truck full of linens from in front of a hotel in a small hamlet twenty miles outside of Atlanta.

Sax finally had good news from Bumpy. Bumpy had called the jazz club where Sax worked. Sax had given him the phone number in one of his recent letters. The news was worth taking a chance. He was too excited to write letters and the time was short. He had located Calvin and Haley.

"They are in Atlanta. What a break! Thank you, Lord." Bumpy had indicated this to Sax in their short telephone conversation. Sax was actually staying in a boarding house in Atlanta. He had landed a gig as a saxophonist with a jazz quartet.

On the evening of September 11, 1935, Sax sat on a small stage, blowing away his listeners with the cool sounds of his saxophone. The jazz quartet was hot tonight. Bumpy watched while drinking beer at the bar. At the break, Sax and the other musicians went out back of the club for a smoke. Bumpy stayed put. Sax had one more round to play before midnight.

Madeline L. Nowlin

After the last jazz session ended, Bumpy went straight to the boarding house where Sax stayed. He hid in the shadows in the alleyway next to the boarding house and waited patiently for Sax. Around 1:00 a.m., Bumpy heard Sax whistling as he approached the alleyway. They shook hands and then lit up their smokes.

"I ain't gonna bore you with my travels up 'til now, but I know where the Lucas brothers are hiding out and we can put paid to this tonight, if you wants to. They are hiding out in a boxcar in the train yard on the outskirts of the city. When I got here, I figured that's where they would hole up 'til their next mission. Sure enough, after a night of hanging out there, I saw them coming out of one of them boxcars. They might be there right now so you and I have to move fast."

Sax didn't say anything. He continued to smoke. Bumpy waited.

"Yeah, you right, man. This gig is over in a few days. I want to be heading home by the weekend. Let's go on out to the yard right now and see what's what."

Sax and Bumpy went out to the train yard. They kept low to the ground and crept near the boxcar where Bumpy had seen the Lucas brothers a few days ago. They could hear the brothers talking inside the boxcar. Sax and Bumpy crawled under it. The yard was not well lit but they didn't want anyone to catch sight of their movements.

"Let's get wind of this place, Haley. I feel the cops are getting closer and somebody is bound to turn us in. It don't matter how much we pay people to keep their mouth shut. Sooner or later somebody is going to want more money, which I ain't giving up, and they are going to turn us over to them Atlanta cops."

Calvin continued warning his brother. "They could know where we are right now. They know we are somewhere in Atlanta. The way you been throwing money around, who would mistake us for anything but bank rubbers?"

Haley said, "Stop worrying about the money. These are unmarked bills and can't be traced back to us so shut the fuck up."

The boxcar door slid open and Haley stood just inside. He turned to Calvin and said, "I'm going to the club down the street and have me a beer and a smoke. You want something?"

"No, you go ahead and when you get your dumb ass picked up by the cops, please don't tell them where I am. You stupid mother-fucker," Calvin yelled from inside the boxcar.

Haley chuckled and jumped down to the dirt floor of the yard. Calvin slammed the sliding door shut. Haley went crunching along the gravel in his path. Bumpy and Sax waited a few minutes then caught up to Haley when he went in between several of the boxcars that could not be seen from the front of the train yard.

Bumpy removed his shoes. The gravel hurt his feet but he wanted to make as little noise as possible. Haley stopped walking for a moment, hearing what sounded like soft footsteps in the dirt. When Haley paused, Bumpy sneaked up behind him and put his arm around his neck, twisting him around and throwing him off guard. Haley hit the ground with Bumpy on top of him. Bumpy outweighed him by 100 pounds or more.

Watermelon Road

The two men struggled on the ground, rolling over several times. Somehow Haley ended up on top and punched Bumpy in the face. He didn't recognize Bumpy and thought he was someone out to turn him in for the reward on his head. Bumpy punched back and knocked Haley off him. He got Haley in a chokehold and whispered in his ear, "This is for Joel and all the others." Haley suddenly bent over, which caused Bumpy to go over Haley's back and land on his back in the dirt. Haley jumped on Bumpy and hit him several times in the face. Bumpy tried to block the punches and throw Haley off of him. Neither man wanted to scream in pain or call for help because they had their own personal reasons for not attracting attention.

They ended up rolling over and over on the ground until they were an inch away from the railroad tracks. Bumpy was on top again. He put both his hands around Haley's throat. While on his back, Haley caught sight of Sax standing over Bumpy's shoulder. He recognized Sax. He knew then there was no hope of surviving, but he fought on. He beat and scratched at Bumpy's face, ears and head. Bumpy held on. Haley's hair had grown out long, which put him at a disadvantage. Bumpy grabbed a hand full of Haley's hair and pulled his head up and down, slamming it on the train tracks. Haley was knocked unconscious.

Sax and Bumpy carried Haley to where they heard a train leaving the yard. They placed Haley's body across the tracks of the oncoming train. They hid so they would not be seen in the lights of the engine. The train picked up speed coming through the yard and the conductor felt a slight bump on the tracks but assumed it was some animal he had run over and kept going. He had a tight schedule and didn't have time to stop and look at somebody's dog on the tracks.

"It's 2:30 in the morning. We might have to wait a few hours until Calvin comes out to look for Haley. He just might sleep through the night and if he does, we'll have to leave before daybreak so we won't be seen. There will be cops all over this place once Haley is found. We might never get another chance with Calvin if he goes off to jail for robbery or worst," said Sax.

Feeling exhilarated from the kill, Bumpy followed Sax back to their hiding place under the boxcar where the brothers had been hiding. They decided to wait until just before sunrise. It was 3:00 a.m. when they heard the sliding door to the boxcar open. Calvin jumped down and started across the yard. Sax walked in his stocking feet ahead of Calvin on a parallel path on the other side of the boxcars. Calvin heard the gravel crunching and stopped to look around. Sax came from behind one of the cars to face Calvin. Calvin recognized him instantly. At first Calvin was stunned to see a colored man he knew from Horace Graves facing him on a dark night in a train yard. A second later he became frightened and then mad. He ran full force into Sax and knocked him to the ground. Sax fell backwards and landed on the hard surface of the yard. He was winded and couldn't move. Calvin put his knee in Sax's chest. He started choking Sax. He didn't hear Bumpy coming up behind him. Bumpy hit him in the head with an iron pipe he had found near the tracks. He hit Calvin with such force, that the iron pipe bounced off of the man's head and flew out of Bumpy's hands. Calvin's eyes rolled back in his head and he was dead before he hit the ground. Bumpy whispered, "That's for Joel, you dead cracker."

Sax got his breath back and the two men went back to the boxcar the Lucas brothers had used as a hiding place. They searched it and found what was left of the stolen bank money. Seven thousand dollars and some change was rolled up in one of the brother's shirts at the back of the boxcar. They split the money and left the train yard unnoticed.

"I'm leaving on the first bus out of town this morning. When you coming back?" Bumpy asked Sax.

"I'm going to finish my last session with the quartet tomorrow night and then leave for home on Friday morning. I won't be but a day or two behind you."

They were back in the alley on the side of the boarding house where Sax was staying. The two men shook hands and hugged each other.

In a trembling voice Sax said, "When I first read Earl's letter that Mirabelle and her daddy had died on the same day, I thanked God that my promise was coming true. Now I stand before you Bumpy and say, with your help, the promise I made two years ago has been fulfilled. I will never forget what you did for me. God bless you, my friend."

Bumpy left on the first bus out of Atlanta that morning, knowing that Bertie would be happy to see him and the money when he made it home. He'd make up some story about the money. He doubted Bertie would care where the money came from.

Sax slept late that Thursday morning and went to work at the club that night. There was talk in the club about two white men found dead in the train yard. The two dead men carried no identification, but were eventually confirmed as the two bank robbers the police had been pursuing for some time.

Watermelon Road
Chapter 33
Reginald Philips Comes Home

Bertie wasn't home when Bumpy walked in his front door the day after he left Atlanta. The children were home from school and told him their mother was out cleaning houses. He washed off and put on some clean clothes. He made the children clean up the house. They were so happy to see their daddy that they obeyed without making a fuss. Bumpy helped by taking out the trash and sweeping off the front stoop, whistling as he worked.

He gave Sissy a $20 bill and told her to go over to Olivia's Diner and bring back dinner for the family. Sissy took the children's wooden wagon with her when she left. She returned with a container of baked ham, two large boxes of fried chicken, seasoned collards, macaroni salad, and corn pudding. Olivia threw in a homemade chocolate cake and two dozen of her honey butter biscuits for free to celebrate Bumpy's homecoming. He had been gone longer than usual and she had been worried about him. The children set the table and Sissy went out back to the well to draw water for the sweet tea.

Bumpy sat by the window and watched for Bertie. Presently he saw her walking up the path to the front steps. He hurried into their bedroom, closed the door, and threw the $3,500 of his share of the Lucas brothers' stolen bank money on the bed. Then he tried to hide himself in the tall wardrobe in the corner of the room. He couldn't close the door fully around his belly.

"Mama, daddy home," said Sissy.

"How long has your daddy been here?"

"He been here a good little while. He come 'bout 3:30. He made us clean up and I fixed dinner. Daddy's in your bedroom taking a nap."

Bertie looked at the set table and the food in bowls on the sideboard. "You fixed dinner all by yourself?" She was doubtful that Sissy had prepared dinner because the girl couldn't boil water. However, she didn't want to hurt the child's feelings so she said, "No wonder it smells so good in here." She kissed her daughter. "Thanks, baby."

"Weren't no trouble," lying Sissy said, sticking her chest out and grinning.

Madeline L. Nowlin

The other children kept quiet. They knew what would happen to them if they told their mother the truth about the food. Sissy would punish them and it wouldn't be pretty. Bertie didn't let on that she had seen the empty boxes from Olivia's Diner stacked on the side porch for trash day.

Bertie headed for her bedroom. She opened the door slowly and saw the money on the bed. She let out a loud scream and then slapped her hand over her mouth.

Sissy and the other children came running. "What's wrong? Is Daddy sick?"

"Everything is all right. I was just shocked that he had cleaned up the bedroom. You know your daddy don't do nothin' round this house." Bertie winked at her daughter and slipped into the bedroom, locking the door behind her.

"You better show yourself. Don't think you hiding 'cause I can see your fat belly sticking out of that wardrobe. You come on out and tell me where all this money come from. Is you been robbing banks?" Bertie was happy to see her husband but also very much shaken by the sight of so much money. She couldn't imagine what trouble Bumpy had gotten himself into.

Bumpy eased out of the wardrobe and danced on his toes like a ballerina across the floor to Bertie. He took his wife's face in both his hands and looked into her eyes. Her eyes sought his with a questioning gaze. He knew he loved that pretty face with the smooth skin and that ring of nappy cropped hair framing her face. Bumpy kissed Bertie hard on the lips.

"You stop that Mr. Reggie Philips. You stop this before my man comes home and finds you here." They both laughed at that.

"Baby, your man is home." Bumpy lead his wife to the bed and sat her down on top of the money.

Bertie said with a sigh, "Oh, Bumpy, what have you done?"

Bumpy went around and sat on the other side of the bed and fingered the money.

"I've been following a floating poker game all over the place for weeks now. I lost track of time and I still don't recollect how long I been gone. I got caught up in drinking and binging and gambling like I never done before. Sometimes I'd wake up in a strange place with no money in my pocket and then I would get a job so I could come home. But I'd hear about another damn poker game and pick it up again. I wasn't coming home to you and the cheerin without nothin' in my pockets. This here's what's left of my winnings. Should be 'bout $3,500 or so."

Bertie yelled "Lawd have mercy, you done hit the mother load. For the first time in our married life we are gonna have enough money to get us through the winter and maybe, just maybe, have some left to put in the bank."

"You come sit by me," she said as she patted her side of the bed. "I ain't welcomed you home proper yet."

Watermelon Road
Chapter 34
Time Runs Out

On Thursday night, September 12, Sax told his jazz musician friends that it was his last night with them. He was leaving on Friday morning for home. "I miss my family," he said.

"I know you guys can find a sax player in New Orleans as soon as you get there. I want to thank you for this opportunity to work with such great musicians."

"If you need to work again, look us up," said Joe, the base player. Ricky, the piano player was banging out a new sound. Something Sax had not heard before. It was a different kind of jazz tune. Sax listened to the music for a moment. Things were changing and swing music was ushering in a new era. He knew there would always be a place for jazz because people would always love it no matter what changes it went through. Ricky kept on playing the piano and Sax walked over and accompanied him on his saxophone. "You jive turkey," said Ricky.

"Yeah," said Leon, the drummer. "Mr. Jive had a sound everybody was digging and now he's splitting on us." He picked up the tempo and joined in. The last set had begun and the customers smiled and clapped when they started the music up again. The men on the dance floor stretched out their hands to the women in anticipation of a spin around the floor. "Willy's Peachtree Jazz Club" was swinging that night. Sax had never felt so good.

Sax thought a great deal about what was waiting for him back home as he packed the next morning. He had to get home. He had left Esther and the boys alone for too long. Esther was drinking herself to death before he left and for all he knew, the boys were probably drinking with her by now. Who knew what was going on back there? It was his fault that he didn't write to them or send them money for over two months. He hoped Esther had found enough work to support the boys and herself.

When I get home, I'm gonna have a long talk with Esther. I'll tell her I've been seeing another woman, but it didn't mean nothin'. She knows I love her. I'm telling her things will have to change or I'm moving on.

Friday morning found him at the bus station. He brought with him an egg sandwich, a cup of coffee and a newspaper. Sax settled down at the back of the bus for the long ride home.

Watermelon Road
Chapter 35
Dreams

On Wednesday night, one day before Sax said goodbye to his musician friends, Petey was having a dream. He went to bed thinking about his 13th birthday coming up on Saturday. *Soon, I'll be a man.* Petey thought while lying in bed.

He began to dream. In the dream he was celebrating his birthday with Jesse and Mimi in the backyard of the Worthy house. Mrs. Worthy had made him a birthday cake and Bonnie Worthy helped him blow out the candles. Jesse and Mimi clapped. Bonnie's blue eyes sparkled. Her blond hair shone so bright in the light of the cake candles that Petey had to turn away from the brightness. The music started to play "Tain't Nobody's Biz-ness If I Do." He held her close to him and began to rub his groin against her. The smell of baby powder was overpowering. He began to rub against her faster and faster until something in him burst open. When he woke in the morning, he thought he had peed on himself. The dream was still vivid in his mind.

School was unbearable now that Mimi would have nothing to do with him. He tried to catch her eye in class but she wouldn't look his way. If they passed in the hall or out on the school grounds, she avoided him. Her abandonment hurt him as much as losing Jesse. He had no one to talk to, no one to tell about his dream. He wished Uncle Sax were home.

He went out to the shed after school to get some money from his hiding place to buy Mimi a nice gift. He knew girls liked gifts and giving Mimi one might make her like him again. He found the floorboard, removed it and reached in for the money. He noticed the stack of $20 bills was not arranged the way he had left them. He looked under the money and saw that the pocket knife was missing. At first he panicked but then he realized that Peewee must have found the hiding place and had taken the knife. He reasoned that if an adult had found his hiding place, the man or woman would have taken the money and the pocket knife. He counted the money. It was all there. He took a twenty-dollar bill from the stack and replaced the board, thinking, h*e'd find Peewee and get the knife back, but not before he beat the shit out of him for stealing from his own brother.*

In the meantime, he took the $20 of Grandmother Mimi's money over to Mr.

West's General Store to buy Mimi a gift. While he was there, he decided to buy a gift for Bonnie Worthy. After all, she was a girl and he wanted her to like him too.

He took so long looking over items in the store that Mr. West thought he was trying to steal something. "Are you trying to steal something, boy?" He asked Petey.

"No sir. I got $20 for my birthday and I want to buy some gifts with it for my girlfriends."

"Well, ain't that just like a nigger, got to have more than one woman and then you have to spend your little bit of money on them." Petey ignored him. "We have plenty of stuffed animals and other toys and games. Why don't you look over there," Tim West said, pointing at the toy section. When Petey walked towards that section, he noticed the jewelry counter. The cheap shinny jewelry caught his eye.

He walked over and looked through the glass case. He spotted some charm bracelets with cute miniature charms of shoes, hearts, crosses and other sundry items attached to them. Petey loved the shinny silver painted bracelets and asked Mr. West if he could look at them out of the case.

"Them's five dollars each, boy."

"I wants two of them, sir."

Tim West rang up the two bracelets and told Petey he owed him $10.10 because of the tax. He gave Petey the correct change from his $20 bill. He had his standards.

"Now get the hell out of my store."

Petey was so happy with his purchases that he let Peewee slide another day before he confronted him about the pocket knife.

Thursday night he had another dream. Only this time he and Bonnie didn't dance. He was a snake in Bonnie's bed. He hissed and twisted himself under her covers, waiting for her to come to bed. When she pulled back the covers, he coiled and leaped for her throat. This frightened him and he woke up in a sweat, breathing heavily and shaking all over.

Friday morning dawned bright and beautiful. It was quite warm and would break a record by 3:00 pm that day. During lunch at school, Petey went to Mimi's table where she was eating with Peewee, Danny and Jimmy. *She's like a mother hen,* Petey thought.

He grabbed Peewee, squeezing his arm as he pulled him up from the lunch table. Peewee's heart was pounding in his chest. He was afraid of his brother but he couldn't let it show in front of his friends. Petey dragged him a little ways from Mimi and her brothers.

"Where's my pocket knife, you fuckin' thief?"

"Ouch. That hurts. Stop squeezing my arm. All right, I took it but I ain't got it with me. I wouldn't bring it to school. Can I keep it until Sunday when I come home from the Beaumonts?"

"Hell no. You give me that knife back right now before I kick your butt across this lunch room floor. See what your friends say then." Petey searched

Watermelon Road

Peewee's pockets, jerking him from side to side. Mimi and the twins watched in fascination as Petey nearly turned his brother upside down to search him.

"Stop that. Everybody's looking at you. You acting like a crazy person," Peewee yelled, fighting back tears.

"I don't give a shit 'bout what people think. I am crazy and if you don't give me my knife, I'm gonna kill you," Petey threatened.

"Ok, I'll give it to you right after school. I promise."

"I'll be waiting for you."

"What the heck was that all about?" Mimi asked Peewee when he came back to the lunch table.

Peewee shrugged his shoulders and said, "Petey thinks I stole some money from him. I told him I ain't take nothin' from him."

"I heard him say he's gonna kill you," said Danny.

After school, the twins hid Peewee so Petey couldn't find him and kill him.

Petey didn't run into Peewee after school but he came upon Mimi as she was walking to the parish house. "Mimi, please talk to me. It's my birthday on Saturday and I want you to come to my party. I'm doing it all by myself. I'm gonna have cake and ice cream and presents for everybody."

Mimi stopped walking and turned to look at him.

"I'm scared of you, Petey. I don't know who you are no more. You are a bad person. You've done some bad things. You let Jesse get blamed for something you did and now he's dead and you can't make it up to him."

"Please, just leave me alone," Mimi begged.

"Things are going on inside my head and I can't stop it. Please talk to me. Help me." He reached out and touched Mimi's arm. She pulled away from him.

"Here, take this." Petey handed her one of the bracelets.

"What is it?"

"It's a little gift. It's a bracelet with little things hanging from it. I got it from Mr. West's store. You can buy more things to hang from it if you wants to." He gave her his most brilliant smile. The smile frightened her even more.

"I don't want it. I won't take anything from you. You stay away from me."

Feeling dejected, Petey went to the secret place. Once, after Jesse died, he had made a half-hearted attempt to run after the watermelon cart, but it wasn't the same any more. He didn't love watermelon the way he used to and it was no longer fun. Nothing was fun any more without Jesse.

He gathered up dried leaves and began rubbing them between his hands. He hadn't done that in awhile. Even the dizzy spells had stopped. Rubbing the leaves stopped him from feeling sad.

Petey needed time to think over how he was going to approach Bonnie Worthy and give her the bracelet he bought for her. He hoped she wouldn't be upset because he had bought the same kind of bracelet for Mimi. When he talked to Bonnie, he'd make her understand that he and Mimi were just friends.

Mimi wouldn't accept his gift or his friendship. He felt he should give Mimi's bracelet to another girl but he didn't like other girls and he had no other friends. That's why he and Bonnie had to be friends now.

Madeline L. Nowlin

Petey thought about Uncle Sax. They hadn't heard from him for over two months. He missed him. Uncle Sax had been a good father to them. Now the family had learned to get along without him.

"I'm the man of the house now," Petey screamed in the woods. "We don't need nobody else."

He picked up more leaves to rub and sat down by the bald cypress and closed his eyes. He felt tired. He'd thought he'd catch up to Peewee tomorrow and beat the shit out of him then for stealing the pocket knife.

Petey had planned to take some of the money from the shed and give himself a birthday party but that would not have been fun without Mimi being there. He didn't feel like giving the party any more. He was afraid no one would come. If Esther didn't have to work on Saturday, he would ask her to make him a birthday cake just for the three of them.

Watermelon Road
Chapter 36
Snake

He thought he was dreaming until he felt the cool night air on his arms. The sky was packed with stars. He looked up at the stars and smiled and they smiled back. He reached up to touch one and nearly lost his balance on the tree branch. Petey caught himself and wedged his body into the nook of the massive oak tree outside Bonnie Worthy's bedroom window. He rubbed his arms to keep warm. The day had been warm but now it was cold. It felt like fall. Then he remembered something and laughed. It was his birthday, September 14. It was after midnight and he had turned 13.

I know mama, Peewee, Mimi and everybody in town is waiting to celebrate my 13th birthday. Oh, everybody but Jesse. But he one of them stars looking down at me. I miss you, Nightshade. I see you shinning at me. Thanks for being my friend. I got a new friend now.

He raised his right hand to the sky again but was surprised to see that he was holding his mother's kitchen butcher knife. The one Esther used all the time to cut up meats and vegetables. He stared at the knife in his right hand and wondered how it got there. It wasn't the right knife. This was a big knife, not Jesse's pocket knife with the snake handle. *Why don't I have that knife? Oh, I remember now, I ain't never got it back from Peewee. I guess I forgot,* he thought, giggling at his mistake. Wearing only his underpants, he started to shiver. He heard a jiggling sound and looked at his left wrist. The charm bracelet was on his arm. He shook it to hear the jiggling sound of the charms again but this time it made a hissing sound.

Still holding the butcher knife, he put his hands over his ears to keep out the hissing noise. He could see Bonnie through the screen in the open window. She looked like Sleeping Beauty waiting to be kissed by her prince. The hissing grew louder and the voice came. "Yessssssss. We have another one to kill. Another Mirabelle. We've got to kill her before she grows up and hurts somebody like Joel got hurt. You remember Jooooeeel, your brrrrooootheeerrr? Yesssssss."

Petey whispered "Stop it, stop it. I love her. I can't be no snake and hurt her. I won't listen to you. You make me do bad things. I ain't gonna listen to you no more. I remember my brother. I loved Joel but sometimes he was mean.

Madeline L. Nowlin

He put a garden snake in my bed one night and it crawled up on me and got in my pajamas. I screamed and Joel laughed 'til he cried. I took that snake and slammed his head against the wall. I threw it out our bedroom window. Is you the snake I killed?"

There was no answer from the snake but the hissing came back, filling his head with the noise. He crawled close to the window, reached out and stuck the butcher knife into the screen, slashing it repeatedly. He kept at it until there was a hole big enough for him to slide through. Petey swung himself over onto the window ledge and slid through to the bedroom floor. All the while the hissing was in his head. "After you kill her," said the snake, "you will be a real snake yourself. You will have scales and no arms or legs and you can slither around on your belly just like me."

"I don't want to be no snake. I ain't gonna harm Bonnie. I'm gonna take her some place safe so you can't get at her," he hissed back.

He tipped toed over to the sleeping child in the bed. Bonnie was lying on her back, holding a small doll in her arms. Petey leaned down as if he was going to kiss her. He put his face close to hers and watched her as she slept. The baby powder was sweet in his nostrils. It made him swoon.

Petey walked around the room to get his head straight. He found a stack of children's books in a bookcase against the far wall. It was dark, save for a lit small lamp on her bedside table. He took a book from the bookcase and eased himself onto the floor. Petey softly tore the pages from Bonnie's favorite book, "Alice in Wonderland."

He put the butcher knife down and scrunched up the pages and rubbed them between his hands, thinking this would drown out the hissing sound in his head. Picking up the knife again, he searched the bedroom for something to put over Bonnie's mouth so she wouldn't make any noise when he woke her.

He found a roll of wide clear tape sitting next to her schoolbooks. He picked it up and went over to the bed and leaned over her again. Her eyes fluttered. He tore off a piece of the clear tape and placed it tightly over her mouth. Bonnie's eyes opened. She saw a Negro boy staring down at her. There was a look of confusion in those blue eyes of hers and then one of complete fear. She struggled to sit up. Petey put is hand on her chest and gently pushed her back down on the bed.

He said, "Bonnie, can you hear me?" She nodded. "Look at me. You know me. I'm the boy that was at Miss Olivia's that fainted the day you and your mama come to eat. Don't you remember me? My name is Petey. I ain't gonna hurt you. I put some tape over your mouth so's you don't holla and wake up your folks. Do you understand?"

She nodded again, her body shaking with fear. "You can sit up now."

Her plan was to run for the door and down the hall to her parents' bedroom but she saw the butcher knife. It looked huge. Petey had the knife in his right hand but was not waving it in a threatening manner. He had forgotten about the knife. "Get out of bed and put your slippers and bathrobe on, baby girl. I don't want you to catch cold while we travel to a secret magic place in the woods."

Watermelon Road

It wasn't just what he said, it was the way he said it that frightened Bonnie even more than the knife. To her, each word ended in a hissing sound. She did as she was told.

"Listen to me, my angel. You are going to have to climb down to the ground from the tree outside your window. I know you can do this 'cause you are an angel and you can fly if you wants to." Petey smiled his brilliant smile and nodded his head to assure Bonnie that she would be all right. "Here, gimme yo slippers 'cause you cain't get a good grip on them branches if you got these slippers on. It's cool out and I forgot the rest of my clothes. They hanging on bushes in the woods so I can find my way back home." Petey looked confused for a moment, then he said "Excuse me. Sometimes I don't know what I'm talkin' 'bout. That was another time."

"You go on now and get to climbing down. I'll be right behind you. I can grab hold of you if you start to fall. Don't you make no noise now. Lemme show you what could happen to you if you start to hollering."

He reached out and took her hand. He turned it over to the backside. She tried to pull away. "Be still now. You be still, my angel." Petey put a little pressure on the knife as he stuck it in the back of her hand. He made a small nick in the flesh, just enough to draw blood. She moaned and tears rolled down her cheeks. She wanted to rip the tape off her mouth and scream for her mommy.

"There, there, now, that ain't hurt none." Petey kissed the back of her hand where he had nicked her with the knife. There was blood on his lips.

"Stop that crying. I got a present for you." He took the charm bracelet off his wrist and put it on Bonnie's wrist. "Ain't that pretty?" Bonnie shook her head "yes," not wanting to upset him. The bracelet was much too big for her arm.

Petey tied the belt from her bathrobe tightly around her waist and helped her out of the bedroom window. She maneuvered through and around the tree branches and made it to the ground safely.

Petey jumped down from the last tree branch behind Bonnie. There was a flashlight at the base of the tree, right where he had left it. He handed Bonnie her slippers and she placed them on her feet. He took hold of her hand and started running. It was hard at first but she was able to keep up. They didn't notice that the bracelet had fallen from Bonnie's arm at the base of the tree.

Please baby Jesus, please don't let him hurt me, she prayed over and over again in her head.

They ran in the dark. Petey found Fisherman's Lane and the opening where he entered the woods. He had the flashlight to guide him. On the way there, Petey stopped now and then to let Bonnie rest. It took over an hour and a half to get to the secret place.

A young oak stood to one side of the clearing. Petey took the belt from Bonnie's bathrobe. He backed her up against the tree and tied her to the tree with the belt. The belt was not tied tight and she could have easily slipped through it and gotten away but she was too afraid to run. She didn't know where she was and Petey still had the knife. Bonnie did remember him from the diner. She had felt sorry for him when he fainted and broke all those dishes.

Petey laid the knife down by the cypress tree. He took the flashlight and looked for dry leaves to rub between his hands. He found a pile of leaves and took some back to the tree. He sat with his back against the tree, rubbing the leaves in his hands and thinking.

He stopped rubbing the leaves, picked up the flashlight and let it shine on Bonnie's face. She closed her eyes and turned her head away from the bright light.

He kept the flashlight on her face.

Petey blew air through his lips and spoke.

"Only I knows Joel sneaked out the house most nights after we went to bed. Mama made Uncle Sax look in on us afore she went to bed." Thus began the story. Bonnie listened for as long as she could stand up, not really understanding what Petey was saying to her. It didn't sound like the stories her mother read to her at night. Her legs became weary and she slid down the tree onto the grass. She couldn't stay awake any longer and fell asleep.

She awoke at daybreak. The flashlight had gone out, its batteries long dead. Petey was still telling the story. His voice was raspy and he had drooled on himself. He didn't seem to notice Bonnie anymore.

Watermelon Road
Chapter 37
Lost and Found

At 7:00 a.m., Jenny Worthy went to Bonnie's bedroom to wake her. They had to get an early start if they were going to pick up Mr. Worthy on time. He was an officer at a military base near Birmingham. It was a long drive and Bonnie wanted to ride with her mother to surprise her father. Generally, she hated the long ride and often refused to go, but she had missed her father and wanted to spend time with him on the way home before her brothers monopolized her father's free time when he arrived home. Bonnie's two older brothers had gotten up much earlier and gone fishing with Uncle Fritz, their father's brother. She knew that her father, uncle and brothers would spend most of the day talking about fishing once they returned home.

Bonnie was not in her room, but Jenny was not alarmed because Bonnie's bathrobe and slippers were missing.

"Bonnie dear, are you in the toilet?"

There was no response. While walking across the bedroom floor, she noticed that Bonnie's favorite book was lying in the corner near the bookcase. The pages had been torn from it and scrunched up into little balls. She hurried into the bathroom and found it empty. Back in the bedroom, she called her daughter's name again. "Bonnie, Bonnie?" That's when she noticed the cut screen in the window.

Jenny put her trembling hands to her mouth and slowly walked towards the window. The window was up, but the screen was shredded, leaving a big hole in the center. She unlocked the screen and raised it up to look out onto the grounds. She was relieved to see that Bonnie had not tried to climb out the window and fallen to the ground. Still, the damaged screen confused and upset her.

Jenny ran downstairs and out the front door. She walked around the grounds, calling her daughter's name. She saw the gardener and asked him if he had seen Bonnie and he told her that he had not. She thought about Suzy Fletcher. Fear gripped her throat and she let out a low moan. Then she saw Viola, her cook and maid, coming up the walkway toward the house.

Viola stopped short when she saw Mrs. Worthy outside in her nightgown and robe, standing in the middle of the front lawn. The look on the woman's face was bordering on hysteria. Viola put down the two bags of groceries she was carrying and went over to Mrs. Worthy.

"What in God's name has happened?" Viola asked. "Miss Jenny, what's the matter with you? Why you standing out here half naked like you is?"

Jenny Worthy put her arms around Viola and burst into tears. "I can't find Bonnie. I've been looking for her since 7:00 and I haven't found her. Where would she go? She knew we were going to pick up her daddy at the base this morning. Something bad must have happened to her."

"Come on back in the house, Miss Jenny, and we'll decide what's best to do 'bout finding Bonnie." She called to the gardener to bring the bags of groceries to the kitchen. They went to the kitchen where Viola made Jenny sit down at the kitchen table. She asked her to tell her all that had happened that morning. This kept the woman talking and she soon calmed down. Viola handed Jenny a cup of coffee from a pot she had made while Jenny was telling her about Bonnie's disappearance. Jenny also told Viola about the torn screen in her daughter's bedroom.

"I tell you what, I'm gonna walk for a couple of blocks and see if I can find Bonnie. If I cain't find her then you got to call the Sheriff over to Bison. I could go knocking door to door and ask the neighbors if they seen her but I know you don't want me doing that. You sit here and drink your coffee while I go look for our baby girl. Besides, she might come home while I'm out looking for her."

"Thank you Viola. I'll wait right here."

Viola returned a half hour later. "I done walked four blocks west to Southerland, then east to Mission Avenue and up Rockford Pass, then back here to McKenzie Street. I ain't see that chile no place I looked. I asked a few people if they seen Bonnie but they said no. I told them that she went off to look for her kitty. I told them that so they don't get curious. I think it's high time you called the Sheriff. Is you fixin' to do that?"

Jenny Worthy went to the telephone on the kitchen counter. "I think I should call Randolph first and let him know that our daughter is missing." This was one call she never thought she would ever have to make. She looked over at Viola and Viola nodded for her to go ahead.

Randolph Worthy also told his wife to call the Sheriff. He told Jenny that he would have to catch a ride at the base with someone coming near Horace Graves and it would take two hours or longer before he reached home.

Deputy Cox answered the phone at the county jail in Bison on the second ring. He listened for a few minutes and then told the Sheriff to pick up the phone in his office while he stayed on the line. Forty-five minutes later Sheriff Richards, Deputy Cox and two volunteer deputies were standing in Mrs. Worthy's parlor. The Sheriff's county car and a new Chevy pickup truck, belonging to one of the deputies was in the front yard. Two bloodhounds were standing in the back of the truck.

Jenny invited the Sheriff into her kitchen and offered him a cup of coffee while Deputy Cox and the other men went back out to the front yard. She related to Sheriff Richards everything that had transpired that morning, and especially about the torn screen in Bonnie's bedroom. They also talked about the schedule Bonnie kept on weekends and about her habits and favorite things. He put Jenny at ease for the moment, assuring her that he did not, as yet, suspect anything suspicious about Bonnie's disappearance.

He also had a talk with Viola, whom he had met once before when she was working a party for one of his neighbors in Bison. Viola was a little agitated but that was to be expected when he questioned Negroes. Sheriff Richards knew that most of them felt that they would be blamed for whatever went wrong, whether they were guilty or not. He knew differently after dealing with the county inhabitants that if you wanted to find out who did something, you couldn't just look at one race of people.

The Sheriff called Deputy Cox back into the house and they both went upstairs to have a look at Bonnie's bedroom. They noticed that the room had two open windows, with screens that locked from the inside, like all the other windows in the house. Neither of the two windows had any visual footprints or handprints on the ledges. They investigated the torn screen at the window closest to the oak tree. The Sheriff and Deputy noticed that the screen was cut from the outside. Looking down from that window, they could see several small broken branches lying on the ground near the tree. Something shining in the morning sunlight caught their eye before they stepped away from the window.

Sheriff Richards told Deputy Cox to go down and check out the area around the tree and the rest of the lawn to see if he could find any evidence that Bonnie had left the house from her bedroom window. The Sheriff was thinking that if she was kidnapped there might be footprints or something that the kidnapper might have dropped on the grounds that would be a clue to finding Bonnie. He also wondered if the shinny thing near the tree was something that belonged to Bonnie or the kidnapper. If, there was a kidnapper.

First Mirabelle's baby went missing and was never found. Now Bonnie is missing. The Sheriff was wondering if someone had put a curse on Horace Graves.

He continued to search Bonnie's bedroom. The room was tidy except for a small pile of balled up paper on the side of the bookcase. It gave him pause as he tried to remember where he had seen rolled paper like that before. He had never met Bonnie but he somehow knew that she was not the type of child that would destroy a book like that. The little pile of paper was so familiar to him, but he could not place it.

The memory came back to him. He remembered back in June when the boy, Jesse, had drowned in Baltimore. Jesse was to come back to Horace Graves to be questioned about a pocket knife. The boy had a close friend named Petey who was the same boy he had questioned about Jesse not being on the train with him and Reverend Beaumont. He thought back further to when he had first laid eyes on Petey. He had questioned Petey about his brother Joel's murder over two years before.

He recalled seeing Petey a third time when he went to *Upon This Rock Baptist Church* the day he heard from Mrs. Laurent that Jesse had drowned. He went there to tell Reverend Beaumont what had happened and to ask a favor of him. He wanted Reverend Beaumont to go with him to the Hammond house to comfort them when he broke the bad news. It was late on a Sunday evening, but the Reverend was still at the church. While he was talking to Reverend Beaumont, he heard a scream coming from the side of the church. The boy, Petey Creek, had been listening somewhere near them and stepped out from his hiding place. Reverend Beaumont ran to the shaking child and tried to calm him down. The boy was crying uncontrollably. The Sheriff had felt bad about not speaking to the Reverend in private so that no one could hear what he was saying. Reverend Beaumont took Petey inside the church and Sheriff Richards followed them.

Sheriff Richards looked on in amazement when the Reverend handed the boy a handful of printed church programs. He looked on as Petey ripped the programs apart and rolled the strips into balls between his hands. After a few moments, Petey calmed down just like the Reverend said he would.

"It brings the boy peace," the Reverend said when he noticed the questioning look on Sheriff's face.

"What's wrong with him? The Sheriff had asked.

"I don't know of any medical term for what is wrong with him. He's been this way ever since his brother was killed two years ago. Otherwise, he's normal but just can't handle certain things that upset him."

"Well, I can drop him off at his house on our way to see the Hammonds. I hate this part of my job."

"I can understand that," said Reverend Beaumont. "I feel the same way when I have to do what you're doing. Sometimes our professions are quite similar."

The torn paper in the corner did not mean that Petey had been in Bonnie's bedroom, but it was evidence that someone had been in the bedroom with Bonnie before she went missing that morning. Petey and Jesse had been best friends. The Sheriff knew that best friends share everything and maybe Jesse had given the pocket knife to Petey for safekeeping.

Damn, why didn't I search Petey back in June when I questioned him about Jesse?

Another thought occurred to him. *Could it have been Petey that killed Suzy Fletcher all along?* The hairs on the back of his neck stood up. He felt a chill. *What if Petey had Bonnie now and was going to do the same thing to her?* At that moment he felt he may have made a huge mistake that could cost Bonnie Worthy her life.

Then Sheriff Richards felt he was grasping at straws. There was no evidence that Petey had the pocket knife. There was no evidence to tie the boy to the Fletcher murder. There was certainly no evidence that Petey had anything to do with Bonnie being missing. Nothing made sense.

He didn't want to alarm Bonnie's mother or get his deputies all worked up. At this point, there was no reason to suspect foul play. Bonnie could have just walked away from the house. There was also the possibility that the child had been kidnapped to extort money from the family. The Worthy's were not filthy

Watermelon Road

rich but they had more than most people in town.

He went back downstairs to the kitchen to have another talk with Viola. Mrs. Worthy sat alone on her front veranda, hoping that Bonnie would soon return.

Sheriff Richards found Viola frying bacon in a pan on the gas stove. She jumped when he entered the kitchen. "What is it Sheriff? Has Bonnie come home?"

"Not yet. Can I have some of that coffee?" He sat at the kitchen table, clasping his hands together in a prayerful position.

"Sure, and I made a batch of fresh biscuits. I just took them from the oven. You want one"

"Can't nobody in the South turn down a homemade biscuit, Miss Viola," he smiled, attempting to put her at ease.

Then he asked, "Has there been anyone in the house other than you and the family lately?"

"Oh here it comes," Viola thought to herself.

"Not that I knows about. I've been here most every day, 'cept for one time a few weeks ago, afore school opened. I had to go to Birmingham for a short time to attend my mama's funeral. She died of cancer. It was almost a relief 'cause she suffered so." She handed the Sheriff a cup of black coffee and a biscuit. Small bowls of cream and sugar were already laid out on the kitchen table.

He picked up a spoon from the table and measured out sugar for his coffee.

"I'm so sorry for your loss. I know what you're going through. I lost my father a few months back.

He continued with his questioning. "When you can't come to work, who does the cooking and cleaning in your place?"

"Mrs. Bertie Philips comes in and do for the Worthy's when I have an emergency. She's real good and dependable. Miss Jenny likes her. She come here when I had to go to the funeral. Sometimes she works over at Olivia's Diner to make ends meet. Miss Olivia is her sister."

"Now that's one colored gal that can cook. As far as I'm concerned, Miss Olivia is the best cook in the whole county."

Viola agreed with the Sheriff.

"When I get a chance, I'll go have a talk with Mrs. Bertie. Thank you for taking the time to talk to me."

Viola nodded her head in response. She was impressed at how well the Sheriff treated her because she was seldom shown any respect by the white establishment in town.

While Sheriff Richards was drinking his coffee, Mrs. Worthy came running into the kitchen yelling that Bonnie was home.

"Thank you, Jesus," Viola screamed, forgetting she was in the kitchen with the Sheriff. She was relieved that the girl was home safe and she was not a suspect anymore. She took the bacon off the stove and followed the Sheriff out to the front yard where Mrs. Worthy was standing.

Mr. Miller tipped his hat at the Sheriff and Mrs. Worthy and helped Bonnie down from his cart. Mrs. Worthy, crying and praising God, gathered little Bonnie in her arms. Bonnie was a sight to behold. She was incredibly dirty from head to toe. Her hair was matted to her head with pieces of forest debris in it. Her face was dirty and smeared with tears. The nightgown and bathrobe she wore were dirty and ripped in several places and her slippers were caked with mud.

Mrs. Worthy put her daughter down and took a good look at her. "My God child, what happened to you? Did somebody hurt you? You look like you've been dragged through a briar patch."

The Sheriff gently took Bonnie from Mrs. Worthy's grasp. The child was whimpering a little but not flat out crying. He took Bonnie a little ways from her mother and the others, including Deputy Rudy who had just whispered to him that he had discovered two sets of footprints leading away from the tree on the side of the house and out back of the lawn.

He also mentioned he had found an inexpensive charm bracelet near the tree. He handed it over to the Sheriff.

Sheriff Richards wanted to hear Bonnie's story right away before she got caught up in her mother's excitement and forgot most of what had happened to her.

"Listen to me Bonnie. I'm the Sheriff and I'm not here to harm you or punish you for running away from home."

"I didn't run away from home. That colored boy made me go with him," she whispered to him because she didn't want her mother to hear.

"Did the boy hurt you? Did he touch your body in a strange way?" He asked, hoping she would take his meaning.

"No sir, he didn't touch me, except to tie me to that tree in the woods. Then all he did was rub leaves on his hands, and shine a flashlight in my face. He talked and talked until I fell asleep. He was still talking when I woke up this morning and I ran away from him. I got lost and kept falling down. I found a road and then I saw Mr. Miller come down the road with his horse cart and he gave me a ride home." Bonnie didn't mention the butcher knife.

"What did he talk about?" He asked the child.

"I don't know. All I know is he kept saying somebody named Joel shouldn't go some place. I didn't understand his words."

Sheriff Richards took the bracelet out of his pocket and showed it to Bonnie. Her eyes lit up.

"That's the bracelet that boy put on my arm. I didn't have it when we got to the woods."

"It must have fallen off your arm," said the Sheriff. "I'll keep it just in case he stole it or something."

"All right," said Bonnie.

He took Bonnie back to her mother. He turned to the housekeeper. "Viola, you take Bonnie into the house and get her cleaned up. Make sure she hasn't been hurt and check for any cuts or scratches she might have. Hurry up now. Mrs. Worthy and I need to have a talk with Mr. Miller."

Watermelon Road

Viola took Bonnie into the house for a hot bath.

The Sheriff and Mrs. Worthy turned and looked expectantly at Mr. Miller. The Sheriff beckoned Deputy Cox to come over and listen in. He put up his hand for the other two deputies to stay put. "I saw her walking along Fisherman's Lane. At first I couldn't even tell if she was a boy or a girl she was so dirty. I slowed down the horse when I got to her because she was standing there waving at me. I asked her how she come to be there looking like that and she burst into tears. I got down and picked her up and put her on the seat next to me. I remembered she lived here because I've seen her now and again when I delivered fresh fruit to Mrs. Worthy. She told me that a colored boy was in her bedroom and made her follow him to them woods near Fisherman's Lane and that he tied her to a tree and talked all night," Mr. Miller reported.

"Thank you for bringing her home. Now I don't want you going about town telling people what Bonnie said to you. She ran away from home to avoid being punished for something she did and probably made up that story so you'd bring her back." The Sheriff's story was convincing. He winked at Mr. Miller and patted the old man's shoulder. Mr. Miller nodded in agreement.

"Please, Mr. Miller, if you would stay a moment I'd like to give you a token of my appreciation for bringing my baby home," Jenny Worthy offered.

"There's no cause to give me anything. I did what anybody would have done for a child. I ain't no hero."

"I know you did it because you are a kind man, but this is for me. I want to show how grateful I am for you being such a responsible man. Please, please let me do something for you. If you won't take money, please come in and let Viola fix you the best breakfast you ever had," begged Mrs. Worthy.

"Well now, I could do with a nice plate of food." Mr. Miller tethered his horse and followed Mrs. Worthy into the house.

Watermelon Road
Chapter 38
Esther

The two hound dogs were led off the truck and onto Fisherman's Lane. The Sheriff and Deputy Cox didn't have anything of Petey's to sniff but Mrs. Worthy had given them a piece of Bonnie's clothing so that the dogs would have a starting point. Sheriff Richards gave the dogs a whiff of Bonnie's nightgown. The dogs became confused and circled the ground for awhile, pressing their noses down. One dog wanted to follow the trail where Bonnie came out of the wooded area and the other dog wanted to follow the trail leading into the woods. The men finally got both dogs to go in the same direction and they all headed into the woods off Fisherman's Lane.

It took only ten minutes for the dogs to find Petey in the clearing. He was sitting in the same spot he had settled in that early morning. Petey sat on the grass hugging himself and rocking back and forth. He was working his mouth, still telling the story but no sound came out. The child had drooled on himself and peed in his underpants. His eyes were vacant and he took no notice of the dogs or the deputies approaching.

"Jesus Christ," Deputy Cox whispered as they came near the boy. Sheriff Richards still held the barking dogs on the leash. Deputy Cox and the two other deputies saw the large butcher knife on the ground beside Petey. Deputy Cox picked up the knife and handed it to the Sheriff.

One of the other deputies found the belt to Bonnie's bathrobe on the ground around a tree trunk nearby. Sheriff Richards took off his lightweight jacket and placed it around Petey's shoulders. Petey took no notice of his surroundings and did not respond when the Sheriff called his name. He picked up Petey and carried him back to the pickup truck and laid him in the truck bed. The dogs stood watch over the child as the men drove off.

It was 10:00 a.m. when Esther and Peewee came out to the front porch after seeing the Sheriff's car and the pickup truck pull into the front yard. Sheriff Richards got out of the old Plymouth police car and went up the steps to the porch. He addressed Esther as "Mrs. Creek," and told her to go into the house so he could talk to her without the neighbors watching. Peewee followed them but went to the kitchen to listen to the conversation that was going on in the parlor.

Watermelon Road

While Esther kept shaking her head in denial, Sheriff Richards continued with his narrative of what had happened up until he ended up at her house. A frightened Peewee listened from the kitchen doorway. No one noticed him. Esther kept repeating the same sentence over and over, "You got the wrong boy. Petey been upstairs sleep all night." Ain't that right Peewee? Peewee didn't respond. He knew Petey's bed was empty when he woke up this morning and Esther knew it too.

"You just trying to pin something on my boy."

Sheriff Richards asked Esther to come out to the truck and look in the back. At first she would not move but he took her by the arm and led her to the truck. They walked around to the back of the truck while the deputies looked on. The dogs were on the lawn. Peewee followed them to the truck. Petey was asleep in back of the truck.

"Lawd Jesus," Esther cried out when she saw Petey. He had on only his underpants and was dirty and smelled of urine, like a drunk that had fallen by the wayside. Tears rolled down Esther's face. Peewee was sad but he didn't cry. At first he thought Petey was dead.

She turned to Deputy Cox and said, "Sir, please put my son in the kitchen so he can get warm." Esther steeled herself for what was to come. Deputy Cox picked up Petey and started for the house with Esther and Peewee walking behind him. Sheriff Richards told the two other deputies to take the pickup truck and go back to Bison and that he and Deputy Cox would use the Sheriff's car to transport the boy.

He said to the two men, "I will hold you both personally responsible for any consequences if word gets out in Bison County about this situation. The girl was unharmed and we did not find the boy with any weapons that would tie him to the Fletcher murder. I don't want a mob scene at the jail because, if that happens, the four of us could not handle it. You know that hate group would use this as an opportunity to stir up a lynching mob. I'm asking for time to investigate this situation and you men will be the first to know the outcome. Now go." The two deputies drove away with the dogs barking in the back of the truck.

Esther and Peewee had a good look at Petey as he was laid out by the Sheriff upon a blanket Esther had placed near the wood stove in the kitchen.

"I need to boil some water and clean him up," she said, not looking at anyone.

"Peewee, you go get some clean clothes for your brother and bring me a towel." Peewee bounded up the stairs to look in the bureau in their bedroom for clothing for Petey. He was badly shaken by his brother's condition. Petey's mouth and chin were caked with dried spittle. His torso was covered with insect bites, whelps and debris from the forest floor. The worst thing for Peewee was that his brother smelled like urine. Just like he used to smell when he wet the bed. Peewee cried a little while he picked out clothing for his brother.

Then he remembered he had Petey's pocket knife in his pants pocket. Peewee was thinking, *What if the Sheriff wanted to search me?* He took the pocket knife out and put it under Petey's mattress, thinking that Petey would find it there later when he felt better. Maybe then Petey wouldn't hurt him for stealing it. He took the clean clothes for his brother down to the kitchen along with the towel his mother had asked for.

Esther had planned to make Petey a birthday cake today. Peewee thought about his own birthday in a few weeks. The Beaumonts had promised him a birthday party when he turned eight. He was frightened that this might not happen since Petey was in trouble. He prayed that the police would not take Petey away because his mother might use that as an excuse to start drinking again.

I'm too young to be the man of the house, but I gotta help mama take care of Petey 'til Sax comes home.

Esther poured hot water into a bowl from a pot on the stove. She dipped one end of the towel into the scalding water and began to clean her son. She hummed while she held Petey in her arms and washed the dirt from his limp body. Petey remained quiet, a vacant stare in his eyes. The Sheriff and Peewee looked on in silence.

When she was done, she dressed Petey, sat him in a chair and tried to force hot coffee into him to warm his insides. He stirred and started to sip, sucking noisily on the cup, drooling some of the liquid onto his clothing. His eyes opened and he looked at Esther for a long time.

"Mama?"

"I'm right here baby. You've been dark for a long time, this time. You back now. You want something to eat?"

Peewee reached over and touched his brother's hand. Petey smiled at him.

Sheriff Richards handed the butcher knife he had found over to Esther. "No need for anyone to know about this." She had a confused look on her face as she accepted the knife. He went on to explain that it was lying beside Petey when they found him in the woods.

"I know word got out that the Fletcher girl had been stabbed but this was not the knife that was involved. According to the coroner, the killer used a knife with at least a four inch blade that could have been a pocket knife. Mr. West had given a knife like that to Jesse's father. Mr. Hammond might have passed the pocket knife on to his son who was a friend of Petey's. Jesse is dead and we never found the pocket knife. However, I need to take Petey with me for his own safety. He did kidnap the little Worthy girl and he did have a weapon."

I don't know if what happened today is going to come out in the county but I know somebody will talk, most likely one of my deputies. You know how worked up people can get around here, especially white folks. I'll take him back to Bison and let him stay with my family, which is the least likely place folks will look for him. Mrs. Creek, you and your other boy can come with me if you want and I can have someone bring you both back home tomorrow."

"Oh, Sheriff, I'd like that. That is real kind of you, sir. Please give me a few minutes to get dressed and to get some more clothes for Petey. I won't take long, I promise. Peewee, I want you to go over to the Reverend's place and stay there 'til I come back home. Tell them that me and Petey had to go to Bison to see 'bout Sax. Say we heard from him and that's where he is at the clinic 'cause he hurt his leg. Yeah, I want you to lie 'cause I don't want them folks to know noth-

Watermelon Road

in' 'bout Petey and what he done this morning. You say what I tell you to say and keep your mouth shut 'bout everything you know."

Peewee nodded "yes." He wouldn't tell anyone the truth. The truth was too bad to tell.

"You tell them that I might be a few days and I would be grateful if you could stay with them."

"All right, mama. Don't you worry none 'cause you know I stay with them a lot and they don't mind one more time."

Peewee would be glad to get out of the house. He had listened to what the Sheriff had told his mother about the pocket knife and he was scared for Petey and for himself. He would have to hide the pocket knife in a better place now that he knew it might be the knife that killed Suzy Fletcher. *Maybe Petey was hiding it for Jesse when he found the knife in the shed*, he rationalized. He looked over at Petey who had a glazed look in his eyes, as if he were slipping away again. Just then, Peewee had a horrible picture in his head of Petey hanging from a tree branch.

"Petey, Petey, don't go dark again," he whispered with the Sheriff looking on. "I'm gonna help mama take care of you 'til you gets better. I ain't know your head was sick. I just thought you was crazy."

Esther went upstairs to get dressed, thanking God that the Sheriff was a kind man. She put on an old dress, put a pack of cigarettes and a book of matches in her pocket and slipped into her shoes. She went into the boys' room to get more clothes for Petey just in case he would need them later. She snatched the blanket and pillow off Petey's bed so he could rest easy in the police car on the ride to Bison. When she pulled at the blanket, it got caught on something under the mattress so she yanked it harder and something clattered to the hard wood floor. Half way to the floor to pick up the object, her hand shook. Her whole body was numb with fear. Esther slid to the floor and caressed the pocket knife in both her hands.

She said out loud, "I knew it." "I knew things were gonna get worst. They always do. Somehow I knew deep down that there was something real bad going on with Petey. Oh God, why couldn't Sax be here to tell me what to do? Why do I have to go through these bad times all by myself?"

"You all right Mrs. Creek?" Sheriff Richards was standing in the doorway to the bedroom. She didn't hear him come up the stairs.

"It sounded like you had fallen over so I come up here to….." His eyes went to the pocket knife she held in her hand. He reached for the knife and Esther handed it to him.

"I swear to God I didn't know nothin' 'bout no knife like this being in my house. You gotta to believe me," she pleaded. "I just found it under Petey's mattress when I was getting the blanket off his bed. That boy Jesse could have given this to Petey to hide for him after he killed that Suzy girl. Besides, you ain't got no proof that this is the knife that done it."

"You are right. All I got is coincidences and suspicions. All I know is that the wounds might have fit this blade. Suzy is dead and buried now and I'm never going to have any real proof. But, your boy was caught with a white girl around Suzy's age and he had a knife. I know you want to know the truth as much as I do."

Esther covered her face with her hands. When she took her hands away her eyes were dry. "You do what you need to do, Sheriff. I know my Petey ain't no killer. He's been confused ever since he seen Joel murdered. That's all that's wrong with him."

"I need to talk to the boy now," said the Sheriff. He went back downstairs.

Peewee froze when Sheriff Richards entered the kitchen, carrying the pocket knife in his hand. Esther entered the kitchen a few minutes later with two pillow cases heavy with clothing. "Peewee, you go on over to the Reverend's house right this minute."

"Wait," she said. "Come give your mother and brother a bug hug." Peewee put his arms around his mother. She held on tight for a long time. Ester whispered in his ear, "You mind Miss Lydia and the Reverend. Always remember I love you." She kissed him on his cheek. "Now, give your brother a big hug and a kiss." Peewee hugged his brother and kissed his cheek.

Peewee left the kitchen. He went to the front door and opened and shut it and then hid behind a chair in the parlor. Deputy Cox was outside sitting on the front porch steps, smoking a cigarette.

The Sheriff placed the pocket knife on the table in front of Petey. Petey looked at it and smiled. Picking it up, he touched the snakeskin handle and pulled out the blade. He made a hissing sound and glanced at the two adults in the room. "That's the snake noise," he said. "He lived in my stomach and then my head but he gone now. I don't hear him no more."

"Did the snake tell you to hurt little Suzy?" Sheriff Richards asked Petey.

"It weren't me. The snake did it. He turned me into a snake so no one could see me. He took her behind the rock and put her to sleep. She was so ugly. Ugly girls like her cause somebody else to die that's why snake killed her. Sometimes girls are ugly on the inside and you can't know that if they look good on the outside."

The Sheriff took out the charm bracelet and laid it on the kitchen table in front of Petey. Petey looked puzzled.

"Where this come from? He asked. "I give this to Bonnie. Did she tell you she don't want it? I tried to give one to Mimi too but she don't want it either. I thought girls liked presents."

"Mimi?" The Sheriff asked.

"Reverend Beaumont's 13 year-old daughter," Esther answered.

Esther walked over to the cabinet drawer and took out a set of keys and placed them in her dress pocket. "I'm going out for a smoke," she said. The Sheriff ignored her and continued questioning Petey.

Her heart could take it no longer. Amos and Joel were dead. Sax was gone. The future looked uncertain. Petey and Peewee belonged to her and they were all she had. And now, Petey would be taken away. That is if he lived long enough. She knew that there was a possibility that Petey might be the youngest child to hang for a crime in the state of Alabama. He would be hung either by the state or by an angry mob of crazy whites bent on their so-called justice and the need to teach other Negroes a lesson.

She went out the backdoor and over to the shed. Deputy Cox could not see her from the front porch and Sheriff Richards was busy with Petey. Esther lit up a cigarette when she came out of the shed. Back in the kitchen, Petey was telling the Sheriff why he had kidnapped Bonnie Worthy.

"She made my legs feel funny. I dreamed 'bout her and then I peed in the bed. Her name should have been Angel 'cause she was so pretty and looked like an angel. She smelled like baby powder. I loved the way she smelled. Snake tried to make me hurt her but I was stronger than him. I beat him this time. I killed snake. I had to tell her the story. I had to tell her about the night I seed Joel die. She had to know my secret." The Sheriff did not speak when Petey stopped talking.

Petey smiled as he looked over at his mother. Esther smiled back. She went over and hugged him and kissed his forehead.

"You ain't kissed me in a long time," her son said.

"I know baby but you needed a hug and a kiss just now. After all today's your birthday."

Petey's face brightened. "I forgot. I been so tired. I forgot all 'bout my birthday. Ain't that somethin'?"

Sheriff Richards said, "We need to get going. You gather your things and bring Petey out to the car." He wanted to get out of Horace Graves as soon as possible.

Esther locked the front door and led her son down the porch steps. "We're ready to go," she said. She handed the two pillow cases stuffed with personal items for Petey and herself to the Sheriff.

Peewee came from his hiding place and watched from the parlor window.

The Sheriff had Esther and Petey lie on the floor in the back of the police car. He covered them both with the blanket Esther had brought from the house.

Sheriff Richards gave instructions to his Deputy.

"We'll do as I said before. You drive us to the county jail. I'll drive them on to my house and they will stay there until I can get this whole thing straightened out with the authorities in Montgomery. In fact, I might have to ask them to send some of their people up here for backup, just in case things get out of control. This boy needs to talk to someone else before I hand him over to the state."

"You mean like a head doctor?" Deputy Cox asked the Sheriff.

"Yes, somebody like that. There must be somebody I can get to talk to a 12-year old child and determine if he is mentally stable or not," was Sherriff Richards reply.

Yeah, like anyone is going to believe a Negro boy is mentally ill after killing a white girl, Deputy Cox mused as he looked out the car window.

Halfway to the town of Bison, Sheriff Richards and Deputy Cox heard Esther crying from under the blanket. The dam had finally broken and she was already grieving for her son. While Deputy Cox drove onward, the Sheriff reached back under the blanket and handed Esther his handkerchief. Esther thanked him.

Watermelon Road
Chapter 39
A Mother's Love

After they arrived at the county jail in Bison, Sheriff Richards made a phone call to his wife, Katie. "Honey, I'm bringing some people over to the house that need a place to hide out for awhile. I want you to take the girls to your mother's tonight to babysit them for a few days. Then I want you to come straight back home after you drop them off. I'll explain everything when I see you. Please, just trust me. You know my job can be very trying and I need you by my side tonight. There's nothing to be afraid of. I just want the girls out of the house tonight. I'll see you soon."

Katie Richards put the phone back on the hook in the living room. She called to her two daughters, Jane and Myra, together and told them they were going to surprise their grandmother by showing up for a sleep over. The girls, five and eight, were delighted and helped their mother with the packing.

The Sheriff dropped Deputy Cox off at the county jail and reiterated his warning to the Deputy to keep his mouth shut. "I'll hold you responsible if word gets out," the Sheriff sternly repeated his promise.

When he reached his house, Katie and the girls were gone.

He drove to the back of the house and brought Esther and Petey through the backdoor into the kitchen. It was a good-sized house with a modern kitchen for the times with running water and a gas stove. An open porch stretched along the length of the front of the house. The Sheriff had been meaning to screen in the front porch but there was little time for that project. The back porch, although smaller, was enclosed with screens on all sides. The brick house had three bedrooms, indoor plumbing and two fireplaces.

He escorted his two houseguests up to the second level and into the back bedroom that was used as an office and a guest bedroom. His two daughters shared a bedroom.

The room did not have a closet. There was a small desk and chair against one wall of the room. "You two can bunk here on the cot. I'll get you some sheets and a coverlet."

Esther nodded in response and pushed the twin sized cot closer to the wall so she and Petey could both fit on it.

Watermelon Road

Petey had been silent the whole trip. She could feel his eyes on her under the blanket in the back seat of the police car.

The Sheriff handed her the sheets and coverlet and she made up the cot while Petey watched. Esther wondered if he had slipped further into his own world. While her back was turned, she felt his hands touch her braided hair.

"I love you, mama. Please don't leave me here with that man." Petey put his arms around her and clung to her.

"I'm never going to leave you, baby."

Esther set her son down on the mattress and said "You know what? Since it's your birthday today, I'm going downstairs to the kitchen and make you some hot cocoa. That is, if Sheriff Richards has any. Maybe I can find a sweet downstairs too and we can have us a little birthday party." Petey smiled and lay down on the bed. "You stay here and I'll be right back."

Sheriff Richards was in the kitchen pouring a large can of soup into a saucepan on the stove. "It's almost five o'clock in the evening and I bet you and your boy are famished."

"Don't trouble yourself, none. I come to see if you got any cocoa so's I can make Petey some hot chocolate for his birthday."

"His birthday? Oh, that's right. I did hear you say it was Petey's birthday today while I was in your kitchen. I'm surprised you feel like celebrating, Mrs. Creek."

"I ain't celebrating, I'm being a mother," was Esther's response.

He showed her where the cocoa was in the kitchen cabinet, and put a pan on the stove to boil milk. Esther searched another cabinet and found cups. She found spoons in a kitchen drawer. The Sheriff handed her the can of cocoa.

"I don't know how to thank you Sheriff Richards for your kindness to me and my boy. I don't ever remember a white person being this good to me. I know you keeping us safe from the crazy people that will come to this house tomorrow and drag my boy out into the street and hang him on the nearest tree they can find. I know this for sure because one of your deputies will talk tonight. You won't be able to stop those folks tomorrow no matter how many deputies you got."

"Anybody who took the time can see that Petey is sick. He ain't been right since his brother died. He's been getting sicker and sicker a little at a time until it all came down on him today." Esther lightly touched the Sheriff's shoulder than pulled her hand away."

"No need to thank me. I take my job seriously and I believe in protecting everybody under my jurisdiction, Negro and white. My father taught me well. He always said, "Allan, you got to love all people because God loves them." He wasn't a church-going man but he was God-fearing and fair and I'm proud to be like him. He passed away three months ago but I still remember everything he told me and I try to follow his example. Now, you fix your hot chocolate and take some of the gingersnaps from that jar over there and go on upstairs to your boy. I'll be up with the soup and jelly bread in a few minutes."

"Yes sir."

Madeline L. Nowlin

Esther went up with the drinks and helped Petey into his pajamas. The hot chocolate was too hot, so she let it cool off a little. The Sheriff came up with two soup bowls, and slices of bread slathered in grape jelly and placed them on the desk in the corner of the room. He stood there for a moment looking at Petey, then he walked out and closed the door.

Esther blew on a bowl of the chicken soup and spooned some into Petey's mouth. He opened his mouth obediently and swallowed. She did this a couple more times, but then he placed his hand over his mouth and said "I'm tired mama. I want to sleep."

"Wait a minute. Don't you want some hot chocolate and a cookie? It's your birthday and you gotta have something nice to eat on your birthday." Esther took a cup of the hot cocoa and drank almost all of it. She left a little hot chocolate in the bottom. When Petey wasn't looking, she took a jar of corn liquor from one of the pillow cases she brought with her and poured it into the cup until the cup was filled up.

"Here Petey, drink some of this and then take a bite of the cookie." Petey drank from the cup and winced.

"This taste funny, mama. It don't taste like no hot cocoa."

"Here, drink it all down and bite the cookie. It's a gingersnap, one of your favorites." Esther prodded her son until he drank from the cup again. She placed the cup in his hands and he screwed up his face but finished it, gagging and coughing until he was done. He took the cookie she handed him and ate it quickly. She sang happy birthday to him and that made him laugh. Petey yawned and lay down again.

Esther waited until he was asleep. She removed Petey's pajamas. She reached into one of the pillow cases and pulled out an old striped shirt of Joel's and a pair of his suspenders. Joel's shirt was way too big for Petey, but Esther put it on him anyway, along with the suspenders. She put the long pants Petey had been wearing back on him, along with his socks and the sneakers Sax had bought him back in June. He loved those sneakers and wore them everywhere. There was a sound of change jingling coming from Petey's pants' pocket.

Esther put her hand in one of the pockets and pulled out a charm bracelet (the one he had brought for Mimi), a $10 bill and 90 cents in change. She put all of it in one of the pillowcases she had brought with her.

Petey never woke up the whole time Esther was dressing him. Esther watched him as he slept. She watched his thin chest rising and falling with each breath he took. She kissed his forehead. He smiled in his sleep.

Esther took out her best dress from one of the pillow cases. It was the black lace dress, the low cut one with a fake red rose pinned in the center. Next she took out a pair of sheer black nylons and a pair of shinny black earrings from her purse. She laid the dress and the nylons carefully over the back of the chair at the desk. Wearing only her slip, she went down the hall to the bathroom and washed the dirt and sweat from her body.

When she returned to the guest room, Petey was sitting up on the cot. Esther's breath caught in her throat but she smiled at her son and asked him if he

Watermelon Road

was feeling sick.

"Mama, I got to tell you the story. I done told everybody but you the story 'bout Joel."

She made him lie down again. "I know the story, but I tell you what, when you wake up tomorrow morning, you can tell me the whole story while we're having breakfast. Okay, baby?"

"All right, mama."

He went back to sleep. The corn liquor had finally done its work. She waited another ten minutes. She put on her good dress and the black nylons. Then she got down on her knees and prayed.

"Dear Lord, I ain't been no follower of yours but I'm sending my son to you tonight and I'm coming with him. I can't let him face tomorrow by himself. They gonna kill my boy. I just know it. You got Amos and Joel up there so you got to let me and Petey in the gate too. If you don't let us in, you ain't the God I been hearing 'bout all these years."

She got up and took the pillow off the cot and placed it over Petey's face. She removed the pillow ten minutes later and checked his breathing. He no longer breathed nor did he have a pulse. Dry eyed, Esther took out the jar with the remainder of the corn liquor and dumped in six small packets of the rat poison she had taken from the shed before they left the house. She drank all that was left in the jar.

She put out the light on the desk and lay down, pulling the coverlet over the two of them, holding her son close to her. A memory came back to her of a psalm she learned as a little girl sitting in the Sunday school class at the missionary church. She began to recite: "The Lord is my shepherd, I shall not want . ..."

Katie came home around eight o'clock that evening. She parked their car out front and came in the front door. "I'm home," she yelled.

"I'm in the kitchen."

"I wanted to stay and get the girls settled and then I had dinner with them. I helped my mother get them ready for bed. When I left, she was reading them a bedtime story," his wife reported as she sat across from him at the kitchen table.

The Sheriff studied his wife's face, the freckles across her nose. Katie kept him grounded. He liked the way she wore her light brown hair in a short style, framing her beautiful face. She was a good wife and mother. Katie was always cheerful and full of hope. She made an inviting home for him. He respected her opinion but never talked about his work, unless he felt it necessary, like tonight. She would be involved in whatever happened next.

He knew that he was lucky she had picked him. What he loved most about Katie was that she was fearless and she would have to be, come tomorrow morning.

Her parents had objected to the marriage because he was 10 years her senior. She wouldn't listen to them and married him anyway. They had proved everybody wrong who thought the marriage wouldn't last. At 35, Katie still looked like a school girl to him. She sat across from him at the kitchen table, waiting patiently for what he had to tell her.

She smiled at him and reached out for both his hands. "Tell me," she said.

When he was done, they both climbed the stairs to check on Esther and Petey. Sheriff Richards opened the bedroom door just a crack and noticed the room was dark.

"They are asleep," he said.

Watermelon Road
Chapter 40
A Time to Mourn

At 11:00 that Sunday morning, Sheriff Richards and Katie, stood on their front porch and watched anxiously as the angry crowd of white people stood in front of their house. One of the deputies had talked. The Sheriff had his rifle by his side and told the crowd that the first person who stepped into his front yard would be shot down. He made it clear that he would do anything to protect his family. Deputy Cox stood beside him, keeping quiet about the part he played in the angry gathering in front of the Sheriff's home.

Two hearses from the Birchwood Funeral Home were parked in front of the house, courtesy of John Birchwood as a favor to Reverend Beaumont. Four men from the funeral home were preparing to bring out the deceased bodies of mother and son. Sheriff Richards had found the bodies around 8:00 that morning. He and Katie were devastated by what had taken place in their home. He felt helpless because he wished Esther had said something to him about what she was planning to do. It was appalling to him that Esther felt her way was the best way out of the dilemma. But, deep down, he understood her decision.

After finding Esther and Petey dead that morning, he called Olivia's Diner, thanking God that Olivia had answered the telephone. He told her what had happened. It was a long time before Olivia could speak. He waited patiently. She pulled herself together and thanked him for calling her. The Sheriff didn't know the parish house had a telephone. Olivia ran over to the parish house and recounted to Reverend Beaumont what the Sheriff had told her about Esther and Petey. She couldn't trust herself to phone him. The Reverend took immediate action and called John Birchwood and asked him to please send someone to pick up the bodies before they were torn apart or dragged through the streets of Bison. Mr. Birchwood got his drivers together and they were able to get to the Sheriff's house by 10:45.

The crowd, pumped up by Bobby West, would not leave until they had proof that the boy who had killed Suzy Fletcher was dead. There was complete silence when the bodies were brought out of the house and placed in the hearses. The Sheriff and Deputy Cox got in the Sheriff's car and provided an escort for the deceased all the way to Horace Graves.

Madeline L. Nowlin

Tim West stood away from the mob of angry people in front of the Sheriff's house. He had a satisfied smirk on his face. Deputy Cox had told Bobby where Esther and Petey were staying and about the pocket knife the Sheriff found at the Creek house. Bobby told his father what Deputy Cox had said.

Bobby got busy spreading the news around Horace Graves. The story of Bonnie Worthy had already become legend. Bobby got the members of the secret society together and they ignited the townsfolk's rage so much that they jumped in their cars and trucks and showed up at the Sheriff's place.

Tim West wanted the boy's body dragged from that so-called safe haven and strung up and beaten until the skin rolled off his nigger bones. Although he did not get what he wished for, he was glad to hear that the boy's mother had the good sense to do what needed to be done. His body shook with anger when he yelled into the crowd, "That damn knife."

Watermelon Road
Chapter 41
The Long Road Home

Sax reached Birmingham Saturday morning on September 14. He hitched a ride from the bus station to the Jackson sisters' farm. He wanted to let Patty know that it was over between them.

"I'm going home to keep my family together," he told Patty as they sat in her kitchen and drank coffee. "I know Esther needs a lot of help but I'm up to it and I'm going to do whatever it takes to make a decent home for them boys."

"Stay for awhile," she said. "Just let me have some of this day before it's over." He kissed both her hands then got up and poured himself another cup of coffee. He stayed the night.

When he came home on Sunday, he found Mrs. Bertie and Bumpy waiting for him.

As soon as they heard about Esther and Petey, Mrs. Bertie and Bumpy rushed over to the Creek house to see if Sax had returned. When they did not find him there, they decided to wait until he showed up. Sax had told Bumpy that he would be a few days behind him after he left Atlanta.

Sax was surprised to see his two friends when he opened the door and walked back to the kitchen. He stood looking at them with a puzzled look on his face. Bumpy said, "The backdoor wasn't locked."

Mrs. Bertie said, "Welcome home, Sax. Sit down. You look tired. I got something to tell you. Bumpy, you pour Sax a drink."

When they told him what had happened, he ran out the backdoor, screaming and ripping his clothes. He circled the house repeatedly until he fell in the front yard from exhaustion. His tear-stained face lay in the dirt. He was half naked, his clothing shredded. Mrs. Bertie held her husband back from stopping Sax. "Let him get it all out," she said.

Later that day, Sax went to see Peewee at the Beaumont's. Mimi opened the door for him. Her face was wet with fresh tears. Peewee sat in one of the kitchen chairs, his feet not touching the floor. Sax picked him up and hugged him. They both cried a little. Lydia and Reverend Beaumont waited for Sax in the parlor.

Sax left Peewee in the kitchen with Mimi and went to face the Beaumonts. He was dreading the encounter because he felt they blamed him for not being there when Esther and Petey needed him. No one could blame him more than he blamed himself. Lydia hugged him and the Reverend shook his hand. Reverend Beaumont began with the funeral arrangements. After the arrangements were taken care of, Sax thanked the two of them for all they were doing and had done for Esther and Petey. He also praised them for the way they had taken Peewee into their family as if he were their own.

There was silence in the room after that, Lydia broke it by stating that she and the Reverend had something to discuss with Sax when the funeral was over. Sax knew it had something to do with Peewee and he was not ready to talk about that. He was glad they were waiting until after the funeral was over to broach the subject. He had enough to deal with at the moment.

Sax looked up to see Peewee standing in the doorway to the parlor. "I got something to show you."

Sax told him that whatever it was, it would have to wait until after the funeral. He thought it best that Peewee stayed with the Beaumonts until after the funeral. He went home alone.

The funeral was held two days later. People came from miles away just to get a glimpse of the two caskets being laid to rest. There was nothing to see. The service was a memorial to the beloved memory of Esther and Petey. Esther and Petey had already been cremated so that their gravesites could not be desecrated later. Their ashes had been given to Sax to keep until Peewee decided what should be done with them.

Mr. Birchwood had arranged for a doctor to issue death certificates on the day of their deaths to avoid confusion in case there was any trouble with the county officials.

"The Pointer" reported that Suzy Fletcher's murderer had been found and that his mother had the good sense to kill her son so that he would not have to stand trial. They didn't report Petey's age or the fact that he had seen his own brother murdered, which had caused the child to have a mental breakdown. The truth was not important, just the facts.

A few whites showed up at the memorial service out of respect for the family and for Miss Olivia and other Negroes they knew personally. Mrs. Worthy was one of them, along with the Sheriff and Deputy Cox. The Jackson sisters, Junior Rocket, Earl, Freaky Joe and Lewis were in attendance.

Sax and Peewee sat on the first row on the left side of the church. Lydia sat with them to greet people as they filed past them. Peewee had drawn a picture of Esther and Petey together. He did it for the funeral since there was not a photograph of the mother and son together. Esther was sitting in her favorite rocking chair on the front porch of their house and Petey was kneeling beside the chair. He was looking up at his mother and she was looking down at him. He colored the picture beautifully and it was placed on a table in the church lobby for all to see when they signed the guestbook.

Peewee remained dry-eyed throughout the service. No one knew what he was thinking. Only he knew that he could not let himself think. He had to keep his mind clear. He would be eight years old in three weeks. He had to grow up

Watermelon Road

fast. He needed all his energy and concentration to keep memories of his mother and brother from rushing into his head. That took everything he had.

Lydia called her mother in Baltimore the day they found the bodies. She wanted her mother to let the Hammonds know of the deaths. Grandmother Mimi was the only person who knew how to get in touch with the Hammonds.

The service had a solemn beginning but people were soon lifted up by the righteous words of the Reverend when he reminded them that God knows best. "Maybe it was part of God's plan that they should go the way they did," he told the congregation. "Don't blame Esther for what she did. She'd lost so much already and it would have killed her to see what that mob would have done to her boy." Sax sobbed through the whole service. He had to be taken outside before it was over. Everyone felt for him.

Lydia felt that, because of the circumstances of their passing, a repast would be inappropriate. She had food at the parish house for anyone who wanted to come by for a meal and to talk about their experiences with Esther and Petey. A few mourners came by the house, but most who had attended the service went home.

Sax paid all the funeral expenses for Esther and Petey with the money he had taken from the Lucas brothers' hideout in Atlanta. He felt he owed Esther that and more since he had not taken care of her or her boys as he should have over the past few months.

It had been a long day for Sax and Peewee. Neither of them wanted to return to the Creek house, but Sax felt the sooner they went home the faster they would get used to being there without their loved ones. Although, he knew that nothing could make them get used to Esther and Petey being gone.

Peewee made an announcement before he went to bed that night.

"I don't want to be called Peewee no more," he said. "From now on you can all me Simon.

"I understand," Sax said. "Peewee was a little boy, but you ain't that boy no more."

Sax had removed Joel's bed, but left the bed that Simon and Petey had slept in. He told Simon that he would get him a new bed as soon as he could. Simon was afraid to sleep in the bedroom alone now that his two brothers were gone. He sat up in bed most of the night drawing from memory the faces of Esther, Joel and Petey. He drew a picture of Jesse to keep his face in his mind. He also drew a picture of Sax and then he taped all the pictures over his bed. He had taken down all his earlier drawings months ago.

The next morning, Sax and Simon went over to the Beaumont's to pick up the rest of Simon's things. While they were there, they joined the family for breakfast. After breakfast, the three boys went out to play. Sax, Reverend Beaumont and Lydia took their coffee out to the back porch and watched the children play. Mimi stayed in the house and cleaned up the kitchen.

Lydia waited for an opening in the conversation to ask Sax an important question. When there was a lull, she jumped in: "What do you think about us raising Simon? We know that you will be busy with your music and traveling a lot and Simon would be staying here anyway, so we want to finish raising him for Esther. He gets along with the twins as if they were triplets and Mimi loves him as if he were her brother."

Sax said, "Let me think on this awhile. I have to talk about this with Simon. I'm pretty sure he wants to stay with you folks but I have to ask him what he wants. I don't want him to think I gave him to the two of you because I didn't want him. I do want him. I love him like a son, but, like you said, Lydia, I'll be gone a lot. I'll let you know as soon as I can."

"It wouldn't be as if you had abandoned him. You will always be welcomed here and I'm sure your travels will bring you through Horace Graves many times over the coming years. We're not going to adopt him and change his last name to ours, we will just raise him for you, Esther and Amos. He will always be Simon Joseph Creek." Reverend Beaumont wanted to assure Sax that Simon would be all right with his family.

When Sax and Simon arrived home that afternoon, Simon mentioned again that he had something to show Sax. Sax followed him to the shed out back of the house. Once inside, Simon showed him Petey's hiding place and the stack of $20 bills under the wooden plank in the shed.

Sax was stunned. He reached in and took out the bills. He sat down on the floor and started counting. He held $4,980.00 in his hands.

"Where did you get this money?" He asked Simon.

"It ain't mine. I found it under the floor one day with that pocket knife they took Petey away for. I took the pocket knife and played with it a few days. Petey knew I had it and told me to put it back but I didn't. I was going to show it to Danny and Jimmy. When the Sheriff come to the house, I hid it under Petey's mattress and that's when mama found it afore she left with the Sheriff."

Sax said, "I don't know how Petey come by this much money, but since no one has come looking for it, I guess it's safe for us to keep it."

He took the money and put it in his pockets. Then his eyes fell on the cans of rat poison in a corner of the shed. Simon saw where he was looking.

"Let's go back to the house, Uncle Sax."

When they got back to the house, Sax asked Simon if he wanted to live with the Beaumonts until he was grown. He let Simon know that he wanted to raise him but admitted that he would not be living the kind of life that would be good for a child. He told Simon that he loved him as if he were his own child and that his love for him would never go away.

"You know the Beaumonts are good people and they love you too. I will surely come visit you when I'm in or near Horace Graves. You can come visit me when you're older. You and I are going to be best friends. I want you to write me and I'll write you back. I'll let you know wherever I'm staying so you'll have my address. If you get into any trouble or if you need me for something, you know you can always count on me."

Simon was quiet for a long time. He had wanted everything to go on as it was before but that was impossible. Petey and Esther were gone. This house didn't belong to any of them anymore. He loved the Beaumonts, and the twins

Watermelon Road

were like having his two brothers back again.

"I think you right, Uncle Sax. And, like you say, we can write each other and visit each other whenever we want to. I think I want to live with Reverend Beaumont and Miss Lydia until I'm a man. Then you and me can live together if you wants to."

"I know I'll want to," said Sax.

The next morning Simon moved in with the Beaumont family for good.

Sax spoke to the Reverend in private. He told him about the money he found in the shed. Then he handed all the money over to the Reverend for him to use to raise Simon.

Watermelon Road
Chapter 49
Jesse

I know these things happened. I know because in 1949, a year after I graduated from Morehouse College, majoring in English literature, my parents turned over to me all the correspondence, including photographs and newspaper clippings they had from those times. Mrs. Bertie wrote to my mother regularly about the happenings in Horace Graves. My mother also received letters from Lydia Beaumont, Miss Olivia and the Jackson sisters.

Grandmother Mimi had rented an apartment for my parents when they arrived in Baltimore in early July. Mimi and her brothers were still with Grandmother for the summer so my parents couldn't live with Grandmother Mimi. She never brought my parents to her house while Mimi and the twins were still in Baltimore.

I had been in the basement of the whorehouse for a month when my parents came to live in Baltimore. They stayed in the rented apartment for a full month before they came to get me in August.

Grandmother Mimi took them to visit my gravesite a week after they arrived in Baltimore. While they were standing there weeping, she told them that I was still alive.

Of course, my parents were overjoyed. My mother fell to her knees in the dirt, praising God and thanking Grandmother Mimi. My father knelt beside her, holding her and crying tears of joy. But, when my father came back down to earth, he wanted to hit Grandmother Mimi for putting them through the worst time of their lives. He stood in front of her, shaking his fist in her face and asking her repeatedly why she had done such a thing.

"What kind of woman are you?" He asked her several times.

Grandmother Mimi calmly told them that if they had known from the beginning that I was alive, their grief would not have been genuine. That would have made some people suspicious. She talked to them, and kept on talking, until they fully understood her reasons for letting them think I was dead.

"You both know what the consequences would have been," she reminded them. "Did you want Jesse sent back home to be lynched for a murder he did not commit?" My parents finally agreed that Grandmother Mimi had done the right

Watermelon Road

thing to save me.

They asked her how soon they could see me, but Grandmother Mimi told them they had to wait a little while longer so that she could make arrangements for us to live some place new with a new identify.

My father asked, "You said you had to identify the body. How did you pull it off? How did you make Jesse look like he was dead?"

"Don't worry about that. I just gave him something to put him to sleep. Police don't care one way or the other about a drowned Negro child. They took my word for it when I identified him at the morgue. They didn't even check to see if he was dead. I paid good money so that everything would run smoothly."

"How can we ever repay you?" My mother knew Grandmother Mimi must have laid out a lot of money to save me. "You kept your promise to me, you kept my boy safe. I could never come up with enough money for what you did to save Jesse's life. I don't know how I'm going to go another minute without seeing Jesse. It's going to be so hard to wait.

Oh, I know what I'm going to do to keep myself busy, I'm going to sew you some new clothes before we leave here. That's what I'm going do." This was a way for my mother to show her appreciation for what Grandmother Mimi had done for all of us.

They both took turns hugging and kissing Grandmother Mimi. She tried to push them away, "Now, now, none of that mushy stuff," she kept saying that while she folded them into her arms.

My mother told me about Esther and Petey a month after we were settled in our new town. She said they had been buried beside Amos and Joel in the church graveyard. I think she lied to me about the graves because she didn't know how I would feel about them being cremated. I didn't find out until years later that they had been cremated and had no graves.

They left me alone for a long time after they told me. I cried myself to sleep many nights thereafter. I ached for the boys we once were, for that freedom we felt and our zest for life. I started taking long walks and carrying my writing pad with me. I wrote down everything I could remember about our time together; our life in Horace Graves and the loss of our innocence.

I made new friends and grew into a respectful young man who made my parents proud. I had avoided the draft for World War II because I had asthma and flat feet. I felt guilty not to be able to fight for my country but I was also relieved that I could go on to complete my college education. I graduated with honors and my parents cried through the whole graduation ceremony at Moorehouse.

In 1947, during my last year of college, I attended a spring dance put on by Spelman College. I ran into Mimi at the punch table. She took one look at me and dropped her crystal cup. Red punch went everywhere. Her flowery summer dress was covered in it. I caught her when she fainted.

She kept staring at me while we sat on a bench in a garden on the campus of her school. "I thought you were dead," she kept repeating. "I thought I had lost you both; first you and then Petey, all in the same summer."

I sat staring at her with my eyes bulging, as if I was ten again. She was beautiful. Mimi no longer wore her hair in a ponytail. The bangs were gone too. The back of her hair was swept up and pinned in a French roll with soft curls surrounding her face. I was 22 and she was 24. She was still in school because she kept changing her major but had finally settled on child development. I always knew that somehow she would end up a teacher like her mother.

"You've changed a lot but I knew it was you," she said, smiling at last. I was a lot taller and thinner than she remembered me at age ten. "I grew up," I said. "Jesse had to die back then. My name is Edward Morgan and you have always been the love of my life." Then I kissed her. From then on we were inseparable.

Over the next few months, I told her my story, often reading from one of my notebooks. She was awed by my experiences with Strawberry. That part of my life seemed to interest her more than my rebirth. Mimi had found out about the whorehouse and her Grandmother's illegal activities when Danny and Jimmy told her one summer. The boys had found out in their early teens.

Mimi was also amazed at the kindness of her Grandmother in saving my life. A month after I found the notebooks in the basement my parents came for me. I had been in that house of ill repute for two months.

Grandmother Mimi had arranged for me to leave my hiding place and to be brought back to her house on Bottom Street. One morning Strawberry rushed down the steps to the basement and told me to pack up my things so she could take me upstairs. I asked her what was happening, not thinking that I was going to see my parents. She told me to keep my mouth shut, get my shit together, and get my ass upstairs. I loved that girl.

I did as I was told and she took me out the back way and put me in a taxi. She kissed my check before the driver pulled away. "Goodbye little gangster," she said, grinning that beautiful girlish smile at me. I put my hand to my cheek where she had kissed me and kept it there, all the way to Grandmother Mimi's house. I asked the taxi driver once where were we going and he ignored me and kept on driving and didn't stop until he pulled up at 337 Bottom Street.

I could never describe to you what my parents felt when they saw me. I can only tell you what I felt and that was pure joy. My mother, thinking I was dead all that time, had lost weight and looked as if she had aged ten years. She hugged me so tight, I couldn't breathe for a full minute. It was the first time I had ever seen my father cry.

The day after I was brought to Grandmother Mimi's, my parents and I were taken to the train station to board a train heading north. Grandmother Mimi had arranged for us to live with her cousin in the small town of Port Mayfair, Massachusetts. A few Negro families lived there and they helped us with our transition.

Grandmother Mimi's cousin worked on the ships that came and went in the port. The cousin, Mason, got my father a job as a carpenter on one of the ships. News of his excellent work got around, and he worked as a carpenter on many of the ships heading for other parts of the world. He was gone for long periods of time but my mother and I bonded again, and were good company for each

Watermelon Road

other. She started sewing again and got a lot of business in the small community. Grandmother Mimi had given us new identities and we were now known as the Morgan family.

Phoebe and Robert Morgan were eventually able to rent a house of their own and lived with their son, Edward, near a harbor that opened onto the Atlantic Ocean. Edward's mother insisted he learn to swim.

Sometimes Mimi would speak of her life after my faked death and Petey's actual death. Many were surprised that Esther had taken her son's life and her own, but everyone felt she had no other options. No one wanted the same end for Petey as his brother, Joel. Everyone believed that would have been the worst end for Petey, especially if he had known that's how he would die.

Talking about the past brought Mimi pain but she wanted to talk so that the pain would lessen in time. Peewee, I meant Simon, was a great joy to their family. Mimi's parents treated him like their own son. Mimi, Danny and Jimmy doted on him. The children continued to spend their summers with their Grandmother and Simon was always included. He was always given the room that Petey and Jesse had stayed in that one summer in 1935. Mimi kept herself busy with her studies and followed her dream to attend college. The growing boys also kept her on her toes.

Danny and Jimmy were still living with their parents in Horace Graves. Simon and the twins had finished high school by the time Mimi and I met as adults. Reverend and Lydia Beaumont let the three boys spend their teen years living with Grandmother Mimi in Baltimore so that they could attend a better school, and have a good chance of getting into college if they chose to go. Lydia taught up to the 8th grade in Horace Graves. Mimi did not want to live in Baltimore with her brothers and Grandmother, so her mother home schooled her through her high school studies.

Mimi continued to visit her Grandmother during the summer months, but found it hard to relax in that house. Her mind would always go back to Petey and me and the summer we were there. She missed the three of us hanging out together. She even missed Baby Boy. They could never mention the dog's name in earshot of their Grandmother.

The twins, now grown, were both studying to become a veterinarian. This gave everyone pause. Simon always knew what he wanted to do when he grew up. He now had a degree in art and worked at a firm in Atlanta, specializing in commercial art.

Mimi told me why she thought Petey had killed Digs. I had not noticed the things Petey had picked up about Digs and his attention to Mimi. When she told me what Digs was doing to her, I knew it was wrong of Petey, but I was glad he had taken it upon himself to end it. I believed as she did, that no one would have believed her had she told what Digs was doing with his hands whenever he came near her. She was ashamed to tell her parents or even her Grandmother. She did tell Grandmother Mimi before she passed away a few years after Mimi and I were married. Grandmother Mimi felt the same way I did about what Petey had done to protect Mimi. Although, Grandmother Mimi could forgive Petey for killing Digs, she couldn't forgive him for killing Baby Boy, even though it might have been an accident.

Grandmother Mimi never got another dog after Baby Boy died. Lucky, the cat, was her only companion after that.

Mimi and I married two years after we met that night at the dance. We had the wedding in Port Mayfair. My mother made Mimi's dress, Lydia's dress, and the two bridesmaids' dresses. The bridesmaids had been Mimi's college friends. It was a small gathering in a Baptist church in the town. All the Beaumonts were there and Reverend Beaumont gave Mimi away. Grandmother Mimi's cousin, his family and the friends we had made in town came to the wedding. Grandmother Mimi was unable to attend but sent us a very nice wedding present.

Mimi found a teaching position in Baltimore so we moved there. I did freelance writing for several magazines while I worked on my novel. We rented a one-bedroom apartment in the northern part of the city. We visited Grandmother Mimi often and enjoyed many great Sunday dinners in the kitchen or out on the back porch. Althea made all our favorite dishes we had had when we visited there as children.

Three years after we settled in Baltimore, Grandmother Mimi became terminally ill with mouth cancer and Mimi took care of her until she passed. Grandmother Mimi left the house on Bottom Street to Mimi.

A year before Grandmother Mimi died, Uncle Theo was sent to prison for a murder he committed. He had gotten into a fight with one of the customers over one of the working girls. One thing led to another and Uncle Theo stabbed the man to death. William and Franklin, Lydia's two brothers, ended up going their own way. Both men left Baltimore for other endeavors.

I got up the courage once to ask Mimi how her grandmother convinced everyone that I was dead. I told her I had never asked my parents that question.

She was silent for a moment but then looked at me and said, "I asked her that before she passed. I asked her if there really was a body in that casket and had she gotten an unscrupulous Negro doctor to write up the death certificate for the authorities. I was so afraid of what her answer would be and I really didn't want to hear that she had had a child killed just so she could identify it as you.

Grandmother smiled up at me and touched my cheek and said, 'Ain't no use in you knowing that now. Besides they's all sorts of ways to get a dead body.'

I truly believe that Grandmother and her band of criminals made the authorities think you were dead because you had been drugged or something like that. Who knows? Back then the authorities didn't care if a colored child had drowned. I don't know if anyone from the police station came to view the body and if they did, Grandmother probably had one for them to see. In any case, yours was a closed casket service."

"It doesn't matter," I said. "Your Grandmother had a soft heart and I don't think any grandmother could have loved her grandchildren as much as she loved you, Danny and Jimmy."

Sometimes I have dreams that I am 10 years old again and back in that basement. I often wondered what happened to Strawberry. I never saw her again.

Watermelon Road

Mimi always laughed at my description of some of the costumes Strawberry wore. I even confessed that twice I painted her fingernails for her to help her get ready for the night. One of those times she was dressed in green with green eye shadow and orange lipstick and a big fake mole on her face. I told her she looked like a witch and she said, "You guessed it." Life in that basement would have been unbearable without her.

I hated Grandmother Mimi for what she did to my parents and I loved her for what she did for me. That woman was tough.

Peewee, I meant Simon, came to our house once. This was before our girls were born. Mimi was four months pregnant with twins. He was passing through on his way to an interview for a job in New York City. Simon stayed with us a couple of days. The first night we stayed up until dawn, talking about the past.

"Do you ever hear from Uncle Sax?" I asked Simon out of curiosity.

"He kept in touch with the Beaumonts and wrote to me at least once a month while I was growing up. He never forgot me at Christmas or my birthday. When I started college, my parents gave me $4980.00. It was all of the money Petey had hidden in the shed, along with the pocket knife I stole from him. I told you about the shed last night. Sax had given the money to the Beaumonts for my rearing. The Reverend and Lydia had saved all of it for me. I was blessed to have them for my adoptive parents. They actually did adopt me in spite of what they had told Uncle Sax. It was all right with him, though, since I still kept the name of Creek.

I heard from Mrs. Bertie that Uncle Sax died of lung cancer two years ago. When he took sick, he went back to live with Patty and Desiree on the farm. He made Patty swear not to tell me that he was dying. I guess he didn't want me to suffer through the death of another loved one. I had wondered why I hadn't heard from him in awhile, but then he moved around a lot. He died in Patty's arms. Speaking of Patty and Desiree, they stopped at seven children. I guess no one knows which one of the sisters birthed the 7th child. Some people thought it was Patty and Sax was the daddy. In any case, the sisters weren't talking."

"Do you know who I missed most when we moved from Baltimore to Massachusetts?" I asked Simon.

Simon shook his head.

"I really missed my dog, Rufus. My parents told me that they gave him to Mrs. Bertie when they moved from Horace Graves. I hope those eight children of hers didn't kill my dog."

We both laughed at that.

"I think what I miss most now are Miss Olivia's honey butter biscuits," said Simon.

"Lord, have mercy! How could I have forgotten those biscuits?" I said, smacking my lips.

The second night he and I went to a neighborhood bar and drank our fill of beer. After that we walked for a bit and ended up down by the Chesapeake Bay. I had often walked this way alone when I wanted to think about the novel I was writing. I thought a lot about how one cruel act of humankind back in 1933 caused a 10-year old boy's descent into madness.

Simon and I stood in silence for awhile, admiring the wide expanse of the Bay. Simon reached in his pocket, took something out and placed it in my hand. I stared down at it in amazement. It was the pocket knife with the snakeskin handle that was given to me by my father all those years ago. "Where on earth did this come from?" I asked in astonishment.

Simon smiled at me and said, "I found it in one of my mother's pillow cases that Sheriff Richards gave to Uncle Sax. I don't think Uncle Sax knew it was there. He handed the pillowcases over to the Beaumonts and they gave them to me. I looked through them a year or so after that, when I thought I could stand it, and found the pocket knife along with two charm bracelets and $10.90. I spent the money on crayons and coloring books back then. I still have the bracelets. I don't know who bought them or why, but I keep them with me all the time."

I stood there staring at the pocket knife. The memories hit me so hard they made my chest hurt.

"You know it really wasn't about the pocket knife." I said to him.

"Oh, I think it was," he said to me. "There are moments in our lives that have sharp edges like a knife and sometimes they cut deep."

I held it in my hand for a long time and then I threw it into the Bay. Simon nodded in agreement.

"It's caused enough harm," I said as we turned to walk home. He left the next day.

A few days after Simon left, Mimi found two charm bracelets in the cabinet where she kept the cereal. She asked me if I knew where they had come from. I told her what Simon had told me about the bracelets. Then she told me what she knew about them.

Mimi is out on the back porch with our three-year old twin daughters, Lily and Lydia. I still write from home and look after the girls while Mimi teaches at a nearby grade school.

I asked her once why she married me. She said it was because we both shared the same first love and that I was the keeper of the memories of her youth.

I've written a book about our time in Horace Graves. I named it "Watermelon Road," because, like the fictitious renaming of the road by Petey and me, it reminded me of the magical time we spent in those woods. The illustrated cover of my novel is by Simon Joseph Creek.

The End